S0-ADM-404

Bolan felt his blood boil

The murder of innocents always inflamed a sense of outrage in Bolan. But when the young were taken before their time by the rage and the violence of evil men, the soldier believed a certain cosmic equation was knocked all out of kilter.

He was a soldier first and last, but he maintained a belief in the divine, in the sanctity of human life, the clear distinction between Good and Evil that cosmic justice could never ignore. There were children beyond the dead who would never be born because of some madman's hate and violence. Viewed that way, Bolan figured the body count was far worse than what the human eye saw.

The Executioner was prepared to go the distance, make no mistake.

DON PENDLETON's
MACK BOLAN®

SCORCHED EARTH

A GOLD EAGLE BOOK FROM

WORLDWIDE®

TORONTO • NEW YORK • LONDON
AMSTERDAM • PARIS • SYDNEY • HAMBURG
STOCKHOLM • ATHENS • TOKYO • MILAN
MADRID • WARSAW • BUDAPEST • AUCKLAND

If you purchased this book without a cover you should be aware
that this book is stolen property. It was reported as "unsold and
destroyed" to the publisher, and neither the author nor the
publisher has received any payment for this "stripped book."

First edition January 2001

ISBN 0-373-61476-4

Special thanks and acknowledgment to
Dan Schmidt for his contribution to this work.

SCORCHED EARTH

Copyright © 2001 by Worldwide Library.

All rights reserved. Except for use in any review, the
reproduction or utilization of this work in whole or in part
in any form by any electronic, mechanical or other means,
now known or hereafter invented, including xerography,
photocopying and recording, or in any information storage
or retrieval system, is forbidden without the written permission
of the publisher, Worldwide Library, 225 Duncan Mill Road,
Don Mills, Ontario, Canada M3B 3K9.

All characters in this book have no existence outside the
imagination of the author and have no relation whatsoever to
anyone bearing the same name or names. They are not even
distantly inspired by any individual known or unknown to the
author, and all incidents are pure invention.

® and TM are trademarks of the publisher. Trademarks indicated
with ® are registered in the United States Patent and Trademark
Office, the Canadian Trade Marks Office and in other countries.

Printed in U.S.A.

If the military leader is filled with high ambition and if he pursues his aims with audacity and strength of will, he will reach them in spite of all obstacles.

—Karl von Clausewitz
Principles of War

Be bloody, bold, and resolute.

—William Shakespeare
Macbeth, IV, i

My pursuit of those who prey on the innocent, who engineer wholesale death and destruction, will never end. I have no sympathy for the Devil.

—Mack Bolan

Waiting was the hardest part. Even a soldier with miles of combat to back him up still couldn't help but chew on nerves a little when riding out the standby before an ambush. A number of factors could even tweak a seasoned vet, cause him to act before he was ready, or worse, force him to reveal his position to unsuspecting enemies. For one thing, the adrenaline rushed to what felt like new extreme heights with each eternal minute of utter immobility and quiet, muscles stiffening the whole time, cramping up even, making a man want to scratch, stretch, move around. Then the slightest noise could be amplified to a pitched roar as blood pressure throbbed in eardrums, the sound of his own heartbeat in the silence maybe fraying nerves even more. And every shadow, real or imagined, posed a potential threat. The mind tended to wander, also, if a soldier didn't stay focused, if he let waves of prestrike jitters drumming up all the "what ifs" filter into his resolve to get the job done.

The true professional, though, knew that lying in

wait all came down to patience, a virtue often learned through pain, loss and suffering.

Colonel Milak Zadar counted himself among the pros who knew that the virtue of patience often rewarded itself in the killing grounds. Patience fused with skill, experience and a heart that screamed he wouldn't fail, no matter what, would see him walk on, victorious to fight another day. With that in mind—and despite his own ironclad rules of pre-engagement—he began to envision his enemies, slayed before him, perhaps even wondering in their moment of dying what manner of supernatural wrath had just overwhelmed and hurled them into oblivion.

Yes, the waiting had worked on his nerves, thoughts slipping into fantasy all of a sudden, as he believed his cotton mouth needed to taste blood to get him right with the moment. If hate and rage alone could light him up, Zadar believed all of Croatia, Bosnia and Serbia might behold a human supernova. He could see them now, the gathered masses of his countrymen spotting him clear across the Adriatic Sea in this remote pocket of Italy while he launched a holy mission of revenge on their behalf. A burning star from the neck down, the oppressed and punished throngs of his own people would see his face, shrouded in light, then they would gape in awe at his weapon of doom chugging out its lethal prototype payload. Finally, the sight of their enemies dying in agony would carve grim smiles that would show NATO, perhaps even the entire world, there was no defeating a people who had twenty centuries of warfare to back up their defiance, their unyielding resolve to claim the Balkans as their land, theirs alone.

Dreams of returning an avenging hero given up to cold reality, Zadar remained one of four unmoving black-clad shadows on the hilltop. They were stretched in prone positions beneath the umbrella of moon- and starlight, weapons ready, holding back their lust for revenge until their targets disembarked the Chinook transport helicopter, assembled on the helipad near the east wing of the compound.

The Apache gunship had already made its flyover, forty-three minutes earlier. Zadar and comrades had stayed hidden in the village to the south while the Apache went through its surveillance maneuvers, then the four of them had moved out. At the village Zadar had paid an old winegrower enough lire to provide them with refuge and to watch their vehicle, the old fool gladly giving them all the cover hunted men could ask for. The Serb colonel knew the Apache reconnoitered the foothills ten minutes to the second before the VIP party arrived, the gunship's infrared and heat-seeking state-of-the-art systems searching out anyone who might break the restricted perimeter. Well, Zadar had a spotter near the Aviano Air Base, a fellow Serb brother-in-arms who had sounded the alert when the Apache lifted off, which was trailed shortly after by the VIP entourage. Better still, the organization he was part of maintained a pair of eyes and ears inside NATO. With their man on the inside—who reported to Zadar's superiors—he had learned one week earlier about this secret NATO compound. Their targets were high up the pecking order in NATO and the U.S. military. They met here once a week, a different day and time, of course, to map out a strategy for complete occupation of the Balkans.

A grim smile slashed Zadar's lips. The Balkans belonged to no one but the Serbs. And the NATO mansion and its perimeter below weren't only about to become a contaminated lake of death, but trumpet a message to the world at large that the gates of hell yawned wide to accept any and all who would violate a sovereign people and their land.

Zadar gave their firepower a mental tally: two sound-and-flash-suppressed Dragunov sniper rifles to pick off any of a dozen standing U.S. Marines who might somehow steer clear of the lethal cloud, break their way in with M-16s blazing; then they had the four homemade M-56 submachine guns, the Tokarev TT-33 pistols as side arms, more Russian hardware, courtesy of their Moscow sympathizers. Enough, Zadar hoped, to get them unmolested to a seashore evacuation.

Checking the troops for signs of jumpy nerves, Zadar felt a flush of pride, seeing only the lean faces of soldiers who had lived off the land while being hunted as alleged war criminals. Triglava, Citnec and Zipidu looked as hard as mountain rock, their gazes narrow, slits in a tank turret. But the eyes seemed to glow, these warriors looking as hungry as tigers smelling wounded prey. Oh, they were ready to taste the first blood of retribution, all right, but this would only mark the beginning.

And why should they deny themselves their sacred right to retribution? How long had it been since they had managed to slip themselves in among the refugees flooding out of Kosovo? Holed up in the squalor and filth of the refugee camps in Albania, fearing they would be found out by some woman whose family they had slaughtered? It didn't matter; it seemed so long ago it could have been another lifetime. The plan to get them out of Kosovo and to this stage was a stroke of genius, Zadar reflected. Of course, it helped to have nerve, money, connections.

Their strike point was situated at the edge of a rise that spined down from the foothills of the Apennine Mountains. This was wine country, with small villages and vineyards scattered here and there, from their current position all the way to the fishing village, some twenty miles east where their boat was docked. South, Zadar took in the distant lights burning from the closest village, then surveyed the broken terrain on his flanks. They were alone, with no one but their hated enemies down there in the valley, four hundred yards away.

Well within range of the warheads.

Zadar listened to the wind, sweeping over their backs, twenty miles or so per hour, and from a dead-on southwest course from the Adriatic. Given what was packed in the 85 mm warheads—one each fixed to fly from the two RPG-7s—Zadar couldn't have dreamed of a sweeter setup, the stiff, steady breeze blowing directly for the target compound. Almost, he decided, as if a divine wind were aiding their cause that night.

Satisfied they were on track and counting down, Zadar turned his attention back to the compound. The Apache was grounded, its rotors slowly spinning to a stop. It was a massive estate, two stories, all white-washed stone, plenty of wood with gold-gilded trimmings. The stone wall encircling the compound was twelve feet high, the front gate guarded by two Marines. It might have been enough to stop a frontal assault, but nothing they had down there by way of security and firepower could stand against what they had on tap.

It was game time.

The Chinook was touching down, landing lights on the helipad strobing around the massive transport chopper. Zadar counted six Marines on hand to secure the area for the VIPs. The rear landing ramp came down, and shadows began marching into Zadar's sight. Ten, fifteen, twenty shadows and still growing as the Chinook emptied its belly of VIPs.

Zadar lifted the RPG-7, the NSP-2 infrared night sight already adjusted for the range to target. He slipped a finger through the trigger, as the ghostly gray-green shapes materialized in his scope.

Zadar heard Citnec, their spotter with the night-vision binoculars, muttering, "Yes. Yes. I recognize them.... Excellent, I see the British mouthpiece for their NATO, I have that lying mouth from their Pentagon who is always on CNN—wait a second. Oh, yes, this is good."

Zadar pulled back, read the laughing expression on Citnec's face. "What?"

"We have ourselves a five-star catch, sir."

It was too good to be true. "Cromwell?"

Citnec chuckled. "The hawk who would be NATO's next Allied Supreme Commander."

Heart pounding with a fresh surge of adrenaline, Zadar hefted the rocket launcher, settled in for his moment of victory. "Ready!"

The wind seemed to gather renewed strength, howling past Zadar like a thousand wailing banshees.

"Now!"

Zadar squeezed the trigger, heard the warhead chugging away, the same familiar and sweet music sounding from Zipidu's RPG. Both rockets were fired off, locked in sync. Zadar watched, his eyes widening as his fin-shaped warhead streaked over the wall and blew, dead center in the helipad. West, just beyond the ring of Marines, Zipidu scored his own doomsday strike. There were no thundering fireballs downrange, as Zadar would have heard and seen had the RPG been fitted with its usual HEAT round. Instead, there were two loud thuds, followed by twin clouds that mushroomed before the Chinook's rotor wash began quickly flinging the sarin nerve gas over and away from the helipad.

Zadar observed the horror show, fascinated. It played out just as he had hoped, almost too outstanding to be true. They began to clutch at their chests and throats, shadows staggering this way and that, rubber legs giving out within seconds, eyes bugged, to be sure, gaping mouths gagging back drool. The Americans and their allies had never even dared to dream something like this could happen, and Zadar wished he could stick around when the decon teams and the media showed up. Down there they were clearly one-hundred percent unprepared. Meaning no antidotes, no ingesting oxime tablets every six hours on the hour, as the only preventive medicine against a nerve agent. Arrogance alone could be a killer.

And they died hard, fast and ugly.

A few of the Marines tried to flee the cloud, but the lethal vapor swept over them, flung at them by rotor wash like a sneeze from some giant. Two heartbeats later, their weapons fell from their hands as their limbs began to twitch as if they were puppets jerked on a string by a raving drunk. The symptoms, Zadar observed through his scope, were instant and hideous. The Marines were collapsing all over the helipad, convulsing, bladders and bowels no doubt emptied out, shaming the uniforms the men donned, central nervous systems shredded as if a raging fire were exploding apart their innards.

Standing, Zadar dropped the spent RPG-7. He gave

the shadows writhing in the lights and the gas clouds a final approving look. Tough justice for them, message delivered. Laughing as he moved off with his men, Zadar listened to the wind, the distant screams of men dying in agony and said, "Now, that's what I call some real ethnic cleansing."

CHAPTER ONE

Mack Bolan, aka the Executioner, was tired of waiting. He sat behind the wheel of his dark blue Taurus
rental, nursing a time bomb of white-hot anger in his
gut as he recalled the terrorist attacks of the past
forty-eight hours. Given what little intelligence had
been gathered so far, the soldier couldn't help but
wonder if Hal Brognola and the cyber team at Stony
Man Farm had steered him in the right—or wrong—
direction to even begin tracking the savages believed
responsible for giving the orders to massacre U.S.
military brass, NATO officials and innocent civilians.
Only hours earlier a terrorist group had created chaos
and destruction at a Florida university.

Whatever the suspicions, Bolan knew he was staring at a riddle coated in blood, one way or another.

Parked curbside, the Executioner watched as the
two big men exited their black sedan, roughly two
blocks down. Like the predators Bolan suspected they
were, they gave the grimy avenue—chocked full of
bars, strip joints and run-down apartment buildings—
a long search, trying to appear casual in their paranoia

as they checked the loitering shadows of bums, crack dealers and the few scantily clad hookers braving the chilly air. All was clear, judging from the slight softening of their expressions, faces gone unpinched, the subtle relaxing of shoulders, shortening of the strides.

Bolan read their act, loud and clear.

They both had shoulder-length dark hair, lean, hard faces, and moved with military bearing. Identical twin thugs, the soldier thought of them as Frick and Frack. And it was something in the way they moved—a sort of controlled angry energy, as if they were braced for sudden violence—that flared Bolan's instincts that these two were inclined to criminal activity, and then some.

That was just one item tipping the Executioner into deeper suspicion.

It was their fifth stop in ninety minutes, as they had moved all around Pittsburgh proper and vicinity, finally stopping there, just northwest of Three Rivers Stadium, close to the Ohio River. They hit each rendezvous empty-handed, but reemerged with one, sometimes two large black duffel bags. By now the trunk and back seat of the sedan were stuffed with so many duffel bags, Bolan imagined it was beginning to look like the locker room of a pro sports team packing up after a game.

What the hell were they picking up? Cash? Guns? Drugs?

According to the Executioner's chronometer, they took no longer than five minutes out of Bolan's surveillance, whether it was a venture into a bar or strip joint, a trip inside a seedy-looking apartment building or a riverfront office along the Allegheny or Monongahela rivers. The two mystery men in black trench coats had even vanished for a longer stint inside a new high-rise in the Golden Triangle, the heart of downtown Pittsburgh where all the new movers and shakers had launched industrial inroads into commercial pharmaceuticals, nuclear technology and state-of-the-art computer upgrading. The City of Steel, Bolan could see, had undergone a massive face-lift in recent years. No longer the grim, soot-covered town, nestled in the wooded slopes of the western Appalachians, with belching smokestacks and a tough blue-collar workforce sweating out the days in factories or coal mines, Pittsburgh was now home to a number of Fortune 500 power players. The town also boasted itself as the Northeast's mecca of art and culture, next to the Big Apple, of course.

Another curious, even ominous change in the refurbished concrete-and-glass jungle was the sudden emergence of a growing Serbian community in and outside Pittsburgh. Even more strange, this Serb immigration was largely male, and between the fighting ages of eighteen to thirty-something, according to Hal Brognola's sources inside the FBI. The big Fed informed Bolan the FBI had recently launched—in joint cooperation with the DEA and the ATF—an ongoing investigation into suspected Serbian criminal activities in the Pittsburgh area. Several Serb nationals had even been busted for assault, drug and gun possession, only to post bail and disappear off the face of the Continental U.S.

Was the sum total of this picture so far just one big fat coincidence and happenstance? Bolan wondered. Right. Something smelled in Pittsburgh and he knew it wasn't the polluted waters of the Three Rivers.

So the Executioner had been turned loose to find out, up close and personal, if a Serbian Mafia or Serb terrorist organization was headquartered in Pittsburgh, and mete out the appropriate response.

Which, of course, was a call to arms, Bolan-style.

In keeping with any campaign that might see the Executioner at loggerheads with the law, Brognola had passed down the order to other law-enforcement agencies to give one Special Agent Mike Ballard a twenty-four-hour window of unrestricted solo movement in Pittsburgh. And Brognola had the clout, Bolan knew, to shut down any interagency interference if they squawked too loud about a one-man Justice band shoving them off center stage. Well, Brognola knew the Executioner could get things done in a way that only legitimate law-enforcement officers could fantasize about, bound as they were by red tape and rules of engagement. If forced to, Brognola could go all the way to the President of the United States for sanction.

Bolan watched as Frick and Frack disappeared into the bar. The soldier knew he had to get the ball rolling if he was going to find out what kind of party he would be crashing in the hours to come. One idea in particular began to take shape in his mind, but he had been pondering a course of action since arriving in town, armed as he was with little more than guess-work hanging out there in a limbo of unanswered questions. Sure, he had the intel pack beside him on the passenger's seat, along with a couple of tracking goodies in the pocket of his black jacket. And he had a shopping list, complete with all the Serb outposts and names of all the "unusual" suspects in Pitts-burgh. But the hard reality was that any mission Bo-lan undertook always required overwhelming force of action. The who, what and why was always flushed out by the barrels of the Executioner's guns.

While a plan of attack gelled in the back of his mind, Bolan mentally ran down what the Farm knew. There had been three separate attacks. One was a nerve gas strike on a secret NATO meeting compound in Italy. More than three dozen U.S. top brass, NATO higher-ups and Marines had been killed, the killers vanishing into thin air. Perimeter was secured now by decon teams, no media allowed anywhere near the scene. Two spent RPG-7s were found in the Apennine foothills south of the compound. The educated guess was that the nerve gas was packed into the RPG war-heads. If that was the case, then Russia had developed a prototype weapon of mass destruction, something frontline troops could use, but only if they engaged the opposition in biohazard suits.

That particular item was kept from the media, since relations between Washington and Moscow were shaky enough, given the current state of affairs in the Balkans. But would Russian commandos attack U.S.

military and NATO officials? On behalf of their Serb comrades, perhaps, or acting in some sort of alliance? Bolan didn't think so, but he'd been around long enough, seen enough hidden agendas and traitors along the way in his War Everlasting to know anything was possible. And if there was a Serbian-Russian alliance, then even Bolan had to shudder inside at the potential nightmare that could pose to the West.

The next item Bolan mulled over was the suicide bombing on the Capitol steps. The main target had apparently been a highly visible senator who paraded his anti-Serb rhetoric before the media, and was killed while chairing a special committee outlining the complete occupation of the Balkans. Two men had apparently just waltzed right in among the pack of reporters, touched off twin explosions, but not before a civilian close to the scene heard one of them scream something to the effect of ''Long live Serbia!''

And the third incident? Three men in black trench coats, their remains yet to be identified, had marched into a university in Boca Raton, almost at the same moment a hundred-plus civilians were blown up on the Capitol steps. More than two hundred had been killed, countless wounded, and the body count was still in question, growing by the hour. SWAT teams had eventually taken down the killers, but not before the attackers had maimed about a dozen lawmen, going for ankles and knees that weren't protected by body armor. It was clear to Bolan the suicide mission was undertaken by professionals, assassins either hired out or belonging to some foreign group looking to take revenge on America for some perceived injustice. Survivors reported hearing the ski-masked shooters talking to one another in a foreign language.

Bolan felt his blood boil, his mind conjuring up all the horror and death, and the aftermath of parents in agony over the senseless slaughter of their children. The murder of innocents always inflamed a sense of heightened outrage in Bolan. But when the young were taken before their time by the rage and the violence of evil men, the soldier believed a certain cosmic equation was knocked out of kilter. When youths were murdered, their future potential lineage was also wiped out.

No mystic, soothsayer or prophet, Bolan was a soldier, first and last, but he maintained a belief in the divine, in the sanctity of human life, the clear distinction between good and evil that cosmic justice could never ignore. There were children beyond the dead who would never be born because of some madman's hate and violence. Viewed that way, Bolan figured that the real body count was far worse than what the human eye saw at that Florida university.

Enough. What was done was sadly, tragically done. The soldier was there, ready to root out any vipers, crush them underfoot if they even had an inkling about the trio of murderous attacks. His favorite side arms were hidden beneath his jacket, but the Beretta 93-R in shoulder rigging and the mammoth .44 Magnum Desert Eagle riding on his hip were merely small firepower compared to what was housed in the black nylon war bag in the rental's trunk. If what Bolan and Stony Man Farm suspected played out there, then the Executioner had come to the City of Steel prepared to give new meaning to the term urban warfare.

Of course, his phony Justice Department credentials would go under the microscope if it went to hell and the cops and the Feds cornered him, zipped open that war bag. Inside they would find a combat harness, fitted with a mixed pick of fragmentation, flash-stun and incendiary grenades. Under his combat blacksuit the eye-popping firepower would be revealed—an Uzi submachine gun, then a Heckler & Koch 33 assault rifle already fitted with a telescopic sight for long-range kills, as well as a dozen spare clips for each weapon. Finally, the aluminum briefcase with its satellite link and fax would raise federal eyebrows, to be sure.

The Executioner abruptly shut down his mental assessment. He opened the manila envelope, slid out one of the black-and-white 8 x 10 photos of a man he hoped soon to confront face-to-face. The pictures were courtesy of FBI surveillance, handed over to Brognola. Bolan looked at the face of the man calling himself Roman Kowalski, the passport and paperwork identifying the man in the picture as a Polish immigrant.

Bolan knew better, and Kurtzman had his own suspicions. The computer expert vowed to get back to Bolan on Kowalski after he worked his magic in cyberspace.

The face staring back at Bolan was that of a stone-

cold killer, that much he was sure of. The eyes were
slate-gray, cold, lifeless. The head was shaved, revealing an odd ridge of skull bone that ran back from
his forehead. The nose was long, nostrils flared,
cheekbones high, jaw like a jack-o'-lantern. The thick
white mustache was another eerie touch to a face that
looked more suited to a gargoyle. Finally, the thin lips
were slashed in a grimace, revealing two front teeth
that were chipped in such a way, the mouth looked
as if it belonged to Count Dracula.

Roman Kowalski was one spooky-looking character, Bolan decided.

Bolan dropped the Taurus into Drive and traveled
another block. He killed the engine, feeling the eyes
of watching shadows boring into him. He took the
keys and dropped them in his coat pocket, well aware
that no amount of face-lifts by architects and engi-
neers in any American city could ever hope to remove
the human acne of crime. He hopped out and hurried
to the sedan. One quick move, in a crouch, and he
fixed the magnetic homer to the front bumper. Next
he pinned the face of Count Dracula beneath the
windshield wiper.

He was retracing his steps, glancing over his shoulder, when Frick and Frack emerged on the sidewalk.
No duffel bags this time. Instead, they were manhan-
dling a short beefy guy, jacking him along, taking
turns slapping him on the back of his head. Bolan
heard Frick and Frack bombarding their punching bag
in a language that sounded Eastern European in ori-

gin. The Executioner wasn't familiar with it, but he was betting on Serbo-Croatian.

Whatever, it was obvious there wouldn't be any black bag pickup at this stop. The soldier was back behind the wheel, watching as the men in trench coats shoved their beefy prisoner into the mouth of an alley. Beefy was all gesticulating hands, imploring eyes. Frick and Frack weren't buying whatever he was trying to sell. A couple of backhands to his face, a fist buried into Beefy's substantial gut, and their guy folded at the knees. Frick's finger-pointing told Bolan they were simply warning the man. It eased some of Bolan's tension, knowing he wouldn't stand by and watch them execute this man in cold blood, regardless of who or what he was.

Bolan fired up the engine, deciding it was time to make his presence felt. He rolled the Taurus slowly ahead, touching a button to electronically drop his window. He closed on the alley and tapped the brakes, his stare neutral as he made eye contact with Frick and Frack.

"What are you looking at?" Frick barked, his words forced.

Bolan paused, putting on a disarming smile. "I'm not sure. Maybe you can tell me."

"What?" Frick snarled. He started to take a step toward Bolan but stopped for some reason. Maybe he was wondering if Bolan was a cop or competitor. No matter.

Bolan raised his hand, the smile holding, as he formed his trigger and middle finger into a V.

"Peace," the Executioner said, and drove off. He looked into his side mirror, saw the confusion on their faces, which were shrinking in the glass.

The Executioner rounded the corner, cranking up the window to drown out the calls from the creatures of the night attempting to buy him, body and soul.

Something told Bolan the wait was just about over.

Next stop was the killing zone.

"I UNDERSTAND. Yes, I understand."

Vidan Ceasuvic didn't understand, at all, but went ahead and played the game for their sponsor. After all, it was Russian money that had gotten him safely out of Yugoslavia several years back, when he was a wanted so-called war criminal. It was Russian ingenuity that saw him go under a knife in Moscow for a little fine-tuning on his face. Finally, it was Russian financing that had gotten him safely into America, where his sponsors from Brighton Beach had an idea to expand their empire. They were moving west, opening up new markets. A businessman had to expand or face going under to stronger, more ambitious competition. The Serb colonel owed his sponsors a debt, but he also wanted in on the action. No problem, the sponsors had said. What was one more Mafia on the American landscape. Besides, Ceasuvic needed money, a lot of it, in fact, if he and his fellow Serbs were to achieve their ultimate goal.

"I see. Yes. I see."

The big, bald Serb, dressed in black from turtleneck to combat boots, felt his hand tightening around the cellular phone. He didn't see a damn thing, except red. He listened to the voice bleating out its angry demands in no uncertain terms. The line was supposedly secured, the phone equipped with the latest in state-of-the-art scrambling, courtesy of Mother Russia. Just in case, knowing the Feds may be listening in, he spoke to the voice in Brighton Beach in Russian. Most Americans, especially the Feds, he thought, were lazy, bringing to mind some joke about the difference between a foreigner and an American, something about Americans being able to speak only one language, while the foreigner knew two, three, even four.

The colonel had heard enough about what his sponsor wanted. He clenched his jaw, ground his teeth and ran a big, long-fingered hand over the ridge of his skull. He felt the blood pressure cooking his brain.

He was sitting in a leather recliner in the office of the warehouse they maintained along the Allegheny River. He glanced at the bulk of his soldiers through the window. They were gathered out on the large floor, which was crammed with furniture, refrigerator, bar, all the trimmings to try to make their lives on the run as comfortable as possible. Ceasuvic then smelled the cigarette and looked at Vuk Cviic. The lean, crew-cut Cviic sat on the couch, puffing away. The colonel glanced at Karina, the only woman on his crew. She was his angel, all legs and breasts, silken blond mane tumbling to her shoulders. He took a moment to admire her classic beauty, anything to distract his anger toward Brighton Beach. He snapped his fingers at

Karina, gesturing with his hand for a drink and cigarette. She got right on it, building a double Scotch whiskey neat, from the wet bar, lighting him a cigarette. He smiled at her, experienced the sudden rise of heat in his loins he always felt when he stared at her beauty, recalling all the passion shared between them. She smiled back, handed over the drink and cigarette, then returned to her chair.

Ceasuvic killed the whiskey, smoked, then heaved a breath. "Problems, comrade? Yes, there are problems. I will go ahead and meet with your people, but I must tell you this town is finished.... What do I mean? I will explain soon.... I understand...I understand. No, I have not forgotten all you have done for myself and my people. Until we meet."

He signed off and found himself suddenly fingering the butt of the Glock 17 in his shoulder holster. He needed action to relieve the stress, but knew all of them would get all the action they could handle, and within the hour.

"They are sending some of their people to pick up their payment," he announced. "Of course we will be long gone from here, but I will contact them once we are safely on the road."

Karina crossed her long legs. "Our sponsors will not be happy when they learn what we have done."

Ceasuvic shrugged. "I do not think they will cry too much over the deaths of a few minority criminals."

Cviic built himself a whiskey to deal with the news. "We have established a strong, ongoing network for them to be able to move merchandise. We have even moved our own organization into Cleveland, Detroit, Milwaukee. We had a deal with the Russians. Must we throw it all away now?''

''There will be other networks for us and for them. And need I remind you, Vuk, this is not, and never was about money?''

''And you are going to assure them we have not damaged their organization?'' Cviic wanted to know.

''They will listen. They know what I have wanted all along. I was clear from the beginning. They have used us as much as we have used them. And, yes, I can be most persuasive when I put my mind to it.''

Ceasuvic picked up the phone and punched in the numbers. Three rings later a deep bass voice on the other end growled, ''Yeah.''

''I wish to speak to your boss.'' While he waited, hearing what the Americans passed off as music pounding in his ear, he looked Karina up and down. ''Karina, I want you to go put on that black leather miniskirt. I need you to show these animals a lot of leg. I'll explain on the way.''

In his ear he heard, ''Yo, you got my party favors?''

Ceasuvic scowled at the aggressive tone of voice. ''I'm on the way.''

''Yeah, well, this time how 'bout not bringin' a small army up here. Makes the homeboys nervous, not to mention your trench-coat convention don't quite fit in with the scenery. Know what I'm sayin'?''

''I'm on the way,'' he said, and hung up.

"Your mind is made up?" Cviic asked.

"There can be no other way. There never was. Now," he said, smiling at Cviic and Karina, baring his chipped fangs. "What do the Americans say? It's show time."

SOMETHING WAS going down. Bolan could hazard a strong guess a meeting was set to take place, somewhere in the high-rise condominiums that loomed before him.

A light drizzle had begun to fall, as Bolan watched the last of four vehicles swinging off Bedford Avenue and rolling into the sprawling parking lot. The homing device had worked like a charm, allowing him to quickly pick up Frick and Frack after what was their fifth and final stop. From there he had followed them to a warehouse complex on the north bank of the Allegheny River. A small army of trench-coated goons had rolled out of the warehouse, maybe thirty minutes into his surveillance. Then they piled into an assortment of vehicles before taking Bolan on a ride across town, finally moving across the 6th Street Bridge, driving northeast to the Schenley Heights area.

Bolan's problem at the moment became twofold as he guided the Taurus into the lot, peeling off from the convoy, searching for a spot from where he could maintain his surveillance. First, Frick and Frack had seen him, but that was part of Bolan's play. He wanted them nervous, looking over their shoulders, adrenaline rushing but their minds maybe distracted from whatever task they were about to undertake. Second, this was a secured building, meaning the trench-coat army would have to be buzzed in. And Bolan didn't have the first clue as to what condo they were going for. Did he buzz the desk, roll in behind the enemy, flash his Justice ID? Then what? And what if the FBI hadn't decided to play ball with Brognola? Bolan had kept hard vigilance on his back the whole ride there. No sign of a tail. But what if the Feds had a raid planned on his subjects right then and there?

Forget it. There was no time to what-if the situation.

The soldier watched the vehicles disappear from sight as they rolled in behind several vans on the distant opposite side of the lot. He slid in by the curb, parked it at an angle where he could watch the front doors. Moments later, shadows began marching for the front steps. As light spilled over them, Bolan recognized the unforgettable ghoulish visage of Roman Kowalski leading the troops. He counted ten men, three of whom carried large black duffels. And there was a woman among the crew, her long and bared legs sweeping out from the fold in her trench coat. It was a little chilly for the woman to be showing off so much leg. And there was no sign of Frick, even though Bolan had earlier clearly seen him take the wheel of the black sedan. Maybe they had left a few troops behind to watch the vehicles, or alert their comrades going in to any sign of unwelcomed surprise guests.

Something felt wrong, either way. Bolan was beginning to get a bad gut feeling about the whole setup. The small army moved as if it were on some mission.

A hard play was going down.

The soldier made the call on the spot to move in behind the trench coats. No time like the present to start crashing the party, whatever it was. He needed some answers, meaning he needed a live one.

Bolan killed the engine. He was pocketing the keys, reaching for the door handle when he glimpsed sudden movement in the side glass.

And one look at Frick's grim face was all Bolan got. The big goon was quick, right on top of the door, rushing up out of nowhere. He was digging out hardware, his face contorted with savage determination, when Bolan made his move.

CHAPTER TWO

Life on the run came with one, maybe two distinct advantages, but it also screamed for sudden fatal disaster. A man learned to live in each moment, the simple pleasures in life—eating, drinking, making love, even a walk through the park—sending the senses soaring to new and magnificent heights, the hunted one aware each and every hour could be his last.

One day at a time was good enough.

Even still, he knew the minus column ran longer than the plus side. And Vidan Ceasuvic often became angry that he was always forced to look over his shoulder, sometimes jumping at shadows; even the sound of a car backfiring burst his gut with fear and paranoia, making him think he was being shot at on the street.

It could happen.

He had left behind many enemies, in many places, more than a few of which were still alive. And he knew he wasn't someone who could simply melt into the crowd, vanish unnoticed, when all hell broke loose. As he waited with his crew for the elevator to arrive, he caught a glimpse of the ghoul in the mirrored door, became bitterly aware the plastic surgery hadn't altered his face that much. If anything, his face could be mentally filed away, to be recognized at some future point by potential hunters. The filing down of the angles of two front teeth, he'd been told, was an added bonus, but to this day he believed it was meant to be some sick and sadistic joke—or a red flag, in case his sponsors needed to track him.

No, he had never fooled himself he was anywhere close to handsome, but what the Russians had done to him was almost sinister. The new face made him wonder if they really wanted a different version—a specter of his former self—or if there was some hidden motive on their part to make his a face that could have been cast for a horror movie.

A sudden knifing pain tore through his face. Thank God, the invisible dagger slashing beneath the skin came on less and less these days. Either way, he had long since come to accept that he would never be completely free of the pain and the itching. More than three years later, though, his face still ached where they had cut, gouged, dug, attaching bone implants along his jaw, the laser surgery to trim the ears of their former elephantine flaps. Then, what he thought of now as death-camp instruments, sucking out flesh and fat from skull to jaw and around the throat, carving his upper face to razor sharpness while the jaw jutted out, grotesquely huge. A portrait of a nightmare, indeed. Months after those endless weeks of surgery, he recalled then floating away on painkillers, the antibiotics and constant injections to ward off possible infection. The pain, always the pain to fight off. Maintaining half a bellyful of whiskey or vodka helped in the beginning, but he knew the worst way to lose control of himself and his people was to use any crutch that would undermine his ability to lead. So he had determined to simply use the pain as fuel for the fire, viewing it as some sort of divine inspiration that would help guide him toward reaping his ultimate vengeance on those he sought to destroy.

The doors opened, and they piled in, gathering around their leader. The colonel held the black bag low, tight in his hand. It felt much heavier at the moment than the seventy pounds or so of ninety-plus pure cocaine stashed inside. Chalk it up, he figured, to prekilling nerves.

Ceasuvic took a moment to admit he harbored some regret over what they were about to do. This was the first of three stops. They were about to sever a trio of major pipelines they had established for both themselves and the Russians to move drugs, guns, porn and whole prostitution rings into Pittsburgh and cities west and northwest. A lot of money would never be made, and the Russians would most certainly view this as an act of treason. Which left everyone's future in doubt. As far as he was concerned, it was the only call to be made. If the Russians didn't like it…

They stared straight ahead, as the doors slid shut, the elevator car lifting off on a brief lurch. It was fifteen floors to the top, and Ceasuvic was aware he would find a roomful of heavily armed black thugs at the end of the ride. This would be his third and final trip to this condo. With that in mind, he allowed himself a degree of comfort as he felt the weight of his mini-Uzi, slung beneath his trench coat on its special webbed shoulder rigging. His people were likewise armed with a hidden mix of the compact Israeli subguns and Ingram MAC-10s, Havel with the room-clearing Mossberg 500 riot gun beneath his coat, a 12-gauge round already racked up the snout. Ceasuvic almost smiled, as he believed he could feel the adrenaline all around. To a man and woman, all of them knew what was at stake.

Life or death, for starters. Second, but hardly last or least, there was the ultimate goal where he intended to live long enough to insure the survival of Yugoslavia, witness the reclaiming of his country's former republics. And by such a terrible and awesome force he believed the world would hold its collective breath, shake as one people in utter terror.

It was the least he could do to avenge NATO atrocities against his countrymen.

He glanced up, the numbers silently lighting above him. He took from his pocket the black-and-white picture Radin had handed to him at the warehouse. He felt Cviic's eyes drilling into him with concern.

"Do you believe Radin? Just one man?" Cviic asked. "He even followed us here. Radin spotted him even as we left our warehouse. A Fed?"

Under different circumstances, he would have

blasted Cviic for his lack of nerve and faith. Naturally, there was always the possible horror of a DEA or an FBI raid, Ceasuvic knew. It was why he spread their cash, guns and drugs at various pickup and distribution points around the city. If one place was hit, there was always plenty of backup, the well was, indeed, deep. Of course, by the time any of his street-level distributors was scooped up, maybe singing to the Feds, Ceasuvic would hear of it by way of his paid police and his DEA plants. Where merchandise was stored around the city, the proprietors of bars, strip joints and pool halls were used as middlemen to move product out of their establishments. The problem was if one fell, a chain reaction could start, middlemen toppling like dominoes before American law. Apparently someone, a lone stranger by Radin's account, had smelled out their movements, might have already added two and two. It disturbed Ceasuvic that someone had tailed Radin and Vladin all over the city, flagging down the stash sites, then finally leaving the Serb's own face beneath a windshield wiper.

As if it were a message. Or a warning.

Ceasuvic took a Zippo lighter from his coat pocket and clacked open the lid. Someone—whoever—had snapped the shot from cover. How long had he been followed? What did they know? Perhaps even right then Feds were hard at work on their vast network of computers, reaching out to Interpol, the CIA, dredging through the NATO files on Yugoslav officers, both past and present, anything to establish a positive

ID on Roman Kowalski. In time, it would be easy enough for his enemies to discover who he really was.

It would be good to blow Pittsburgh, moving on, even if all of their futures were in jeopardy. Ceasuvic could only take it one day, one move at a time.

First he needed to fatten the war chest.

"Let me know the instant your pager vibrates," he told Cviic with a sideways look. SOP was that he always left two men behind, ready to send out the signal by vibrating pager if it looked as if a raiding party of FBI or DEA agents were storming in behind them.

The car shuddered slightly as it stopped, a soft chime announcing they had arrived. As the doors opened, Ceasuvic fired up the lighter, putting the flame to the edge of the 8 x 10, his face quickly beginning to melt in his hand. He led them off the elevator, then tossed the smoking, half-eaten photo to the carpet. He glanced at Karina as she fell in step beside him. There was a grim and determined set to her stunning Slavic-Teutonic features that made him at once proud and burning with sudden lust. When this night was over, he would need relief.

"To answer your question," he told Cviic over his shoulder, as his people filed into the hallway behind him, "I have complete confidence Radin will handle any problems below."

THE THUG MADE one mistake, and it cost him any edge he might have used on Bolan. Had Frick come up his blind side, blasting away, the soldier knew it would have been over before it even started. Instead, the thug tried to do too much at one time. Apparently, Frick wasn't sure who he was dealing with.

Mistake number two.

Frick was grappling for his holstered piece, trying to clear it from his coat while attempting to fling open the door, his free hand grasping the handle. It left Bolan with his only opening, Frick standing nearly on top of the door, right at ground zero. And the Executioner bulled into the door panel, blasting the door out, driving the edge into Frick's knees. Bolan was rewarded by a sharp grunt of pain, the goon starting to buckle, but his adversary's counterattack proved to him that this close encounter would go the distance.

Fair enough.

A short charge, the thug hurling his weight into the door, and Bolan found himself wedged against the edge of the roof. A white-hot pain shooting up his spine, he glimpsed the Glock pistol flying out from its holster and knew Frick was going for the kill. The soldier found wiggle room, shoving the door back, Frick thrusting, all rage and desperation to keep his opponent pinned before he started shooting.

Bolan whipped up his left arm, cleared the top of the door and spiked Frick in the nose with an open hand. Using the heel of his palm like a battering ram, he slammed the thug again, squelching the guy's nose even more. Hearing cartilage crunch, Bolan saw Frick stagger back, the Glock sliding from his hand, clattering to the pavement.

It was now or never.

Two swift paces, and Bolan was on top of the guy. Again, it became obvious Frick wasn't looking to dance. The haymaker came out of nowhere, and only the slight shift in Frick's shoulders tipped Bolan to a potential blow that would have dropped him for the eight count and beyond.

Crouching, the soldier still felt the knuckles bang off the top of his skull, with enough behind the blow to set a fire racing through his brain. But the home run swing left Frick off balance long enough for Bolan to launch a pile driver into the thug's gut, a punishing blow with so much force behind it, he thought he'd gone all the way to the spine. A growl of pure rage sounded two heartbeats after Frick belched air. Bolan knew he had to end it then and there, grimly aware the man was like some rampaging bull that wouldn't go down, no matter how many swords gored it.

The man's elbow flew up, but Bolan twisted enough to take the flesh-and-bone spear on the hip, Frick missing again, this time with a blow intended to crush a man's sac to powder. The Executioner felt the pain lance through his hipbone, but used the brief flash of agony as fuel for his fire. Wrenching up a handful of long hair, Bolan jacked Frick to his feet, whirled and ran him face-first into the edge of the driver's-door roof. A kidney shot finally dropped Frick, who hit the ground belly up like a sack of manure.

Bolan pulled out the Beretta, aimed it at the bloody mask staring him back. The light drizzle was threatening to turn into a steady hammering as raindrops pattered off the rooftop of Bolan's rental, quickly washing away any blood smears.

Dazed eyes sought out the tall shadow. Frick hawked out a glob of blood, his tongue flicking away a hanging tooth. His laugh was choked with pain. "You are unusually good, for a man of peace. Who are you? FBI?"

"Let's just say I'm not with the Red Cross."

The Executioner stepped back, checking the lot. There was bound to be some sort of security on hand, but with a thunderstorm set to pound the city, the soldier figured they wouldn't be making the rounds anytime soon. No cars moving around the lot, no shadows. Bolan was as alone as he could hope for at the moment.

He stepped over the thug and twisted the keys from the ignition. None too gently, he took Frick by the hair, pulled the thug toward the trunk, the man growling and cursing as he was forced to crab along on hands and knees. Bolan opened the trunk and zipped open his war bag. Shedding his coat, he took the special swivel rig for the Uzi subgun from the bag, then attached it around his shoulder. Uzi fitted in the rigging, a full clip locked in place, the Executioner palmed a frag and a flash-stun grenade. He dropped the steel eggs into a coat pocket along with three spare clips for the SMG, then slipped back into the long coat. Next he took a pair of plastic cuffs from the war bag.

"Eat some asphalt. Hands behind your back."

When Frick complied, Bolan snapped on the cuffs. A quick but thorough pat down of the thug turned up a commando knife in an ankle sheath. The sheathed knife went into the trunk.

As Bolan fished out a greasy rag, he asked, "I don't suppose you're up to answering a few questions?"

"Such as what condo they are in? Such as what is going on? How many guns, you wish to ask?" Another pained laugh, a curse in his native tongue. "Talk to the front desk."

Bolan shoved the rag into Frick's mouth. Q and A could wait.

"Here's some temporary pain relief," Bolan said, then put out the man's lights with a short slashing right to the jaw. Dumping Frick on the floor behind the back seat, the soldier quickly threaded the sound suppressor to his Beretta. It occurred to him right then that his head count of the small army that had gone inside, which had been off by two, was only out one now. No point in leaving any problems behind. Beretta leading the way, the Executioner moved out.

AWARE THIS WAS the last time he would have to tolerate setting foot in this place made it easier for Ceasuvic to bite down his contempt. But not by much.

As his men spread out along the landing that wound halfway around the sunken floor of the living room and Karina held her place beside him on top of the foyer's steps, the colonel took in the African decor. Some of it was obscene, at least, the statues and oil paintings of naked African tribesmen displaying all their glory, no doubt meant to inflame the fairer sex. Ceasuvic turned his eyes from them to all the trinkets, bone necklaces, python skins and animal-hide shields hanging on dark mahogany walls, the unfamiliar pottery, ivory vases, here and there. Next he took a look at the tangle of vines draped from the ceiling, where several ceramic vipers were coiled to strike, fangs showing. The burning incense and the raging bellow of rap blaring from man-high speakers was the final assault on his senses.

The punks, he thought, had brought the jungle to the city.

Ceasuvic counted nine of them, scattered around the living room, all of them armed, an Uzi subgun, a TEC-9 here and there within easy reach. And nine pairs of dark eyes were right then boring into Karina as if she were some juicy slab of meat about to be made ready for a feast.

If the sum total of all the decor and the drill-bit stares was meant to intimidate some white man, then Ceasuvic wasn't buying any of it. The fact was, he didn't feel the first quiver in his bones. He was a soldier, blooded in all-out combat, while he viewed them as nothing more than common street criminals, at best.

He felt rage, just the same, at their blatant disrespect. He could only imagine what fantasies were burning up their filthy minds at the sight of a lone and stunning blond woman in their presence. Oh, well, Ceasuvic figured, let them indulge in their fantasies. It wouldn't be long, and the entire condominium would make some of the slaughter of Albanian Muslims in Kosovo pale by comparison.

A few of the punks looked a little unsettled at the sight of so many grim-faced strangers, all of them obviously armed, none of them speaking, just watching their hosts watching them. Havel and a few of the others, Ceasuvic saw out of the corner of his eye, were sidling down the landing, their moves slow, deliberate. No sign of intimidation over there.

The Serb colonel waited as Samson moved from the large glass coffee table. The drug crew's leader was wearing a white Japanese *gi,* his muscular pecs rippling under what Ceasuvic figured was twenty pounds of gold necklaces and medallions.

"Yo, my Eastern Euro brothers, nice to see ya again."

Ceasuvic grimaced, pointed at his ear, glanced at the stereo.

Samson shouted, "Hey, someone turn that shit down! Where's your manners? We got company!"

It took a few more seconds for one of them to peel his eyes off Karina. A big black hulk in a tank top, arms like tree trunks, finally waddled over to the stereo. He twisted the knob, lowering the noise enough to make conversation possible.

"See you brought the party favors. Talkin' about the bags," he said, and laughed. "Everything beautiful?"

Ceasuvic smiled in the face of the obvious insult. "One hundred kilos. Just like last time."

Samson ran a fat tongue over his lips, glancing at Karina and sweeping a hand over his bald dome. He was edged out, jumpy, a few beads of sweat mottling his forehead. But the Serb colonel had already noted the glass pipes, the silver tray with its scattered rocks on the coffee table. He knew Samson and some of his crew had a habit of giving the merchandise a lengthy taste test before it was stepped on, packed up and moved out.

Samson obviously couldn't help himself, grinning at Karina. "Hey, baby, maybe you stick around for the party later. Case Vee-lad and his homeboys here got business somewhere else?"

Ceasuvic watched as Karina stood her ground, looking the punk right in the face. She showed him a smile. It was an act, of course, but Ceasuvic felt his face flush, his chest tighten. What the hell? He had just felt a stab of something he didn't think himself capable of. Jealousy.

"Perhaps," she said. "Would you mind if I went to the bar for a drink while you do your business?"

Samson lit up with another hopeful grin. "Make yourself at home, baby. Sample anything here you like."

"Quite the gentleman, you are," she said.

"And then some, baby, then some. And we won't be long, right, Vee-lad?"

"No, not long at all."

"Yeah, we one big happy family, right. Share the wealth, booty, too, maybe."

The Serb colonel smiled. But the smile did not reach his eyes.

Samson chuckled, turned his back and headed for the coffee table. "I like you, Vee-lad. First time we did business, I say to myself that's one tough mofo. Stuff was so sweet, I been kickin' down paper like I could buy me up a whole Third World country to retire in someday. One with a nice beach, lots of booty, you understand."

"A man needs to dream."

"Hey, no cigarettes in here!"

Ceasuvic turned his head and found Havel frozen, his lighter poised an inch or so from his cigarette. Havel didn't flinch, but his gaze narrowed, a hint of anger in his eyes as he nodded at the coffee table.

"That's different. It's clean, no ashes."

Ceasuvic caught Havel's eye and shook his head. The cigarette disappeared.

"Thank you."

He then saw Karina settling onto a bar stool covered in leopard skin. A punk slowly rolled behind the bar and asked what she was drinking.

"Vodka. Chilled."

Mr. Courteous got right on it, Ceasuvic saw.

The colonel was growing weary of the game. Just a little longer. Ceasuvic then looked at the doorways that led to the adjoining halls, caught still more rap thumping from one direction. The last time he dropped off a load here, Samson had been in a bragging mood. Samson had told him he had bought out the entire top floor. Walls were soundproof, with the walls in the connecting condos knocked down by a brother-in-law's construction crew, another brother-in-law owning the building, allowing the work to be done here according to Samson's specifications and needs. Which meant there would be other punks, maybe party guests spread out, hidden from immediate view, their brains probably tweaked out on crack. No matter. The party was just about over.

"Now how 'bout a taste test, Vee-lad."

Ceasuvic saw Samson rubbing his hands like an expectant child. He tossed the bag away, and it thudded at the feet of the closest flunky. A nod from their leader, and the other two bags were pitched to the living-room floor. The colonel watched as three punks got busy unzipping, hauling out a brick each. Switchblades flicked open and the thick plastic was sliced with a small cut, blades delving in, coming out with white powder, which was then carried to the coffee table and tipped into three separate glass tubes. The whole ritual was performed with all the skill and precision of a heart surgeon.

"And the money?"

While they dumped small amounts of water and baking soda into the tubes then put them to the flame of a mini propane torch, Samson gave the order to bring the money.

Ceasuvic saw that a few of them had stayed interested in Karina. The leg show was working just as he hoped.

Moments later, two large duffel bags were dumped on the landing. Ceasuvic waited as Havel and Mavric opened them, rifled through the rubber-banded stacks of bills. Two nods, and the colonel raised his voice to end the charade.

"I am afraid I have no time for any last requests."

Samson looked up, pipe in hand, his expression a curious mix of amusement and anxiety. "Say what?"

Ceasuvic gave the word. "I said there has been a change in plans. And you do not fit into them."

His look confirmed what his words had warned them; they weren't meant to do any taste testing ever again.

Most certainly the first few rounds of autofire ripping from the weapons of ten men and one woman got their undivided attention.

Uzi out and flaming, Ceasuvic hit Samson across the chest with a 9 mm 3-round burst, the deal-breaker washing the white *gi* in a sudden spray of gore that no amount of bleach would ever remove. Across the way, he spotted Karina's bartender drop from sight as she hit him full in the face with a stuttering blast from her Ingram MAC-10.

Ceasuvic felt like a proud father, but there would be time enough later to celebrate. There was plenty of killing to be done before they broke out the booze.

CHAPTER THREE

They were a brazen lot, as tough as the day was long. After his toe-to-toe dusting of Frick, after watching the trench-coat army march into the building as if they either owned the place or were supremely confident they could handle any crisis, Bolan had to give them their due.

He was going after A-list competition, which meant he could ill afford to leave anything to chance.

Hunched low, the Executioner forged through the driving rain. Unless he missed his guess, a lone pair of eyes was left behind in one of the four vehicles, some thug now clock-watching maybe, impatient for Frick's return.

On full alert, if the man was a decent watchdog.

The soldier stayed away from any light through the downpour. But the lampposts were scattered around the edges of the lot, enough distance between them to allow Bolan the next best thing to invisibility. He skirted west to east at a hard jog, hidden from any car-bound watcher, he hoped. Covered as he was by the back ends of vehicles, he sprinted forward when necessary, across the short distances between the lines of cars and SUVs. On the run he searched the lot, racing adrenaline tuning in his senses to the slightest sound or movement. All clear at the moment, just the soldier and whoever he'd find at the end of his run.

At the next to last row, the soldier took cover behind a Jeep Cherokee. Peering around the back edge, he spotted their vehicles, parked side by side, backed in against the curb. It was the best point of surveillance to monitor the entire front and the east side of the condominium high-rise. Bolan made out a solitary shadow behind the wheel of the closest vehicle—a Lincoln Continental—thanks to the cherry-red glow of a cigarette.

Darting from cover, Bolan made the last line of vehicles, then bolted up behind the parked cars. Closing hard and fast, Bolan saw that the smoker appeared to be looking off in the general direction for his errant comrade, the constant glow of the cigarette's tip warning the Executioner the watcher was wound tight.

The first rule in Bolan's experience was to never underestimate the opposition. If his intended victim was anything like Frick, he knew he'd have to make his first try for the kill his last. Switching the Beretta for 3-shot mode, the soldier picked up the pace, rearing up out of his crouch as he rapidly cut the gap to the Lincoln. He was three cars and counting, heading in at angle on the Lincoln's rear, when the smoker decided to look his way—for whatever reason, and not that it mattered.

Tapping the Beretta's trigger, the Executioner punched a trio of 9 mm Parabellum shockers through the driver's window. Glass shards washed over the startled face a microsecond before Bolan saw the dark mist of blood flying through the interior. He confirmed his kill, then quickly checked the remaining vehicles. The smoker was the last of their backup.

Now what? He looked the building up and down. The only way in was to buzz the desk and announce himself as a cop. It stood to reason this wasn't the first trip here for the trench coats. Assess. Service people—such as whoever monitored the lobby desk, in this case—had a knack for reading all manner of individuals and situations, and were imbued with a peculiar intuition or nosiness for knowing what went on around them that was never part of the job description. Maybe the desk person was even slipped a few crispies in advance to keep a lookout from below, sound the alarm if strange faces came through the doors.

Some sort of illicit deal was in the works somewhere in the building. That much Bolan could be sure of. Short of banging on doors and killing whoever worked the desk, he would do whatever it took to find the right den of thieves. Beyond that, the soldier would call the play on the spot.

Stowing the Beretta, he was angling for the front doors, pondering his dilemma, when he was suddenly blessed with two strokes of luck. He spotted the couple, huddled together under an umbrella. They were moving hard for the front entrance when Bolan called out, "Could you hold the door, please?"

He took a step, then froze. At first he thought he was being pelted by hail. Then another sharp object bounced, slashing off his face. He traced the line of blood across his cheek, then stepped back. Eyelids slitted, he looked up the building. Lights were mounted along the edge of the roof. He heard what he thought sounded like glass tinkling on the asphalt beside him. Scanning the top floor he was barely able to make out the miniature holes bursting out in the line of windows, but he'd seen enough. A hole, maybe the size of a basketball, blowing out a bed of shards and slivers, a silent rain of glass glittering for a moment in the light. The final tip telling Bolan he was late for the fireworks was the brief but chaotic bursts of light striking the curtains up there. Muzzle-flashes.

"You coming in or what, mister? I'm not a bell-boy!"

The Executioner made the door on a surge of adrenaline. He thanked the guy, who was staring at Bolan, taking note of the crimson trickle on his face with a sudden hard eye. The Executioner couldn't spare Mr. Surly the time, even if he had felt so inclined, guessing the guy was probably wondering if he was a tenant or some street character who didn't belong there, conning his way inside.

The Executioner made a beeline straight for the desk. He wasn't about to congratulate himself yet on a job not done, not by any stretch. And he wasn't prepared to tell Mr. Surly a one-man killing crew had just walked onto the premises.

The whole building would know that, and soon enough. The Executioner knew that wasn't any drugged-out rock-and-roll band trashing the place on the top floor.

CEASUVIC KNEW they **were** only getting into the swing of things. This wasn't the first time he had committed wholesale slaughter with this particular group of soldiers.

Everyone knew the drill.

And practice now proved perfect.

Warming up, he swung his Uzi off the bloody mess that was Samson, the head punk stretched out and twitching on his bed of glass. Ceasuvic spotted a punk with a Mohawk in flight, the man apparently having no stomach for this kind of action. Too bad. No one wanted to die, the colonel thought, so he stitched Mohawk from the knee to the thigh, a hard lesson in pain, to be sure. Using the mini-Uzi's own natural inclination to rise, he followed through, drilling a few slugs through the ribs, Mohawk screaming, his curses flaying the air. Mohawk didn't go down—instead, he staggered in a partial whirl, faced front and lurched ahead in a half hobble. Ceasuvic saw where Mohawk was headed, figured he'd keep for a couple of seconds or so while he checked the troops, Karina to be specific.

A quick search of the shooting gallery, and the Serb colonel found the black hulk over by the stereo, bellowing and bringing up a TEC-9 pistol. The hulk was absorbing plenty of lead—his Karina holding her ground by the bar, helping to pour it on with her compact Ingram MAC-10—but the giant wouldn't topple. Ceasuvic figured the giant owed his strength to pure rage, or a brain over-charged by drugs, as his massive torso became matted with running blood in a matter of heartbeats. Finally, Havel put the hulk down with a deafening blast from his riot gun that all but blew the head off his shoulders.

Ceasuvic stepped down into the living room and saw Mohawk go into a desperate lunge, aiming himself for the sanctuary of a pillar that braced one corner of the kitchen. A long burst from his Uzi gave Mohawk the haircut of a lifetime.

It was just about over, in the living room, at least. To the Serb colonel the punks had struck him as a frenzied pack of jackrabbits, darting and hopping all over the place at the first sound of gunfire, damn near a comedy act with their shock and horror, torn as they had looked between flight or fight. Most of them had already been cut down by the opening rounds of autofire, with the roar of Havel's riot gun having swept the room, taking out one, maybe two immediate threats. Hard to tell, since there was now so much blood and shot-to-hell decor, everything shrouded in a pall of cordite.

A few punks were still hauling up pistols or machine guns, but they were mowed down where they tried to make their stand.

If, by chance, they encountered any resistance on

the way out, well, he hadn't survived Bosnia by tossing down his weapon when the going got ugly, his hands up to plead mercy from an opposition stronger in numbers.

The colonel glimpsed the tails of trench coats sweeping behind a few of his men as they vaulted the railing and hit the living-room floor, weapons fanning the carnage for wounded, any punk who might rise from the dead. It was a clean sweep, he thought, nine kills—until he heard Samson moaning and rolling around in the glass. The music, the pounding of feet, the cries and curses sounding from both halls pulled the colonel's attention off the wounded punk. Without having to issue the order, his troops split up, bolted for the hallways, fresh magazines slapped into the SMGs, Havel filling the Mossberg with 12-gauge man-eaters on the way. Ceasuvic saw Karina striding from the bar. She was chucking aside her spent clip, cracking a fresh magazine into her compact subgun and stepping in behind Havel, when Ceasuvic barked, "Karina!"

There was a strange fire in her eyes, but he'd seen the look before. Ceasuvic fought to keep from smiling. Killing always made her especially hot. He understood her burning, her need to cleanse herself of their disrespect. She had been raped by Bosnian Muslims, he knew, and Ceasuvic could well imagine her shame. Even to this day, he sometimes saw in his mind a pack of animals in human skin devouring her defenseless flesh. He was never sure what exactly about that image disturbed him, what made him sometimes wonder if she had put up enough of a fight. Right then he knew what she wanted, but he wasn't willing to risk her life further. If they made it through this night—the next two stops—Ceasuvic knew she was up for some icing on the cake.

Vehement, he shook his head at Karina, as the sounds of autofire roared in his ears. She hesitated, even clenched her jaw at him. Scowling, she broke his stare, swung around, heading back to the bar in her high heels. Only when she settled herself on the bar stool and went to work on her drink, did Ceasuvic relax a little.

He focused his dark hate and rage on Samson, walking up to the dying drug dealer and crouching beside him. From two distant but converging points he heard his troops hard at work, mopping up. Beyond the din of autofire and shotgun thunder, though, beyond the bleating pleas of party people begging for their lives, Ceasuvic still heard Samson cursing him. Ignoring the curses, he glanced left, the mini-Uzi smoking perched over his knee.

He took in the sight, a war dog getting his fix of blood. His people were tried-and-true professionals, and he savored the moment to admire their handiwork. One man would crouch low at the corner of a hall, thrust his SMG, one-handed, around the corner and fire away, while another soldier burst by, his own weapon blazing in sync with the cornerman. It was what Ceasuvic called his bulldoze version of the standard SWAT or military leapfrog assault. A dug-in enemy would be forced to cover by the initial blind firing, while the spearhead charged in, burning up his clip on the fly, but not before the now trailing shooter had reloaded and come in behind him shooting. And so on. With enough spare clips and the right kind of soldiers, it always worked. Ceasuvic had yet to lose a man under his command using the bulldoze technique. He could be fairly certain he wasn't about to lose any people this night, either.

"Why? You...mother...we had the world...."

Ceasuvic smiled at Samson. "You talk too much. You have no respect." He reached down, clamped his hand over Samson's throat and squeezed until he saw the man's eyes bug. He was unmindful of the blood rolling from the gaping mouth, sliming over his knuckles. He didn't care. What was the death of one more drug-dealing scum? There would be plenty of blood on his hands before this night was over. In a way, Ceasuvic figured he was making the world a little better place with each kill.

Samson grabbed at the Serb colonel's forearms, unwilling to give it up so easily.

Tightening his hold, relishing Samson's heart rate pulsing in his grasp, he growled, "And that's Vidan. 'Vee-Don.'" The colonel set down his mini-Uzi, pulled his Glock and rammed it in Samson's mouth. "This one is on the house."

BOLAN DIDN'T PART with the fifty. The deskman had been very helpful when he saw the Justice Department credentials, then looked into the face of death giving him a cold word of warning not to call ahead.

Not that anyone in the condo where he was now headed would bother to answer the phone. The Executioner suspected he was about to bull his way into a war zone.

Bolan had taken the elevator to the floor directly below the penthouse. From there he had climbed the eastern stairwell. Uzi subgun up and ready, the soldier saw the door opened toward him. He grasped the handle, pulled it open wide enough to squeeze his head through and ventured a look down the long, wide hallway. It was free of human traffic. But as he stepped out into the hall, a muffled sound filtered to his ears. He stepped closer to the wall, noting that both sides of the hall were covered in mirrored glass. He listened. It took a little straining, but he caught the muted sounds of autofire, shotgun blasts and screaming beyond. A mass execution was underway.

The soldier was moving up the hallway, taking in the small alcove on his left, ready to arm a frag grenade to lead the way in, when the front doors opened some twenty feet ahead. It was as if the man in the doorway had some uncanny radar, as if he'd seen Bolan coming, through the walls.

Suddenly, the soldier found himself trapped out in the open, dead to rights. Bolan squeezed the Uzi's trigger, spraying the doorway with a flurry of 9 mm lead at the same instant Trench Coat cut loose with an Ingram MAC-10. Leaping away from the tracking line of fire, Bolan was forced to race the few steps across the hallway. On the fly, the Executioner returned fire, the Uzi jumping in his fists, when another compact subgun joined in from the door. With bullets slapping the air above his head and shattering whole sections of the mirrored wall, the soldier flung himself to cover in the alcove.

A voice boomed out in the brief lull, Bolan straining his ears, ringing to near deafness now from the exchange of weapons fire in the tight confines of the hallway. The tone of command was clear, even if the soldier didn't understand the words. Dropping to one knee and placing a spare clip on the carpet for quick access, Bolan went low around the corner, tapping off a quick burst of autofire when he glimpsed the unforgettable face of Kowalski and what looked like the entire trench-coat army sweeping boldly into the hall. At once they cut loose, their lightning barrage of autofire and the ear-shattering cannon roar of a shotgun chasing Bolan to cover.

It was the soldier's worst-case scenario. He was pinned, outnumbered, forced to ride out the relentless hellstorm, the command voice bellowing orders from some distant point in the total assault on the Executioner's senses. It seemed a pointless waste of ammunition, hundreds of rounds keeping one man down. Then, through all the glass and chunks of plaster and stone hurled past his cover, Bolan discovered the method to their madness.

They were good, all right, but the man coming his way seemed to have forgotten all about the mirrored walls, or simply figured in all his brazenness the covering wave of ceaseless weapons fire would enable him to storm into position. Of course, if Bolan could see him...

The man forged ahead, his Ingram MAC-10 sweeping up to draw target acquisition. Bolan backed up, took a step away from the alcove's wall. Forced to brave the ricochets, he unleashed a short burst of subgun fire, scoring flesh on a line of red holes marching across the shooter's chest. The enemy gunner died with a stunned look on his face as he crashed into the mirrored wall, bringing down a wave of glass shards.

The voice of command upped his bellow a few decibels. The respite in enemy firing didn't last long, but this time Bolan weathered a leadstorm he figured was hitting his position from only two, three subguns tops.

They were bailing.

Bolan kept waiting for their clips to burn up, forcing the shooters in those two heartbeats to stand their ground while changing magazines. Then he could make his move, fire around the corner, catch them before they could unleash another volley.

It didn't happen.

The pounding leadstorm would slacken, then come back, full strength. Bolan figured out the strategy. One or two shooters would burn up a clip while another gunman had his SMG locked and loaded, ready to fire the instant the lead shooters ran dry. Oh, they were good, Bolan thought, too good to leave alive and running wild, chasing whatever terror schemes they had.

The SMG storm abruptly ended, leaving behind a

sound like a swarm of angry hornets in Bolan's ears. He waited several heartbeats, made out the faint, far-away voices and a door banging. Feeding the Uzi a fresh clip, he chanced a look around the corner. They were running for the stairwell in the opposite direction, the last of the trench coats right then charging into the doorway.

The Executioner marched out into the hall, his finger curled around the SMG's trigger. He had a full head of steam, and he hadn't come this far to see them just boldly vanish into the night.

Not on his watch, his hunt.

Not ever.

CHAPTER FOUR

When he heard the rap of hard soles on teakwood above, the gray-haired man with a matching goatee pointed the lamp in the direction of the far corner of the cabin. He viewed the shroud of near darkness as one of two necessary evils. Yes, he knew who his visitor was, of course knew all about what office he represented, all the stature and prestige that came with it.

Window dressing.

Too often in this day and age he knew corrupt men held lofty places of power. Such were the times he lived in.

So the Gray Man had used a cutout to summon his contact for this midnight meet. Drop everything, he told the contact in no uncertain terms, something of a crisis was brewing. He twisted the lamp another several inches, casting him in deeper shadow. There, that would work. The lamp's puny fifteen-watt bulb would have left him in shadow regardless, but he simply didn't want to see the contact's fat, smug face. A part of him was disgusted about this business he had fallen into—sleeping with the nation's enemies, so to speak—but he viewed this second of necessary evils as the only way in which to exact retribution, salvage whatever pride he had left in his waning, lonely years. Not to mention that he craved to make a personal statement to those who had stabbed him in the back.

Whenever he met with one of the contacts—these meetings either in total darkness or in deep shadows—he figured it was best for all concerned if no one on either side could come up with a positive ID. Just in case it all went to hell. He had been careless in the past, so burned by the power structure he would never again give up any edge he could find and hold.

The Gray Man drummed his fingers on the top of his massive oak desk, waiting.

A short, paunchy shadow stepped into the cabin. Even in the poor light the Gray Man noted the dark immaculate suit that was most likely, he guessed, woven from Italian silk. He'd seen this waddling ball of self-indulgence and overinflated ego on CNN many times, giving the press the briefings in tailor-made suits that would cost the average working American a month's salary or more. The Gray Man could see his money was being well spent, on the finer things in life at least.

"Beautiful yacht, very nice," the Suit said in a voice as smooth as the silk of his jacket. "She must be your pride and joy."

"*Winston.* He."

"Pardon me. He."

Without being invited, the Suit settled into a wingback chair, his double chin the only part of his upper body that was clearly visible. "I trust you're finding Virginia Beach suitable to your retirement needs."

On the Suit's breath, the Gray Man could smell the veal marsala, a hint of spicy marinara heaped on top of a side of linguini perhaps, and Scotch whiskey. "Only in the off-season."

The Suit chuckled, one of the team. "I understand."

"Do you now?"

The Suit balked but gathered his composure. Always on stage, before the cameras.

"Well, too many tourists, kids, all the traffic from Memorial to Labor."

The Gray Man smiled. "I was referring to how I'm a little out of my element."

"Ah," the Suit said. "It's Navy country down here."

"If we have finished with the small talk…"

The Suit paused, then said, "All this cloak-and-dagger, tell me why that makes me nervous."

"It's only our second meeting."

"It feels like ten. But maybe that's because we have some problems."

"It's why you're here."

"Yes, your intermediary mentioned a crisis in the wings. I have to tell you in all honesty, I see more than a few problems myself."

The Gray Man was always suspicious of any individual who began statements about his being honest and frank, as if they were inclined to lie at other junctures of conversation.

"Why don't you go first, then?"

The Suit hesitated. "Very well. First and certainly not least, I didn't sign on to aid and abet terrorism against the United States and its citizens."

"It came with the package."

Now the Suit showed some fire, his double chin quivering with anger. "But I didn't know that!"

"It's all part of the bigger picture."

"Which a few loose cannons on the deck…"

"Our Serbian connection, you mean, our friends from Moscow."

The Suit stopped cold, the silhouette of his darkened head swiveling as if he was terrified someone he hadn't spotted coming down was standing over his shoulder.

"We are quite alone." Now it was the Gray Man's turn to chuckle. "No bugs, either. I promise, I swept the yacht just before you arrived."

"Don't even mention…Serb or Serbia. Or the Russians. Ever. This is nothing to joke about."

"Relax. Let's shift gears for a minute. I understand you're up for a promotion."

Ego and ambition took over as the man bared his white teeth in the shadows. "Sounds like maybe you've heard the news."

"I have my sources."

"Uh-huh. Well, our residing secretary of defense got caught in a very ugly and compromising situation. I guess you could say…he was, uh…"

The Gray Man finished it when the Suit abruptly stopped, fidgeting with his pudgy hands. "Caught with his pants down, yes, I heard something to that effect."

The Suit didn't know how to react.

The Gray Man shrugged. "Feel free to speak. There's nothing to be uncomfortable about. What happened at the Pentagon is ancient history. At least the Army was kind enough to allow me to retire early. No court martial. Pension in my pocket. Full benefits. All the frills. I can even still go to the Officer's Club up at Fort Meyer, if I swear an oath in advance to some puffed-up numbnuts windbag general who's never heard a shot fired in anger that I'll be a good soldier boy while I'm in D.C."

"Uh, yes, quite. Good for you." The Suit cleared his throat. "Well, at any rate, the SecDef has created quite the mess. Naturally, the White House wants to sweep it all under the rug."

"Naturally. And understandable, in light of what the last Administration put the country through."

"Right. Anyway, the SecDef, this idiot, he not only sleeps with two of his daughter's college-age friends—mere freshmen, for God's sake—but he gets one of them pregnant."

"Sounds like quite the scandalous dish for the inquiring mind to feed on. Oh, well, it will give those talking heads on cable a sure boost in ratings."

"Dammit, man, that's the last thing anyone wants."

"In other words, there will be a quiet resignation."

"With me in line for the job."

"You're that confident."

The Suit grunted, as if a stupid question had been asked. "The President and I are old, old friends. He's done everything short of making the announcement."

"I suppose congratulations are in order."

"The ink's not on the paper yet, but it's as close to a done deal as I could ask for."

Unbelievable, the Gray Man thought, the Suit had no military background whatsoever, and he was in line for SecDef to the most powerful nation on earth. He could only imagine the amount of ass-kissing the Suit had planted on the right butts to land him on the A-list.

"Then we'll have that much more clout."

More throat-clearing, rubbing of hands. "That's something I also came here to discuss."

The Gray Man saw the flimflam coming, had already heard all the whining before it even started. He leaned forward, feeling his blood pressure rising, and put the kind of no-shit look in his eyes he had used in the past on a subordinate who needed a severe dressing-down. "You listen to me, and you listen very closely. If not for me, if not for my connections, which are now your connections, and which are the connections wiring money into your account in the Bahamas on a monthly basis, you'd still be just a fat little pissant mouthpiece for White House propaganda."

The Suit wouldn't take the bait. "Right. The account. Funny you should mention that. On the way down your private pier to your million-dollar *Winston*, I was admiring the estate up on the hill. What, two new Cadillacs, an SUV, I think I even saw what looked like a customized Harley in the drive. Looks like you've done pretty good, retiring on whatever the Army gives a full-bird colonel to be put out to pasture. Is there some bestseller you wrote that I haven't heard about, seeing as I'm such a businessman these days?''

The Gray Man eased back in his chair, softening his tone. ''I had some luck with a few stock investments.''

''I'm sure that's what you'd tell Big Brother.''

''I can't say I care for your tone. Am I hearing a threat?''

''No. But understand, if I go down... Need I finish?''

''Then we have an understanding. I will add this. Should I hear any rumors coming at me from up your way, making me even suspect you're not going to stick with the program, you might find some very large, some very ugly strangers paying you a quiet visit some night.''

''Now I'm hearing a threat.''

''No. I don't threaten. I promise, then I deliver.''

The Suit took a few moments to rethink his position. ''What about 'them'?''

''They're sponsored, as we are sponsored.''

''Not exactly what I wanted to hear. This thing could get ugly.''

"It's already ugly. Show some backbone, will you? Have some faith."

The Gray Man thought he heard what sounded like a whimper as the Suit lapsed into a brooding silence. "What?" he asked.

"The endgame, what is it? Give me some answer."

"It's basic. Money, power, glory," the Gray Man replied.

"Would you mind being a little more specific?"

"Fair enough. In time, myself and a few of the others will prove instrumental in pushing East and West toward a third world war."

The Suit nearly leaped out of the wingback. "What?"

"Settle down. I don't think I have an extra pair of underwear that would fit you. I said 'pushing.' The way I'm reading it, you're an ambitious sort who wants his place in history. Maybe you see statues built in your likeness all over the city, or your own memorial like Lincoln or Jefferson, maybe you want to be up there on Rushmore. Whatever. You want the brass ring, you want it all. You want 'the power.' Fine. But understand that's why you were approached. And let's be crystal freakin' clear on one thing. There is the right way to do this, and there is the wrong way. Now, if we stay the course, I will have what I want and you will be the one in the spotlight who saves mankind from the Apocalypse. With that crowning achievement, who knows? Tomorrow SecDef, later the Oval Office. And it won't matter where the campaign contributions come from. It could end up being all but a lock. But only if no one panics. Only if everyone gives themselves a good squeeze between the legs to remind themselves there's still a few men left in the world.''

The Gray Man could almost feel the Suit relax, dreaming the big one no doubt. Give the Suit hope, promise him the keys to the kingdom, the future bright and beautiful, sweet dreams to see him sleep like a baby at night. Those were the Gray Man's orders.

''Now, we still have some matters to review,'' the Gray Man said.

''I have one more question.''

''Let's have it.''

''What would it benefit you, our sponsors, even myself to drive the world toward a final conflict? If it goes that far, anything could happen.''

The Gray Man smiled. ''It won't. You see, it's very simple, it's even all part of the evolution of humankind. Oh, there will be some bloodshed along the way, but it brings to my mind two things that benefit humankind from war. One—war bolsters the economy.'' He paused, then added, ''Better still, there's the other equation, the one that matters the most.''

The following silence appeared to agitate the Suit.

''The punchline,'' the Gray Man said. ''This is where you're supposed to ask 'what's the punchline?' ''

''Whatever. The punchline.''

''Number two is survival of the fittest. The only

question you need to ask yourself is just how fit are you.''

IVAN CHURYBIK KNEW they were very concerned in Moscow. In fact, the Old Man was so unhappy with recent developments he had sent special representatives Churybik had been ordered to personally greet when they landed. Churybik wondered if they were coming to America as part of the problem, or part of the solution.

Meaning, were they flying in with diplomacy on the mind, wishing to iron out the wrinkles, one big happy family pulling together, or coming to kick ass and take names, with Churybik at the top of the list. It was a question that was a few short minutes away from being answered.

He heard the black executive jet's screaming turbofan engines before he saw the aircraft. He stared eastward, into the darkness, the faint sheen of Manhattan's skyline seemingly a thousand miles away right then. He wished to God he was back in Brighton Beach, safe and sound, nerves in check, drinking vodka, collecting money, a juicy portion of stuffed veal in front of him, his mistress waiting…

Not tonight. This was urgent, even grim business, he knew. And orders were orders.

He searched the black sky hanging over the New Jersey countryside. They were coming in from the northeast, the flight already cleared to land on their private airfield. In just a few more minutes… Churybik's throat felt suddenly sandpapered raw. Even the tailor-made Armani jacket and silk slacks, normally molded to his muscular body like a second skin, now made him feel wrapped as tight as a mummy. He licked his dry lips, smoothed back his fresh hundred-dollar haircut with a trembling hand. Churybik glanced over his shoulder at his lone bodyguard, Lev, standing by the limousine, hands the size of footballs folded over his crotch, no expression. Ygor, his driver, sat behind the limo's wheel, casually puffing on a cigarette, not a worry in the world, either. And why should the hired help give a damn? This was his problem. No matter how this business was concluded, they would still have a job the following day, still see the sun....

He stopped himself and took a deep breath to try to clear his head of all paranoid thoughts. Why get carried away, anticipate trouble that hadn't shown itself yet?

He watched as the black jet touched down at the far east end of the runway, rubber screeching a little, then it began rolling past the scattering of choppers, twin-engine planes, the hangars in the distance. He waited, heart thumping in his ears while the sleek bird kept rolling his way, a dark winged shadow barely lit up by the runway lights. He tried to distract himself by admiring the prototype Tokinov Eagle. Tokinov Aerodynamics, he knew, was only one of several businesses Viktor Tokinov owned back in Russia. The Family had also branched into computers, restaurants, nightclubs, even manufactured video games, ran a magazine and book publishing house. A front, of course, for the real money behind the Family.

Whatever, the shadowy world of Viktor Tokinov had made him a rich man. He could only hope this mess somehow straightened itself out, so he could get on with it, enjoy his wealth, live to a ripe old age.

The Tokinov Eagle slowed to taxi. It was a long flight from Moscow. They would be weary from jet lag, but there was always plenty of food and vodka onboard, even two "stews" on-hand to ease the tension and keep the troops happy if they felt the need for an extended visit to the rest room. But even if they were sated by all the creature comforts, he still imagined he could feel the angry energy swelling the fuselage like an inflating balloon, their dark thoughts about whatever their own orders were working on their nerves the whole flight, pumping them up for the job at hand. Viktor Tokinov wasn't sending him a bunch of tired old drunks.

No, Churybik knew he was looking at a jet full of stone-cold killers, the best of the worst.

Damn right, he was nervous. This wasn't going to be good. Or maybe he could talk himself through it, come out the other side, casting himself as a mere unwitting victim to circumstance. A hundred and one excuses and rationalizations came to mind. Wasn't it the Old Man who had originally brought the Serbs aboard? Didn't the Old Man insist they launch their operations westward, using the Serbs, whom the Old Man had this great affection for, often calling them his misunderstood warrior comrades? Wasn't it the

Old Man who had granted him carte blanche to get the Serb arm of the Family thrust westward and flexing? How was Churybik supposed to know the Serbs had some hidden agenda for unleashing a campaign of terrorism against America and her allies? What the hell, was he supposed to read minds, check the tea leaves on a daily basis?

The jet stopped in front of Churybik, the engines shutting down. He swallowed hard as the door opened and the ramp lowered. Six men in black leather bomber jackets slowly walked in single file down the ramp: two crew cuts, one shaved dome, the other three looking to Churybik as if they hadn't seen a barber in years. They also carried large black nylon bags. By the way the bags bulged and the tight grips he noted they maintained, Churybik could pretty much figure those bags weren't stowed with a month's worth of wardrobe. Churybik's bad read on the moment made his heart race even more, as he noted how none of the six acknowledged his presence, didn't even look at him as they peeled off, three to a side, flanking him, several feet ahead.

Seven, he had been told seven men by Viktor.

He stood there for what seemed an hour, as if he were supposed to bow or something, or meant to brace himself for the Second Coming and all the hellfire to follow.

The shadow rolled into the lit doorway, followed by the emergence of a big man in a black trench coat. This one didn't carry his own bag, then Churybik glanced at the stone figures and spotted that one of the crew cuts had been relegated to bellhop detail. The figure above Churybik was so tall and broad he had to stoop, then turn sideways to squeeze through the door. The man had some sort of flattop haircut that seemed to make his skull appear like a block. But it was the eyes boring into him that quickly grabbed Churybik's undivided attention. After another long wait, the big man moved off the ramp and toward him with slow and measured strides.

"You are Churybik?" he said.

With less than two feet away, Churybik could see the fire burning in the big man's eyes. "Yes. Comrade Churybik, at your service."

The big man nodded. Churybik saw he was smiling. Good, that was good.

"I am Duklov."

"Welcome to America, Comrade Duklov."

The smile disappeared. "Would you care to tell me, comrade," he said, his tone sounding very congenial to Churybik, another hopeful sign, as he slid another inch forward, and roared, "what the FUCK is going on?"

It was all Ivan Churybik could do to stay on his feet. He felt his heart lurch into his throat, the big question all but answered.

They had come to kick ass and take names.

THE SMELL OF DEATH was overpowering, even to Bolan. He stopped in the open doorway, but lingered no longer than two seconds. A look inside, the stench of gunpowder, blood and emptied bowels and bladders spiking his nose, and the soldier could only guess why this slaughter had happened. Most likely it was a drug deal gone bad, or maybe a straight rip-off by the Serbs. He could be sure no one had been left alive in there to explain it all to the cops.

Speaking of police, the Executioner knew all the racket of weapons fire was sure to have the neighbors tying up the 911 line to the nearest precinct. If the police showed up before this was finished—one way or another—Bolan knew the trench-coat army wouldn't simply throw down their weapons and demand a lawyer. Surrender clearly wasn't their style.

No mistake, the Executioner was on the clock, so he beat a hard run for the stairwell door. He crouched, Uzi ready, and grasped the door handle. Some sixth sense warned him he had company on the other side. He thumbed down the handle with a click, whipped a leg around and sent the door crashing wide.

Instinct panned out. He leaped back as a long burst of autofire flayed the doorway, bullets whining and sparking off the frame. Bolan hugged the carpet as wild ricochets slapped off the door while it swung shut on its own momentum.

There was no other way in and down the stairs to nail them up their backsides, he knew, than to bulldog the play.

Bolan took the handle and flung the door open on the fly as he darted for the other side. A glimpse was all he caught, enough to see a head vanish beneath the lip of the top steps, boots drumming concrete, the waiting shooter hell-bent for quick descent.

Bolan was in, Uzi leading the charge. At the rail, he leaned over, heard the furious pounding of more hard-soled boots on concrete, angry and urgent voices slashing the air below. He threw himself back just as the muzzle of a compact subgun popped into sight two flights down. A voice raged behind the autofire in what he figured was a stream of Serbo-Croatian obscenities. Bolan bounded down the steps. He stayed close to the wall, putting quick distance between himself and the wild scream of bullets ricocheting off the metal banister, thudding into the ceiling, slicing off the concrete walls of the stairwell above.

Well, two could play that game of lucky shot.

Once the autofire below stopped, the Executioner went to the railing and held the Uzi over the side. There was enough space between the descending spiral of banister, and Bolan was able to make out the shoulders of a few hardmen down there. Firing the subgun one-handed, he held back on the trigger. He swept the Uzi back and forth, burning through the clip before he was rewarded by a howl of pain. Two faces then poked over the railing into the tight space three stories below. Bolan ducked back as they cut loose, then resumed his hard run down the steps, away from the hornet's nest of bullets raging across the flight of stairs he'd just vacated.

He stopped and put down the Uzi. Time for a power play, turn the tide, shave some numbers. He took both a frag and a flash-stun grenade from his coat pocket. It was risky, but he was gambling any residents using the stairwell right then would bolt through the closest door at the sound of all-out combat blowing their way. He armed the grenades, counted off two ticks as he made the railing. Just as he dropped the steel eggs over the edge, aiming for the narrow space that accommodated his drop, autofire roared up in his face. The shooter began shouting in his native tongue. The way the words were thrown away from him, Bolan figured the shooter had seen the falling grenades.

The Executioner hugged the wall, squeezed his eyes shut and put his hands over his ears as the steel eggs blew. Even covered from the full effects of the twin detonations, Bolan was still jarred to the bone. He could only imagine what had happened below.

Grabbing his Uzi, he charged on, ramming a fresh clip home on the fly. He was glancing at the floor numbers on the doors as he descended, read 6 on the next level when the same stench of death he'd taken in above filled his nose. Wheeling low around the corner, he found his play had scored three hardmen. Judging from the scarred walls, the door leading to the fifth floor blown off its hinges and the railing severed to display two twisted sections pointing up and in, Bolan knew both grenades had blown there. Beyond the property damage, he found three hardmen had nearly been sheared off their backs by shrapnel, exposed flesh resembling something like raw hamburger.

The Executioner caught the hammering booted footsteps, roughly three floors down. They were moving hard and fast, no coughing or gagging, no cries of pain. They had either a two- or three-story head start on the unfortunate trio before Bolan, or they'd hit the deck, riding it out. Probably both.

They were running now, he knew, for the parking lot, no thought to shooting back or standing their ground.

Bolan gave chase, nearly flying down the rest of the stairwell. When he came to the exit door, his decision was already made to bull his way out. Just the same, he was ready if a shooter waited on the other side. But the soldier was banking that his double-bill surprise package on the way down had them scurrying, tails tucked.

The Executioner put his shoulder into the handlebar and sent the door flying open. He missiled through and past, clearing the door and flung himself into a dive. The bullets never came as he landed on his belly, rolled up and swung the Uzi around, searching for any movement.

There was nothing but the rain slashing off his face.

He heard the engines roar to life and jumped up as two of their vehicles sluiced out of their spots, noses aiming toward the front entrance.

Some reckless determination at this point, and he might get lucky again.

On the run, the Executioner held back on the Uzi's trigger. They had to have seen it coming, as shadowy heads dropped an instant before the first wave of 9 mm Parabellum lead started exploding in glass. Tire rubber squealed as the wheelmen gunned the engines, gathered speed.

The Executioner charged ahead, his Uzi flaming, muzzle sweeping left to right, the fusillade drilling into the back windshields of the lead, then the trailing car. He was still running after them when the clip burned out.

The lead car swerved, hammering off a parked vehicle with a tremendous thud. At first look, Bolan thought he'd scored, then watched as the driver straightened his course, before throwing the sedan into a wide sliding turn at the end of the line. Bolan was changing clips, slowing his strides, ready to go at it again, but he knew it was useless to resume firing. Less than a second later both vehicles were blurs, racing through the rain, barging out of the lot. Making a mental note that they had turned right, the soldier headed swiftly for his vehicle.

On the way, he heard the distant but growing cry of sirens.

The cavalry was late.

Fair enough, Bolan thought, finding the way behind and ahead clear of watching eyes.

He owed himself the curtain call.

CHAPTER FIVE

"Watch your eyes!"

With Karina huddled next to him, Ceasuvic sat in the back of the sedan, clenching his jaw when he figured out what his wheelman was about to do. To his left, the Serb colonel found Davic slumped against the door, his worries over.

Ceasuvic shielded Karina's face with his hand, not wanting to see her face marred by even the slightest of superficial cuts. A hail of rain, wind and glass slivers was already whirling around the interior, the back windshield and passenger windows blasted out by their nameless stalker. The nearly constant pelting and infuriating discomfort reminded the Serb colonel that neither nature's rage nor a manmade storm were in any mood to back off. As far as he was concerned, there was nothing left to do but torque it up a few more notches. Professional soldiers and assassins to the man and woman, all of them knew they had to dig deeper now, especially if they thought they had nothing left to give.

There was no way Milenko could safely drive with

the windshield so cracked and pocked with bullet
holes, vision all but completely obscured. Milenko
snarled, then slugged the windshield with a black-
gloved fist. The first attempt took out only half a sec-
tion of windshield. Milenko cursed, then reached over
to start chopping at jagged chunks that didn't want to
give; the wheelman was caught up, it seemed, in his
brief display of rage. Cviic's head lowered in front of
Ceasuvic as shards tumbled to the dash and a new
storm of glass, wind and rain slashed around the colonel's face.

They had just crossed the 6th Street Bridge, he
noted, the great canyon walls of steel and glass loom-
ing above the dark mass of the Allegheny River. Taking his hand off Karina's face, Ceasuvic squinted into
the wind, spotted the Cadillac ahead with what remained of their crew, then checked their rear. Finding
no vehicles behind, he reached over and pushed the
door open wide enough for the task he was about to
perform. Half of Davic's skull had been blown away.
The glistening shards of bone and the exposed brain
matter dribbling down his face were grim testament
Davic hadn't been quick enough when their mystery
shooter had cut loose with yet another long burst of
subgun fire as they beat the final leg of evacuation
out of the lot. A few of the others, he seethed, had
also not been quick or good enough. A number of
questions would need to be addressed in the next few
minutes if he was to shore up their resolve, weed out
any doubt and remind them all, in no uncertain terms,
that lack of faith and determination was unacceptable.

No need to read between the lines on that score. Any waffling or excessive questioning of the program would be handled with a death sentence on the spot.

Ceasuvic braved the angry gust of wind and shouldered Davic out the doorway, sending him tumbling into the night. He glimpsed the body roll off the road, flop from view down what looked like a short embankment beyond the shoulder. He then read the anger on Cviic's face as they passed beneath a fleeting sheen of light. He could well understand his team's rage and fear, the shame over dumping their dead like excess baggage. But they all knew the standing order. If they died they were left behind, the wounded who couldn't go on likewise taken care of with a bullet behind the ear. It was simply part of the operational package: no mercy for slackers or the unlucky. That order included the colonel, who had made that announcement before heading out, just in case anyone was wondering. And at this juncture, if they found themselves facing down American policemen, they were ordered to fire on cops with all the savage skill they could command, even if that meant suicide.

Let the American cops come at them, if they dared. In his experience, Ceasuvic knew a soldier with no options was more often than not the best one to have fighting by his side. He had no problem bringing Bosnia-type slaughter to America's civilians, cops, whoever.

America could kiss his bloody Serbian ass.

Ceasuvic had one of the drug bags on the floor, but now that the car appeared to be unmolested and was on the way to the next stop, he barked, "The bags! Cviic?"

"I have one, you have one," Cviic answered. "The other three I accounted for before we...left."

Ceasuvic grunted, then pulled the cell phone from a coat pocket. He was hardly satisfied with events so far. Five bags, he thought, nearly one for each man he had lost, a million and change per head, not to mention the missing man, Radin. With a fury, he began punching in the numbers to the first of two urgent calls. The cell phone wedged against his cheek and ear, he fed his mini-Uzi the last clip. He heard Juric answer on the other end in Serbo-Croatian.

"It's me. I need backup. How many men can you round up?"

"Ten with me, maybe as many as fifteen with a call."

The colonel felt his rage mounting. On the other end he clearly heard raucous laughter, the heavy metal of American rock and roll, even caught the giggling from some whore.

"I am out here, Juric, my back to the wall, twisting in the wind with a noose around my neck, and you're having a goddamn party?" He waited while Juric bellowed the orders to kill the music, clear out the whores.

Juric came back to the sounds of scuffling feet from somewhere around him, the music dying. "My apologies."

"You know the nightclub off the Allegheny?"

"Our Italian friends."

"Meet me in the alley that runs off the main alley behind their building. How long?"

"Give me twenty minutes."

"You have fifteen. Listen. I need tools, and a shit-load of extra drill bits, do you understand?"

Juric understood. Ceasuvic needed hardware, and plenty of spare clips in 9 mm. There was no need to spell it out over the phone. Certain phrases and code words had long since been committed to memory. The colonel then ordered him to bring what they might need for work on heavy machinery. Again, Juric understood. At the next hit they would not only be beefed up with more guns, but would have grenades and RPG-7 rocket launchers at their disposal. Ceasuvic wanted to be juggernaut strong when they rolled out of Pittsburgh. The night was young, and it was already going very badly.

Thanks to one nameless bastard.

"Bring two extra vehicles, and make sure they are clean."

Juric knew they all used vehicles registered to owners on the fringes of their organization, all of whom took a small weekly fee to allow Ceasuvic's people easy access to transportation for as long as needed. In the event a cop pulled one of them over for a traffic violation, the owner would be contacted to state simply that he had loaned the car to the driver. If the vehicle was abandoned or linked to a crime, the owner would say it was stolen.

"My dogs are also barking. Bring muzzles so I can shut them up." A grunt on the other end, sound suppressors to be likewise delivered. Ceasuvic added, "One final matter. You and the others will be leaving town with us. That is a direct order. We have discussed this matter before. We're bailing. Are we clear?"

"We are clear. I have prepared for this moment, you know that. Anything else?"

"Yes, now that you mention it. As we discussed, you are aware the time would come when I would need all of your available funds. How much do you have on hand?"

"I am looking at the heavy end of a deep six."

Almost another million to bring the Russians. "I expect you to have it when I see you. Will that be a problem for you?"

"No problem."

"Good. You now have fourteen minutes," the Serb colonel said. He signed off and punched in the next series of numbers. "How much farther?" he asked Milenko.

"Ten minutes."

"Pull in the back alley when you arrive, go to the end, past the row of garbage bins. There is an adjoining side alley where we will meet Juric."

"I know it."

"He will have silencers for our weapons, spare clips. Cviic, you will stay outside and transfer the bags to one of two vehicles Juric is bringing for us. We go in even harder on the Italians, silent and fast. No talk. Just shoot. I want this one wrapped inside a minute, then—"

A voice came over the phone's receiver. The sponsor from Brighton Beach, the Serb colonel knew, never went anywhere without his cell phone. "It is me."

Ivan Churybik sounded his usual surly self as Ceasuvic heard him growl in Russian, "We were just talking about you."

"Is that a fact? And who is we?"

"'We' is someone who has come a long way to meet with you. I must tell you, he doesn't smile much, Colonel, and I don't think he came here to discuss your stock options."

Ceasuvic froze. He didn't need a psychic hot line to help him figure out the future. Weeks ago he had anticipated Brighton Beach getting their bowels in an uproar, had figured them to call in the bill collectors. For nearly a month now he had been late in the cash deliveries to Brighton Beach while he put together this night's master strokes. From New York, the cash was always flown back to Moscow. Of course, Moscow hadn't been receiving its full payments lately. Now this, a cleanup crew flown in for a face-to-face on top of everything else.

Ceasuvic needed to take the steam out of any problems headed his way. "I have your payment."

"That's three payments, Colonel."

"Three payments, yes. But there's been a change in plans."

"Why is it I don't like the sound of that?"

"There's no time to explain right now. Send your collectors to the farm. You know the one?"

"Of course, I do. I set it up as part of your operation."

Considering all the stress he was under, Ceasuvic forgave himself that small mental lapse. "I will be there with your money—" he checked his watch, factoring in the next two hits, the driving time to the farm "—four, five hours at the latest."

"Colonel, you better be there by the time my choppers land. You have explaining to do. These men sitting here, looking at me as if I were nothing more than a juicy slab of prime rib to be cut up and chewed very slowly, don't appear in the mood for a nice little sitdown over caviar and vodka. The Old Man sent special representatives, Colonel. You want me to spell out my problem here?"

Ceasuvic felt the knot in his guts. Moscow had sent a killing crew to collect. Well, the good news was he had their money—almost. "I have a fairly good picture of your problem."

"Good. Because my problem is now your problem. We're on the way. Again, if we have to wait on you…"

"Understood. We have much to discuss. One last thing."

"What?" he heard Churybik nearly roar.

"You have not forgotten the items I requested, I hope. The items that all of us—including the Old Man—discussed from the very beginning, I may add, of our joint business venture, comrade."

It was a feeler he had to throw out. A negative response spelled a certain death sentence. Of course, the Russian could always lie just to make sure he got his money, but the Serb colonel knew how to read the craftiest of liars.

There was no hesitation on the other end, no subtle shift in tone, although Ceasuvic wished he could read the body language and face. "It's been in the works, you know that, Colonel. However, there are some glitches on the other end. In time, they can be worked out, but I need some show of faith on your part before I move ahead with what you want."

Some of the tension flowed out of Ceasuvic. "You will have it. Until we meet." He felt their stares, could imagine all the questions they wished to ask, as he dropped the cell phone into his coat pocket. "Listen to me, all of you. From this point on, nothing and no one must stop us. I know we have someone hunting us. One man. No, I cannot tell you who he is. If he was FBI, one of any representing their DEA, ATF or whatever, he would not come up our asses shooting first, throwing around grenades. That is not their style. We have rights in this country, remember that. And it is our right to get what we want, that is the American way. If this shooter was FBI, we would have encountered a swarm of them as we left the building. Enough on this mysterious gunman. He is one man and if we encounter him again he will be dead. Now, in less than twenty-four hours we will be reinforced by two of our six cells. We will be full strength. I'm sure you're wondering about the call just now. Yes, we could have a Russian problem waiting for us at the farm. We deal with each step along the way. The bottom line right now is that we must secure the remainder of the cash from these next two stops. If we die here, the dream dies with us. If we leave without the rest of the money, the Russians will become our next and last problem. Are we clear on what must be done?''

Cviic and Milenko didn't hesitate as they nodded and answered in the affirmative almost as one voice. Ceasuvic turned and found the same fire he'd seen back at the condo now lighting Karina's eyes. She smiled, took his hand and squeezed it. She was so beautiful right then, a vision of his perfect warrior woman.

The Serb colonel resisted kissing her, aware his men were watching. Just the same, he silently savored this moment of bonded spirit among all of them. They were together, he knew, and they would march to glory in and beyond Pittsburgh, or die as one.

Under the circumstances, Ceasuvic couldn't ask for much more.

TIME AND CIRCUMSTANCE weren't on Bolan's side.

By the time he had reached the rental's trunk, hauled out three spare clips for the Uzi and pocketed another frag and flash-stun grenade, the soldier figured they had gained a two-minute jump. Another thirty seconds or so was gobbled up wrestling Frick up and behind the passenger's seat where Bolan could keep an eye on him in the rearview mirror. Then circumstance had called another brief time-out, when he thumbed on his tracking unit only to find the red dot frozen in place.

His homing bug was now attached to an abandoned vehicle. How the hell was he supposed to have figured...? Stow it. Time was running away from the Executioner.

Bolan had put six blocks between him and the condo high-rise, window down and listening to the growing wail of sirens behind, when he decided he would have to grill Frick under the gun and risk losing still more time. He slid the Taurus into an alley between two rows of town houses and killed the headlights. Reaching back, he snatched the rag out of Frick's mouth.

Just to underscore the point, Bolan hauled out the mammoth .44 Magnum Desert Eagle and thrust the muzzle in Frick's face. "One chance. Where are they going?"

Frick took his brazen time. "If I answer, what's in it for me?"

"You stay breathing."

"Some deal."

"It's the only one on the table."

"I help you, I know a lot. If you are some kind of American law, I want deal, protection. You have ways in this country, I see it on the TV all the time. Mafia hit men, turning in their bosses, they go on with good lives, new identities, write bestselling books, sit by pool all day, go dancing in nightclubs with pretty girls paid for by FBI. That's what I want. That's my one-time nonnegotiable deal. So, shoot me. Without me, you will not find the others in time.''

"You want quite the party."

"I take French fries with shake, too. No party, no help. Shoot me."

Bolan wasn't quite sure what he read in the thug's eyes. He didn't think Frick would roll that easily on his comrades, go loudly singing into a Federal Witness Protection Program. But the soldier didn't see where he had much of a choice. A last deep look into Frick's eyes, and Bolan knew the man would take whatever information he needed to the grave.

"What's your name?"

"Radin. Well?"

Bolan holstered the Desert Eagle. "I'm not the one who makes the final call, but I can put in a good word for you. It all depends on you."

Radin nodded. "Drive for the 6th Street bridge. I will get you there. Fear not," he added.

There, that was it. Bolan caught the laughter in Radin's eyes as he backed out of the alley. Where there was life, Radin was hopeful the only party in his future was a song and dance over Bolan's dead body.

Good enough, the soldier decided. If there was any laughing to be done at all, Bolan damn well intended to have the last chuckle.

THE ITALIAN MAFIA in America had undergone a drastic and startling face-lift during the past two decades or so. Gone were the glory days of the true

Dons, those street soldiers who had fought, killed and extorted their climb up the pecking order, those so-called men of honor slaughtering their way up the ranks, holding true to their dreams of someday landing the hallowed status of Godfather at best, remaining men of respect at the least. Between the FBI and the Justice Department stings—which had decimated the Five Families in New York, whose power and connections had once reached to Los Angeles—the Italian Mafia was now a wheezing dinosaur. Any bona fide tough guys who remained after decades of FBI and Justice Department savaging now languished in prison cells, nothing left to do but write their memoirs.

This day and age, those who had eaten up chunks of former Italian turf—Jamaicans, Colombians, just to name the shortlist—respected nothing but money and the power of the gun. Honor to them meant more notches on the bedpost than the other homeboys or hombres, as if a longer string of sexual conquests assured them status as men of respect.

The Serb colonel had seen them all, knew from personal experience their madness and indiscriminate willingness to kill their own and innocent people for more money and power. The newer so-called Mafias were a growing cancer, these more vicious criminal organizations all but flushing the Italian Mafia down the toilet.

Times had certainly changed.

Sure, there were others had who picked up the ball from the old men, and Ceasuvic was well acquainted with the new breed of Italian gangster. These days the crown had been passed to cousins, sons and other underlings, many of whom thought a college degree, or a bar fight or two, bought them stature as men of honor. They were top dogs, more bark, though, than bite. These days the new breed was more worried about holding on to the good and easy life of sex, drugs and rock and roll, even if that meant turning informant when the going got tough. These days they toted cell phones and pagers instead of revolvers. They sipped espresso instead of whiskey or aged fine red wine. They had their fingernails manicured instead of getting blood on their hands. Ceasuvic couldn't even recall the last time he'd seen one of them sucking up a bowl of linguine marinara. They ate other ethnic foods instead, as if mama's home-made veal parmagiana was one more thing to be buried with the past.

Vince Viscardi was at the head of this class of new Italian Mafia. And Ceasuvic was ready to give the nightclub owner a last hard lesson, straight from the old school textbook.

They gathered in the alley. Ceasuvic and the others braved the rain, as Juric began handing out the spare clips. The Serb colonel dropped three magazines into the deep pocket inside his trench coat. He counted the fifteen extra men, now emerging from the vehicles, that Juric had promised. Quickly, everyone began attaching sound suppressors to their compact subguns, Ceasuvic threading one on his Glock. He knew the layout; the club divided into the main dining and dancing room, with the offices and Viscardi's den partitioned in the back by a soundproof wall. He noted two Cadillacs, each with a driver. Cviic loaded their booty into the trunk of a Caddie while Ceasuvic handed out the orders. Karina would stay with Cviic. Juric was to leave seven men with the vehicles, arming three of them with RPG-7s and hand grenades. If a suspicious vehicle showed up, the order was to blow it into a hundred smoking sheets of metal. Cops showed up, likewise a big-bang hello.

When their subguns were tucked away beneath their trench coats, hanging from cords or special swivel rigs, the Serb colonel led them out of the alley. No bags this time, since this was straight butcher work. No conversation, no fuss, he hoped. They were marching down the main alley, the colonel finding mouths at each end clear, when the steel back door opened.

The big Italian in the fancy suit hunched in the doorway, clearly agitated by the thought of getting wet as he scowled at the sky. "You're late! Vince don't like to be kept waiting like this!"

Ceasuvic read the man's look as the Italian noted the visible lack of delivery bags. The Serb colonel brandished the Glock and shot the confusion off the face in the doorway. "My apologies for the inconvenience," he said, then flung the door wide and charged past the sprawled heap.

Class was in session.

THE EXECUTIONER braked the Taurus in the mouth of the alley. He found nothing but rain and an empty alley behind the nightclub called Viscardi's. It felt wrong, and he suspected he was late for round two. He slid the rental car into the alley, turned off the ignition and pocketed the keys. He gave Radin a look in the rearview, but the Serb didn't meet his gaze. Radin had been so busy giving Bolan directions—a left here, no, a right there—there had been no time for the soldier to get a fix on the situation at Viscardi's. Radin had jerked his chain.

Suddenly Bolan saw a door midway down burst open. He was out, Uzi subgun poised and leading him into the rain, when the shadow collapsed in the alley.

The show was over.

Bolan closed on the figure, heard the groaning and noted the expensive threads tattered by bullet holes. As if sensing his presence, the wounded man looked up at Bolan.

"You Serb bastards," he spit. "You want war... with us Italians...you rip us off..."

Bolan palmed his sound-suppressed Beretta. This gig was dead. The Serbs were gone. He caught the stink of death coming from inside the building as the back door swung wide on the squeal of rusty hinges. The soldier was starting to figure out what his enemies were up to, even though he was still left with a slew of questions he needed answered. This wasn't the time or place, but it was clear to Bolan the Serbs were running and gunning, robbing from and killing the links in the chains of whatever black-market pipelines they'd established. But why?

"I'm not Serb," the Executioner said, "and I'll pick up your war from here."

A single mercy shot from the Beretta, and Bolan backtracked to the Taurus. He caught Radin watching him. Bolan felt his blood running hot with anger, knowing the Serb had duped him. He wrenched open the back door, Radin bleating, "They are gone?"

Bolan jammed the Beretta into Radin's sac, looked the Serb dead in the eye and told him, "There are fates worse than death."

Radin started to scream, then looked set to pass out as Bolan squeezed the trigger twice. The expected agony never came, as Radin opened his legs and found the big man had shifted his aim at the last instant, pumping two rounds into the cushion just in front of his groin.

"There's always a next time," Bolan growled.

"Okay, all right. I became confused."

"Is your head cleared up now?"

"Yes, yes. I know right where they are going next."

"I hear one too many lefts here, a right there..."

"I understand. I know a direct route this time."

The Executioner leathered the Beretta. "So do I. And I'm not talking about the drive," he told Radin and slammed the door in his face.

CHAPTER SIX

"Do you know what real power is, comrade?"

At first, Ivan Churybik thought he was experiencing auditory hallucination. With all the worries distracting him, coupled with the fact he hadn't slept in over twenty-four hours, he wasn't sure he'd heard the man correctly. The underboss adjusted himself in the soft leather of the highback chair, peered across the short distance to find Duklov wearing an odd grin. Looking away from the unsettling expression, Churybik listened to the hum of the turboshaft engines and the muted bleat of rotor blades, blinking his tired eyes. Both sounds were muffled by the reinforced walls of the Tokinov Eagle's fuselage, but they had droned softly in his ears since liftoff, quickly becoming like music massaging his tweaked nerves, finally threatening to lull him into slumber. He wondered if he had just been caught napping by Duklov.

The underboss checked the cabin, wondering why he felt so unsure of his surroundings. The six dark shapes were spread out behind Duklov, his troops sitting comfortably, two of them smoking, two napping, two staring out the windows at the passing darkness. Weird, he thought. They did everything in pairs, no wasted or hesitant moves, in total lockstep, as if there were telepathic communication among the six, all of them silently aware of their two-man shifts no matter what they did. Why did that bother him?

Fear, he concluded, was pushing him to the edge. He became aware of just how utterly alone he was right then. His own bodyguard had been ordered by Duklov to fly by himself in the cabin of the other sleek black executive helicopter. Churybik wanted to believe the other near-empty Eagle was meant to fly the Serbs back to New Jersey, all of them one big happy winning team—meaning there would be no bloodshed. Since Duklov hadn't seemed inclined to conversation up to that point, there was no telling how this whole mess with the Serbs would be handled.

Which worried and scared the hell out of Churybik.

Churybik found Duklov running a hand over his bristled hair, as if enjoying the sensation of the porcupine-like needles against his palm. Churybik decided to check his own voice, asking, "What did you say?"

When Duklov repeated the question with an edge to the words, Churybik knew this was no dream. The reality check bolstered Churybik with a degree of confidence that he might pry some answers from Duklov.

Even still, Churybik didn't trust the moment. This was the first time Duklov had spoken to him since deplaning and exploding the awful question in his face. It was confusing, even frightening as he recalled how Duklov had grunted and waved him off as a litany of excuses started rolling out of his mouth as soon as they had climbed into the limo. Clearly, Duklov wasn't there to buy any sales pitch about the Serb problem. In this instance silence certainly wasn't golden.

Then the strange call had come from the colonel, after which Churybik had hung up and attempted to engage Duklov in conversation again, forced to tell Duklov they had to chopper to western Pennsylvania to meet the Serbs. The man from Moscow hadn't seemed the least disturbed by the abrupt change of plans. In fact, Duklov had shown no sign of emotion as Churybik had ordered the wheelman to drive back to the small airport just as they were within sight of the Manhattan skyline. Another hour's drive, sitting in their cold wall of silence all the way back to the choppers, only then to discover both choppers needed to be serviced due to some sort of mechanical failure. During the entire delay, Duklov didn't say a word, just going with the program, the other six smoking in twos, even going off to piss in pairs. Churybik found it all extremely spooky.

Now Churybik watched Duklov, feeling his nerves some more during another stretch of silence. Duklov was waiting for him to speak, Churybik figuring this was where he was supposed to play the confused lackey. The underboss went along with the game, asking what he meant.

Again, Churybik rode out the silence, as Duklov

began massaging his temples, making a strange face as if he were fighting the onslaught of a migraine. Finally, Duklov stopped playing with his face.

"Real power, Comrade Churybik, is the ability, is one man's will to make things happen, and to make them happen his way and his way only."

It was time to get some straight answers, the underboss decided. "May I ask, what things will you make happen with the Serbs?"

Duklov chuckled, shaking his head as if he were talking to an idiot. "Again with the Serbs. I am getting sick of hearing about these Serbs."

"They have the money."

"Indeed. So they told you."

"I believe them. That's good enough."

"For you, perhaps."

"Isn't picking up the money why you are here?"

"What you want to ask is do I intend to kill this Colonel Ceasuvic, this war criminal and his barbarians? The answer is we will see what we will see."

"They have made the Family a lot of money."

"Using connections, I understand, here in America, which you and our other associates in New York were grooming."

"That much is true. Viktor wanted to expand, and he felt our presence in other American cities would draw unwanted attention. The Serbs were his idea. I simply made some introductions through cutouts. I pointed them in the right direction and opened the door a crack. They have been extremely productive.

And as I said, they have made the Family another not-so-small fortune.''

"This is not only about money, comrade.''

"Feel free to clue me in. Is there some power struggle going on back in Moscow I am not aware of?''

Duklov chuckled. "Worried about your own place in the larger scheme of things?''

"Under the circumstances I think you already know my answer.''

Duklov heaved a breath, exasperated. "Viktor Tokinov is an old man. Yes, he is a rich and powerful man, with many important connections in the military, our latest version of the old KGB, the Kremlin. When was the last time you actually saw him in person?''

Churybik shrugged, silently embarrassed he no longer bothered to make a trip to Moscow every six months or so as he used to when he first arrived in America. Briefly he wondered if he had become so seduced by the money and pleasures the West offered that some part of him wanted to sever all ties to his heritage.

"Two years," he told Duklov.

"More like three. I checked.''

Churybik felt the anger flush his cheeks. "I speak with him on the phone. Four times in the past week as a matter of fact. I am sure you checked.''

"That would explain some things.''

"Explain what?''

"If you were to see him now, on a daily basis...well, it is sad to see the Old Man. It can even make sick a heart like mine."

Churybik liked that one. "Oh, kindly stop, before you make this grown man cry."

Duklov ignored the sarcasm. "Where once he was a lion among the hyenas, now he mostly waddles around his dacha all day like a dying water buffalo, his belly hanging out of his robe, scratching himself as if he were afflicted by some agonizing rash he can't get rid of. When he isn't raving drunk or stuffing his face with all the gluttony of starving hogs—are you aware he talks to himself? No, but, of course not. He even answers his own questions. I have heard him tell dirty jokes to himself, then burst out in laughter over the punchlines. Do you know that he will even diddle with himself in very important meetings with business associates? Most embarrassing, to put it kindly. Is this senility, you ask? Insanity? Advanced alcoholism? Some combination of all the above? I regret to report, I do not have the answer."

"That is not the Viktor Tokinov I remember."

"There is no duplicity here. I simply tell you what I see."

"You're telling me he is no longer fit to run the day-to-day business."

Duklov shook his head. "Not necessarily."

"If he was so incompetent, why would he know exactly when and how much the cash deliveries from my end are to be made?"

"He has moments of lucidity, I will grant you that. I still see at times the tiger I once knew in the KGB roaring back, ready to cut an adversary's throat himself, the fire in his eyes telling me he can still clear an entire room of barbarians with his bare hands and his will. That he, yes, still knows 'the power.'" Duklov shrugged, shook his head. "Perhaps he is simply just a tired, sad, old man. You know the history of the Family. Since his wife's suicide he is pretty much alone in that dacha. His only son, educated years ago in some fancy school in England, calls the father on a rare occasion."

"Spare me, I know."

Duklov forged ahead. "The son, this pompous ass, took his law degree and set out to be his own man. But instead of becoming the heir apparent, like Viktor wanted, he builds his own law firm. But since the only law in Russia is the law of Darwin, where brute force rules the day, well, Mother Russia has very little use for lawyers. So his firm folded."

"Tell me something I do not know."

"The son oversees some of the Old Man's business ventures now, only he keeps a discreet distance."

Churybik lost all patience, and rasped, "I know all about Vladin!"

"And the two daughters? Do you know Natasha and Svetlana recently married? Against their father's wishes, they wedded the hired help."

That was news to Churybik. The daughters had married what Viktor would consider nothing more than his common street soldiers. He began to see where Duklov may be headed with his runaround style of Q and A.

"You're saying there is potential trouble in the palace? A changing of the guard?"

"I did not say that," Duklov answered.

Duklov's act was starting to wear thin with Churybik, who felt a surge of sudden and surprising courage. "Why is it I have never heard your name mentioned? You seem to be very close to Viktor. You sit there and claim to know so much that is all news to me."

"Perhaps you should remain more available to Moscow and you would know more."

Churybik clenched his jaw. "I get the impression you are on some fishing expedition, comrade. Now, indulge me, I have some things to say to you. The Old Man built an empire from the gutter, with his own blood, one bullet and one obstacle at a time. I know, because I was one of his first soldiers."

"You were a corrupt policeman who jumped to the other side of the tracks at the first opportunity to make serious money."

"Whatever! I fought many of the same battles as Viktor, by his side and the whole way to the top! I earned my place as underboss in America. No games, no please and thank you and may I, boss. I will remind you we belong to the largest organization in Russia. I will remind you the Old Man has a special place in his heart for the Serbs, whether you care to hear that, whether any of us cares to understand this. Viktor's mind may or may not be what it used to be, but he still has ambitions, some of which I am privy to."

"Such as?"

"He made a deal with the Serbs. If nothing else, Viktor Tokinov is a man of honor."

"I will agree with you on that matter."

"Then we will end our discussion on that pleasant note."

Churybik began to mull over all the questions flaming to mind. First, was Duklov even telling the truth about Viktor and the daughters? Was he there to plumb the depths of his own loyalty to the Tokinov Family? Perhaps return with a scathing report about him, untrue as it might be? Even lie to Viktor that he was stealing from him? He wanted to hash all of this over in quiet contemplation, but he saw Duklov watching him, thought he even saw laughter in the bastard's eyes.

"Obviously you wish to say something else. What?"

Duklov's face hardened. "I am no second-string talent, comrade. I have become Viktor's eyes and ears. I know Viktor has political appointees he has groomed and who are waiting in the wings to take their place in Russian politics. I know he fears for the future of Russia, I know how much he despises America and this abominable joke they call NATO. I know there are VIPs our organization bought and paid for in this country. I know we are connected inside NATO. I know we are prepared to prove ourselves vital in the next American election for their President, with campaign contributions that will make the Chinese look stingy by comparison. Finally, I know precisely what it is the Serbs want to acquire from our organization.''

Churybik began to believe he could see the immediate future. Duklov was the only one who wanted more power. He would take the money from the Serbs, then kill them all, including the underboss. Then he would report to Viktor that Comrade Churybik was stealing. Of course, he would have to manufacture proof, but it would be easy enough to doctor the books in any number of their offices in Brighton Beach, perhaps coerce "collaboration" from one of Churybik's associates, and on tape. Or was it really potentially all that insidious? Was Duklov that devious? Or was he telling the truth about Viktor? Say he was—did it even make a difference at the moment? Moscow could have been light-years away. The more Duklov talked, the more Churybik determined to keep his hold on a life he had worked so hard to build in America, not to mention saving his own hide, if it came down to a them-or-him confrontation.

"I see you sitting there, Comrade Suspicious," Duklov said. "Am I the only one between the two of us who has the balls to stand up to these Serbs? Do you not admit they have had their own hidden agenda all along? They used us.''

"As we have used them.''

"I will grant you that. Item—the colonel contacted one of our competitors while in Moscow, when Viktor could not deliver what Ceasuvic now clearly intended all along to use on the NATO VIPs in Italy the other day. You do know about the three attacks?''

"I do. Say what you mean."

"Those warheads deliver nerve gas. These were prototype, little-known weapons not used since our own Afghanistan fiasco. We will not even sell them on the black market to our Arab buyers. Not even the CIA knows of their existence. Ceasuvic managed to finagle a deal with our competitors, who, I may add, are now permanently out of business. Anyway, these careless bastards who attacked the NATO party left behind evidence. If the Serbs responsible are tracked down and forced to talk, we could all be implicated, simply because the RPG-7s that launched the nerve gas warheads were left behind. Surely you can see they can be easily traced to the source."

"You do not give the Serbs or Viktor enough credit. Before they came to America their trail was covered. All of them, here and in Europe."

"Fool! Do you think forged passports, some plastic surgery, the fact the American authorities found no ID on the dead terrorists in Florida and Italy means they don't know who they are? I have sources in this country who tell me things not even their own media knows."

"Such as?"

"Such as all your vaunted Serbs have a tattoo on their arms of their country's double eagle head, the Yugoslav coat of arms."

Churybik felt his stomach lurch. Dammit, how careless of Moscow to overlook the one signature that could—

Duklov interrupted his thoughts. "So, the problem is more serious than you knew."

"We can work it out."

"'We.' We?"

"Yes, we. I tell you, Comrade Duklov, if you do anything in haste or in anger or in some attempt to further whatever ambitions you have, Viktor will show you just what this 'real power' is you seem to believe you have a monopoly on."

"I will be squashed like a bug, is that it?"

"To use your words—we will see what we will see. Now, if we are finished comparing the size of our balls, I wish to take a brief nap."

"Of course, we will end our discussion on that pleasant note."

But Churybik knew he wouldn't drift off into dark, worry-free bliss. No, he had too much to think about, sort out. Pain then knifed through his stomach as he felt his bowels rumbling, most likely his nerves suddenly working overtime on the two racks of lamb he'd devoured before heading out from Brighton Beach. He stood, felt the queasiness kick in, this abrupt discomfort fueling his anger. He was moving for the bathroom, when he heard the insolent bastard chuckle. "They say some men do their best thinking on the toilet."

Churybik looked away from the bristled blockhead, nodding to himself. Okay, they thought they were in charge of something, in control of all destinies concerned. Well, Duklov obviously didn't know the Serbs like he did, and they didn't know Ivan Churybik either, not by any stretch. If Duklov thought he was going to steal his crown, kick some Serb ass and demand from Viktor quick advancement up the Family ladder...

Well, Churybik could be pretty sure Mr. Smug and company hadn't brought any Tomahawk missiles to this particular party. Because if this turned ugly they would damn sure wish they could launch a few smart bombs from a safe distance. Ivan Churybik was no one's lackey, no man's peasant. He could be damn certain the Serbs felt the same way.

THE SERB COLONEL began to think of his master plan as his three-ring slaughter circus, the Ceasuvic Show. He was the ringmaster, his troops the lions, their victims the clowns. It was an image he wished to further indulge, if only to pump his resolve, keep the fire burning. Then he discovered their convoy was now rolling into the empty front parking lot of the Iranian mini–strip mall.

Time for the encore.

Slaughter ring two had seen Ceasuvic display all the bravery and brilliance of the master lion tamer, only the ringmaster had turned the lions loose on the crowd. In fact, it had been too easy, as he briefly recalled their surge into Viscardi's office, the Italian flustered at first, hands flapping, confusion all over his face. Seven Italian-American hardmen had been on-site, and, incredibly, only three of them were armed. After making a clean sweep, another two million stuffed in duffel bags, they were gone, on their marauding way to this last stop.

Ceasuvic took his handheld radio, raised Juric whose sedan drove point and ordered him to stop for a minute when he was midway down the far north side of the mall.

So far, so good, but it felt too damn easy. No sign of cops, nor any sighting of the nameless shooter. Even the driving rain had slackened to a mere drizzle, as if nature were looking to accommodate expediency. But in favor of whom? Or what? He wasn't sure what it was, but the Serb colonel knew trouble was lurking, some unseen disaster about to erupt in his face. He felt Karina take his hand.

"We are nearly finished here. We have done well," she said.

He held her stare, felt compelled to say something, but he couldn't find any words of assurance. His mental radar for trouble was blipping an angry buzz in his head. He felt a sudden grave concern for her safety, then wondered if he was simply indulging selfish desire.

"This time I come with you."

She said it softly, just a mere hint in her voice that she wouldn't be denied her role in the finale. He was about to object when she squeezed his hand. He saw the fire in her eyes, felt his heart racing, aware of what waited him later when they were alone.

"Stay behind me at all times," he told her and pulled his hand away.

When they rolled into position, Ceasuvic got out

of the Cadillac and began to issue orders. Juric and three others were to drive back and survey the front lot from the south end where there was very little light and raise him by handheld radio the second any vehicles showed up. Spare clips for their subguns were passed out all around, the Serb colonel designating the men who would wait with their vehicles. He ordered and received two frag grenades from Juric, then dropped them in his coat pocket. If it went to hell inside, he anticipated the Iranians might try to barricade themselves in the maze of stores and call for reinforcements. The Serb colonel wanted the finale wrapped up even more quickly than ring two. In and out, exit with a bow.

A last check of the lot behind them, and Ceasuvic settled back into the Cadillac. The strip mall was well off any main road, the closest suburban development a good mile away.

This was it, he thought, the final smashing of a small empire they had built for themselves and their Russian sponsors. In a way he hated to leave it all behind. He had enjoyed the money, the power, this life as—what, a Serbian Mafia boss?

Like the Italians and the blacks, the Iranians had been reliable and savvy business partners. Tabrij always had the cash ready when the colonel rolled in with a semi loaded with Russian grenades, AK-47s and other large and small arms. How the Iranians shipped the weapons out of America and landed them safely in the hands of their brother Islamic fundamentalists in their homeland was none of his concern.

They paid up on the spot, and that was all that really mattered.

The strip mall, he knew, offered the public everything from a variety of restaurants, to a sporting goods and music store, men and women's clothes, and hardware. And it doubled as one massive warehouse for the largest arms exporting operation Ceasuvic believed America had ever seen.

But it was time to move on to bigger things.

He felt the adrenaline rush as their convoy wheeled around the far end of the mall, rolling up into a staggered line near the loading bays. The colonel found two Iranians, armed with AK-47s, standing on a concrete ramp of the closest dock. A door opened from up there, and he saw the slight figure of Tabrij emerge, moving to stand between his bodyguards.

Ceasuvic stepped out of the Cadillac. "You have our money?"

There was something in the Iranian arms dealer's eyes and his stance that warned the colonel there was a problem.

"I do not see any truck. Where is my truck? You always bring the truck."

"The money!"

"The truck!"

Enough. Ceasuvic picked up the pace, cut the gap to the trio to less than twenty feet when he freed his mini-Uzi. His troops were once again in sync with his opening burst. Tabrij bolted through the door as his bodyguards were mowed down before they could cap off the first round.

Bounding up onto the dock, Ceasuvic found that the steel door was locked. He waffled for a moment, torn between fight or flight. How badly did they really need another five hundred large? He had at least that much stashed at the farm.

Screw it, he decided. This had just become personal, and he wasn't about to leave any loose ends behind.

"Stand back!" he ordered Karina and the other soldiers massed on the dock behind.

Ceasuvic armed a frag grenade, backed up and gave the steel egg an underhand lob.

No way, he decided, leaping off the dock as the blast thundered a fiery knockout punch of shrapnel through the door, would he be denied his encore.

Not a chance in hell.

Welcome to the show.

CHAPTER SEVEN

The Executioner almost missed the sedan. Under the circumstances it was perhaps understandable, but certainly not forgivable in Bolan's eyes. After all, the soldier had seen that his enemies were lions in human skin, knew they would show no mercy, hanging back while he pulled himself out of some brief mental lapse or silent hashing over of questions.

Moments before spotting the sedan, Bolan's mind had been burning with questions, just the same, over what little facts he'd gleaned from Radin during the thirty-minute run to the minimall on the northeastern outskirts of what appeared to be a new and fashionable suburb. Getting straight answers from Radin was proving just short of pulling teeth. On top of that, Bolan was considering the possibility some civic-minded suburbanite would dial 911 at the first sound of weapons fire. He had noted the closest homes were scattered up and down the surrounding hills, lights out, well off the beaten path from the minimall. Still, any combat in Bolan's immediate future would more than likely rouse them up there in dreamland.

The clock had already wound off at the alarm stage, the cops out in force, Bolan knew. Luckily any squad cars he had seen on the way out of Pittsburgh proper were flying past him in the opposite direction. The killing grounds were behind for the moment, but how long could his luck hold before roadblocks and drag-nets were thrown up, police choppers with search-lights swarming the skies, and he was nailed as a possible suspect? Of course, there was always Brog-nola to bail him out. But Pittsburgh Homicide was going to be left with more bodies than their morgues could probably store, with mountains of paperwork and weeks' worth of questions from angry cops for the first suspect they cuffed before this night was over. Getting snapped up by the police was the last thing the soldier needed, cooling his heels in jail while the big Fed used his considerable clout to free Special Agent Ballard and get him back on track.

The law problem considered, Bolan knew it was once again balls to the wall.

According to Radin, this was the Serbs' last stop on their killing march, then they were blowing Pitts-burgh, heading east with their loot. But why were they ripping off what appeared to be major distribu-tors in their crime organization? Why were they so willing to throw it all away? Where were they run-ning? Why run at all? What was on the back burner, if anything? How did the Serbs even establish these original underworld connections? Was some other criminal organization backing the Serbs? Those ques-tions—just the shortlist—put to him by the Executioner, and Bolan's hostage stonewalled. The soldier saw right through the smoke screen.

Radin did tell him the owners of the mall were Iranians with big bucks at their disposal, using the premises as a front to buy and export Russian military hardware back to Iran. Russian weapons? To Bolan it made more sense for Russian gangsters to sell weapons to Iranian fundamentalists back in the Motherland, or even to ship them down the Caspian Sea to the Iranian border. Unless, of course, there was a major surplus of Russian weapons housed on American soil. No response from Radin again, the Serb sticking only to the facts Bolan might need to wage war at the minimall, his prisoner glossing over major details pertinent to the campaign.

Radin figured there were as many as ten armed Iranians on-site during a drop of weapons by Kowalski. Kowalski? Bolan had asked. A shrug, a smirk, and Bolan knew Radin wasn't going to lay out the bigger picture without his party on the table. No doubt, Radin had a lot to spill, but the soldier knew the answers he wanted were on hold until he could get the Serb situated in more private surroundings.

Preferably someplace where they couldn't hear the man scream.

Lights out, the sedan was almost perfectly concealed in the deep shadows, wedged between the last store's wall and some shrubbery. Combat senses had the soldier make a quick surveillance as he drove into the empty parking lot. A look at the L-shaped mall, the storefront windows lit by the soft glow of security lights from inside, then he caught the vehicle out of the corner of his eye at the last possible instant before he would have driven past their surveillance corner. Before turning away, Bolan glimpsed dark silhouettes attempting to hunch beneath the dashboard. Two men, or three?

"Don't look at them," the Executioner warned Radin, but caught the Serb looking at their watchers for another moment. Seeing the ghost of a smirk from Radin in the rearview mirror, the Serb facing front, Bolan had the situation pegged.

The Serbs were on-site, possibly beefed up now by reinforcements. Radin had informed him they always met with the Iranians in the back where the loading dock received "Kowalski's" eighteen-wheeler. Comrade Hopeful was easy enough to read, and Bolan knew Radin would have to go into the trunk.

The Executioner rolled into the lot, drove at an angle away from the sedan's line of sight as he made a snap judgment call. He was hunting blind once more, with no fix on enemy numbers, the mall's layout beyond what he saw and knew, and no clear read on the Serbian motive. Why chain the pit bull now?

Throwing the wheel hard to the left, Bolan drove back for the southern edge of the mall. He unleathered the Beretta 93-R with sound suppressor, flicking it to single-shot mode.

Bolan fed the engine some power, sluicing away from the edge of the last store. He hit the high beams just as he whipped the front end around and bored the Taurus straight at the sedan. He jammed on the brakes, heard Radin shouting in Serbo-Croatian, but Bolan didn't have a second to even spare Radin a warning to hold on. The soldier glimpsed the wheelman's shock a heartbeat before he slid his vehicle into the sedan. The impact jarred the three shadows framed in the car's shroud, bouncing around their seats, their eyes blinking, mouths wide in a silent show of rage. Lights suddenly doused, Bolan rode out the impact, hearing metal hammering and the piercing sound of breaking glass. The battering-ram ploy worked, as Bolan's angry intro to the trio of hardmen left his vehicle intact, as planned.

Game time.

The Executioner was out the door and tapping the Beretta's trigger in a fluid now-or-never strike before they could get it together. His first three 9 mm Parabellum shockers cored through the windshield, catching the wheelman full in the face, obliterating that expression of angry surprise to crimson goo. The wheelman crumpled out of sight but not before Bolan saw the handheld radio fall from the splatter of blood.

Had the alert been sounded, or had he taken the wheelman out before he could raise the troops?

No matter.

The Executioner had called the play, and there was nothing left but to follow through. Surging forward, Bolan poured it on at near point-blank impact, tracking the next two shadows with a lightning fury, the Beretta chugging out a barrage that dropped them just as they barged out the doors. A stuttering burst of subgun fire still burped from the rear door gunner's sound-suppressed Ingram, but it was a wild spray touched off by a hardman dead on his feet and falling. Bolan tracked the shooter's fall, burning up the Beretta's clip, just to make sure.

Slapping a fresh magazine into the Beretta, Bolan jumped behind the wheel of his rental car. He bulled through the shrubbery on two leading beams of white, grateful the headlights were in working order. After this night, it would be a sorry slap by fate if a state trooper pulled him over for a busted headlight.

Bolan killed the lights. Rounding the corner, he found a single bulb shining midway down, the sheen casting enough light over the narrow service alleyway to guide his drive, aid him in his search for any moving shadows. He braked the rental in front of a garbage bin and turned off the ignition. The warrior needed to make several fast moves before he slipped into the mall through a side doorway.

The soldier grabbed the Uzi, hopped out, his senses cranked to a state of high voltage, his blood racing hot with adrenaline. Economy of movement, and he had Radin jacked out of the Taurus, trunk opened and the war bag hauled out. He checked both ends of the service alley, detected not even a flickering silhouette from either end. Shoving Radin into the trunk and quietly closing the Serb into the tight confines, Bolan unzipped his war bag. He took his small burglar kit with its lock picks and dropped three more frag grenades into a coat pocket. Finally he slipped the HK-33 assault rifle over his shoulder and loaded his pockets with spare clips. He wasn't about to get caught short this time.

Likewise he wasn't about to lose his war bag, either to his enemies or the suspicious scrutiny of the police if his luck soured. Quietly lifting the garbage bin's lid, Bolan laid the war bag on top of discarded boxes and plastic garbage bags. He listened to the night, but heard nothing to galvanize him into immediate action. He peered into the woods that paralleled the alley. When enemies were present, Bolan knew utter stillness and total quiet were usually the calm before the storm. Or maybe the Serbs were too busy inside the mall, mopping up the Iranians, a skeleton force left out back at the dock. It would be easy enough for a hard force to lay in ambush in the woods, but Bolan heard nothing but silence from that direction. No telltale crackle of feet over leaves, rustling of cloth, snapping of a twig. If they were going to shoot him up from hiding, he figured they would have done it by now.

Moving on, Uzi in hand, Bolan reached the first door on his way. He went to work on the lock, setting the SMG by his feet. There was always the risk silent alarms had been installed, but Bolan figured the Iranian arms dealers didn't desire any direct link to the closest precinct. Apparently, the Iranians provided their own security.

Getting in was no sweat, as Bolan made quick work of the lock. So far, so easy as the soldier glided through the doorway, into the shadows of what looked like a sports store. Easy would change soon enough, he knew. Given what bite the lions had shown him so far, the Executioner knew the Serbs would play true to ferocious.

CEASUVIC FELT it all slipping from his control. No sooner was he leading the way past the crumpled sheet of doorway marking their surge inside to charge down the long hall than he discovered Tabrij had already turned his office into an armed bunker. The familiar bark of AK-47 autofire flayed the colonel's senses, but it was being directed from two fire points, and just like that Ceasuvic couldn't be sure how many assault rifles were blazing away at his people. The doorway he crouched beside was being chewed up by a long fusillade of 7.62 mm lead. Tabrij was maybe all of ten feet away, howling and cursing in Farsi, but with his bodyguard or two in there firing like there was no tomorrow, Ceasuvic might as well have hoped to move in behind the shovel of a bulldozer.

He ordered his trailing soldiers to surge past him, bulldog the action—meaning take care of the gunners out in the mall who had come on the scene out of nowhere, and on the double. The Iranian shooters were blurry shadows in the colonel's line of sight, firing beyond the opening that led out to the mall. There were maybe three or four figures with AK-47s out there, but it was hard to tell with all the lead pounding at them from a sit-down area of benches and cabanas, with some little garden shielding the backup fire team from his invading force.

Then Karina decided to flank the other side of the

door, acting on her own, the colonel knowing full well she knew not to take unnecessary risks. It was all he could do to contain his outrage and horror as Karina bolted past him, his woman sweeping through the wood splinters and plaster dust shower being thrown into the hallway, not to mention braving all the lead shooting up the door.

Somehow, above the shooting and screaming, Ceasuvic heard Juric patching through on the handheld radio. As Karina hunched low and fired her Ingram SMG into the office, Ceasuvic plucked up his radio. Sound suppressors had been removed from all of their subguns for this round, Ceasuvic opting for full stopping power, hoping the mall itself would contain the racket of weapons fire from the outside world. He was forced to nearly shout as Karina's Ingram stammered on across the way. "Report!"

He heard something about one vehicle, which had moments ago rolled into the lot. A Taurus, Juric informed him, two men. It was their mystery hunter, he knew, but now there were two men. He was about to give the order for Juric to fall in behind the Taurus and alert Cviic trouble was coming their way, when he suddenly heard screams of fear and anger on the other end, followed by a short stuttering volley of sound-suppressed subgun fire. The following silence on the other end told the colonel everything he needed to know. He had already seen the lone hunter's work. Juric and company were history.

Just the same, Ceasuvic seethed over the loss of still more irreplaceable soldiers. Then he glimpsed one of his men nailed by wild AK-47 autofire as Vatar's Ingram jammed and he took a burst in the chest. He raised Cviic, told him a problem was on the way and ordered them to throw everything they had at the gunmen—now perhaps two shooters.

Ceasuvic needed this wrapped up, and two minutes ago. He was arming a frag grenade, when he saw his men shoot out the display glass of a jewelry store at the far end of the hall. Like flying eels they slipped between the jagged teeth of glass, firing on the run as they took deep cover inside the store, the Iranian autofire blasting out hanging shards on the heels of his soldiers. Dammit! He didn't need them pinned down, exchanging fire, both sides turning the whole place into a shooting gallery, waking up half of Pittsburgh.

It was going to hell fast, and Ceasuvic knew he had to seize back the initiative.

"Cover me!" he told Karina, who fed her Ingram a fresh magazine, then wheeled low around the corner and began directing SMG spray-and-pray all over the office.

As bullets slapped the doorway from return fire, Ceasuvic pitched the steel egg into the office, pulled back and hugged the wall. He was forced to roar at Karina to pull back and get down, resisting the impulse to hurl himself across the doorway to shield her body. The countdown to detonation had nearly ticked off when Karina flung herself to the floor. Her head twisted away from the wall, her eyes screwed shut a microsecond before the thundering blast spewed dust and countless steel bits through the doorway. He barked for Karina to cover him, but she seemed oddly distracted by the firefight down the hall.

"Karina! Did you hear me?"

"Yes, I heard."

What the hell was wrong with her? he wondered. She acted like she wanted to get down the hall and make some grandstand play against the Iranians. Knowing she would obey him, he braced himself for the charge into the office. The mini-Uzi held low and leading the way, Ceasuvic bored into the smoke and raining plaster, his senses spiked with the stink of blood and innards. He fanned the splintered ruins of the desk, found the walls pocked and scarred by shrapnel. Even if nothing else was going right, he discovered the frag blast had delivered some hope he could turn the tide of battle. It was a clean kill, he observed, with three bodies shredded and strewed before him.

"I'm clear!" he told Karina over his shoulder. She unfolded from her crouch inside the door.

Fax papers floating around his head, the colonel kicked through shards of debris, listening to the relentless autofire beyond the doorway. He cursed the stalemate outside, then found what he'd come killing for. The aluminum briefcase was partially impaled in the wall, hurled there and spiked through plaster by the frag blast. He wondered if it was some fluke of a laughing fate, but wasn't sure who exactly the briefcase might be mocking. He tugged the case out, found it dented and scratched from end to end, but otherwise miraculously undamaged. He flipped up the latches, opened the lid and found the neat stacks of rubber-banded hundred-dollar bills staring him back.

Finally, things were looking up.

He almost smiled, but they weren't close to a clean exit yet. He was shutting the case, about to march out into the hallway and order his people to frag the Iranians when he heard the tremendous explosion just beyond the doorway, so close it rocked the floor, shook the walls and nearly knocked him off his feet.

A brief scream of agony needled through the ringing in his ears. Oh, no, what had he just heard? That was no man's scream.

And he found Karina was no longer in the doorway.

He couldn't make his legs move for a long moment, his heart pounding like a jackhammer in his chest. He slogged ahead, feeling as if he were trapped in some nightmare he couldn't free himself from, his voice bleating with terror in his mind.

Fighting down the bubbling nausea in his gut, Ceasuvic forged into the acrid sting of the frag blast's cloud, his legs wanting to fold beneath him, ice-cold terror clawing through his bowels. He was out the door after what seemed like an hour, pivoting and about to run up the hall toward the firefight.

He froze, felt the wind empty out of his lungs, the air burning like fire past his mouth. He heard his mind scream in silent rage, felt the bile rush into his throat, everything spinning in a haze, the whole world flying off its axis.

He took several wooden steps forward, the din of autofire now sounding miles away in his ears. He breathed in the stink of cordite and blood, unable at first to make out the face beneath him as the bitter cloud ever so slowly thinned, as if to mock what he found. He teetered, felt himself wanting to collapse, heard the howl of rage building in his chest.

Features once so fair in classic beauty were sheared to the bone by shrapnel. He told himself it couldn't be, no way, what manner of injustice was this horror before him? But there was no mistaking the long blond hair, fanned out from the crimson head, soaking up a growing puddle of blood.

Ceasuvic felt his weapon slip from numb fingers as he dropped to his knees.

THE EXECUTIONER pulled the pin on a frag grenade, assessing the situation on the run. He had come up on the blindside of five Iranian shooters spread out in a circular seating area in the middle of the mall. The Iranians were pouring it on three, maybe four Serbs, who were blazing away with SMG weapons fire from the shadowy depths of a store that marked the end of a hall Bolan figured led back out to the loading dock. In all the chaos and confusion no one saw the new player take cover behind a support column.

Bolan gauged the range to the Serbs at roughly forty yards. He had his two opening moves mentally mapped out, but once both sides discovered his presence he knew it could all go to hell in a hurry. His blazing entry would have to be timed to the split second.

The Executioner whipped around the column. A stray Serb bullet sliced off concrete splinters an inch or so above Bolan's head, causing him to dip instinctively—and just as he released the steel egg with all the snap of a third baseman whipping a putout ball to first. He had aimed for the blasted-out opening, hoping to land the frag bomb in the middle of the store. Someone's wild round had temporarily saved the Serbs inside the store as the soldier watched the grenade strike the base of the storefront wall way too hard, then fly down the adjoining hallway, out of sight.

Not exactly what he wanted, but Bolan went right to work with part two.

With the Iranian shooters glued to their task and clearly framed in the overhead security lights, Bolan hit them with a long burst of Uzi autofire. He swept the SMG left to right, hosing them down on their blindside. They screamed in pain and shock, two of them spinning Bolan's way to attempt return fire, but their effort was driven back in faces spattered with blood as the Executioner drilled them with 9 mm rounds across their chests. An Iranian runner was now firing back at Bolan, sidling toward a storefront window, when the grenade broke a fresh wave of ear-shattering chaos across the mall. The smoke-and-shrapnel storm hit the Serb fire point. It wasn't nearly enough to take the Serbs out, but the surging cloud of lethal steel fragments held them down long enough while Bolan burned out his clip and sent the runner crashing through plate glass.

Slipping the Uzi over his shoulder, Bolan took the HK-33 and charged from cover. He didn't expect the going would get any easier as he secured cover behind a retaining wall.

It didn't.

Then something happened to jar Bolan's senses for several heartbeats. The soldier thought his frag blast had scored a hefty pound of flesh as a roar of agony washed over his position, the hideous sound clearly spearing in raised decibels through Serb return fire. Bolan wasn't sure what he heard, as his senses were assaulted by the long salvo of autofire, slugs whining off concrete, chewing up the bench beside him with all the crazed fury he'd seen the Serbs display at the condominium. It sounded more like the wailing of a wounded animal, slowly gored and gutted, than any amount of pain flying shrapnel could inflict on a man. Bolan pinpointed the eerie din somewhere beyond the cloud of smoke and cordite he'd seen pluming into the mall.

While he listened to the hideous noise and hoped for a lull in the leadstorm, he fed the Uzi a fresh clip, knowing he would need quick access to immediate backup.

Fire sprinklers hissed above Bolan, spraying him in cold drizzle as the soldier crawled down the retaining wall, leaving the hornet's nest of slugs swarming behind him. Then he heard several voices shouting in Serbo-Croatian in the lull of shooting. Ears ringing with the echo of autofire, Bolan popped up.

He couldn't believe what he saw as Kowalski rolled into the mall, out in the wide open, as if daring someone to cut him down. Serbian return fire was instant, driving Bolan back to cover before he could trigger his assault rifle. The big Serb was roaring at the top of his lungs, both fists, Bolan had glimpsed, filled with compact SMGs. The soldier scrambled back down the wall, backing up to fire but thinking better of it when he saw the weapons in Kowalski's hands jumping around as he sprayed the wall in mindless rage, the tracking line zipping straight for the Executioner.

Bolan ducked a millisecond before concrete shrapnel could flay his face, bullets snapping the air above his head. It was an incredible display out there of a man hell-bent on a suicide mission. He briefly wondered if the Serb had snapped under the pressure of combat or was blinded by shrapnel, but he couldn't be sure of what he'd seen. Whatever, he knew he had to do something quickly or they would swarm his position.

On his hand and knees, he crabbed to the far end of the wall and delved into his coat pocket. Palming another frag bomb, he listened to the voices beyond the wall shouting, clearly rife with rage and fear.

After another hiatus in firing, Bolan reared up. Four Serbs were wrestling with their shaved-head leader, the man bellowing, firing on, slashing an elbow into the jaw of one of his men. Just as Bolan was about to pull the pin, they managed to tug the crazed Serb around the corner, but he was still sweeping his weapons around even after he burned up the clips.

Bolan shoved the grenade back in his pocket, fisted his HK-33 and rolled over the retaining wall. The shouting intensified even as they were bailing. He anticipated a straggler or two, and a gunman appeared in his gun sights a heartbeat later.

The Executioner unloaded a 3-round burst into the Serb's face then charged up the short flight of steps.

Reaching the corner at the edge of the hall, the soldier took his frag grenade, pulled the pin. They were bailing once more.

This time the Executioner intended to see their exit stick, in blood and guts.

CHAPTER EIGHT

Securing cover near the corner's edge put Bolan's quarry momentarily out of his sight. But the Executioner didn't need to see the commotion at the far end to get a decent fix on the target distance. He figured a few feet here or there wouldn't matter much if he could roll the frag grenade in the general area of the stampede. Beyond that...

The Executioner whipsawed his arm around the corner, letting the steel egg fly. A long burst of subgun chatter added to the human racket, bullets gouging out plaster above Bolan's head. Two eye-blinks later the autofire was silenced by the smoky thunderclap.

Stealing a page from the Serb manual for close-quarters fighting, the soldier flung his HK-33 assault rifle around the edge. Bolan held back on the trigger, raking the muzzle left to right, up and down, using the single-handed spray-and-pray on which his Serbian adversaries had stamped their patent. When the clip burned out, Bolan shouldered the HK-33, grabbed the Uzi backup and bolted into the hall. He was pumped to maximum to wax any Serb—wounded or otherwise—who confronted him, but the soldier found himself charging only into a choking pall of dust. He halted at a doorway that was still framed in smoke. A quick check inside, and he found three bodies strewed around the demolished office. Satisfied his back was secure, he ran on.

Bolan kicked the warped shell of an aluminum briefcase out of his path. Clearing the smoke of ground zero, he discovered it was raining money, most of it shredded. The soldier indulged a grim smile. Mark him down for one Pyrrhic victory, he thought.

Before he reached the ravaged exit at the end of the hall he stepped past two mangled slabs of raw beef. Two more Serbs out of the picture, but it was small consolation, since the bulk of the herd had cleared the building. And how much backup was waiting outside?

Angry voices slashed the night, with autofire rattling on, but for some reason the doorway wasn't taking any hits. Bolan didn't hesitate, sighting a metal bin beyond the doorway. It was a short dash across the dock to his next point of cover, and the soldier didn't miss a step, surging ahead. He charged out the door to a bedlam of revved engines, slammed doors and autofire raking the back lot.

The Serbs knew he was coming, of course, and turned away from whatever they'd been shooting up. Bolan made the cover of the bin. Two heartbeats before another fusillade washed over the dock, slugs spanging metal and whining off concrete, Bolan caught a flash of the Serb leader. He was lumbering into the motor pool, carrying a body in his arms. After only a glimpse of a bouncing head and flowing blond hair, the Executioner understood the Serb leader's death wish. So, his first errant grenade had claimed the woman's life. So, the ante was upped. It was personal now with the Serb.

Bolan knew all about personal.

They were racing out of the lot, splitting up, if Bolan could accurately judge the sound of powerful engines gunning in opposite directions. Sporadic autofire kept pounding the dock but Bolan risked the flying lead, triggering his Uzi as a Cadillac blurred by his post. He had two frag grenades left, but a moment later he found he wasn't going to get the chance to shave a few more numbers.

Nor were the Serbs leaving Bolan any means of escape.

The Executioner was bolting down the dock, their SMG fire withering to a few wild rounds zipping past him, when he looked over his shoulder. He saw figures hanging out the windows of the luxury vehicles, subgun muzzles flashing, but no rounds were snapping his way. Then Bolan saw why he'd been met with token resistance coming out. He watched for another angry moment as they shot out tires on the smattering of parked cars, pumping still more rounds into the grilles for good measure.

Bolan flew off the dock as the screech of tires grabbing asphalt faded and hit the service alley running.

The Cadillac was nearly on top of the Taurus. Bolan saw an arm thrust out the back window and recognized the object in the hand a split second before he triggered the Uzi. Bolan's short burst of 9 mm Parabellum shockers stitched the arm, but the intended damage was already en route. The Cadillac roared past the Taurus, eating up the short distance before the wheelman whipped the vehicle around the far corner to finish the vanishing act.

Bolan bit back a curse. There was nothing the soldier could do but brace himself and hug the wall as the grenade erupted. Whether or not his Uzi fire had deflected the toss at the last possible moment became just another hard lesson in frustration. Had the frag bomb rolled up under the chassis, Radin would have been cooked and diced. As it stood, there was plenty enough ensuing damage for Bolan to curse his luck, just the same. The fireball boiled beneath the rental's bumper, lifted the front end while smoke and flames belched up through the engine block, shearing the hood up and off. Metal was still banging off the wall, flying into the woods for another dangerous moment as Bolan charged for the trunk. The stink of burning fuel and crackling flames choking the air, Bolan knew he only had a few seconds before the gas tank blew. The soldier could only imagine what Radin was suffering, as he heard the pounding of feet on metal from inside the trunk, the muffled shouting between fits of coughing. He keyed open the trunk to a billow of black smoke and grabbed Radin.

After running maybe a dozen steps, yanking Radin

along, Bolan heard the gas tank go in a peal of thunder, superheated flames reaching out, as Bolan flung Radin to the ground and nose-dived.

Moments later the soldier leaped to his feet, his swift backtrack helping to clear the cobwebs as he steered clear of the leaping tongues of fire. He hauled the war bag out of the garbage bin, straining his ears to listen to the night.

"Now what?"

Radin was on his feet, hacking his brush with death out of his lungs.

Bolan couldn't make out any wail of sirens, but with the ringing in his ears and the angry lap of fire he couldn't trust his senses at the moment.

With mounting urgency, the Executioner grabbed Radin by the arm and led him toward the woods. "We walk."

VUK CVIIC WAS spooked.

There was bad news, he thought, and then there was very bad news. Aware his fear was showing, he glanced at Milenko who took his eyes off the interstate long enough for Cviic to read the grim resolve in their wheelman.

Not much fear there at all, Milenko's seasoned nerve under fire was plain enough for Cviic to read. He wished some of Milenko's cool would rub off on him. What was he thinking? Cviic wondered about himself. Had he lost his balls to tackle whatever lay ahead?

As paramilitary commandos trained to charge

through any front door and clear out rooms choked with armed combatants, fear was supposed to motivate them, Cviic knew, to do the impossible, push themselves to the limits of mental and physical endurance when lesser men would fold and head for the showers. Fear as motivator was always a soldier's best friend, next in line, of course, to his willingness to kill his enemies. Right then Cviic felt anything but motivated and willful. All he felt was cold and gnawing fear, the kind of fear that paralyzed, made men second-guess themselves, get themselves killed.

First, he bitterly mulled the bad news. Forget that the skies had opened up once again to now hammer their vehicles in a relentless assault, obscuring visibility to near zero. Never mind that they'd lost still more men, not to mention the little matter of the briefcase with five hundred grand blown to hell by a grenade blast, the last hit on the Iranians just one big face-slapping fiasco. Scratch one badly wounded Pitritic, his shot-up arm bleeding all over the Cadillac next in line, a possible amputation in the man's near future. Stow next to the backlist of worries cops roaring up any second, forcing them into some suicidal showdown. Last, but hardly least, put on the back burner some one-man killing crew, a nameless adversary who was showing up wherever they went, this brazen relentless bastard hell-bent on heaping new misery on their shoulders at each turn.

Cviic again heard the snarling from behind. It was a sound like something he would expect to hear from wild beasts. He shuddered, the snarls growing in angry pitch. He touched the handheld radio, wanting nothing more right then than to talk to his comrades again in the other vehicles. He caught Milenko shaking his head.

"I know where we go," Milenko said. "I-79 comes to Interstate 80. East. Not too far."

"I was thinking about checking on Pitritic."

Milenko shook his head again. "He lost much blood," Vetalic said. "I do not think he will make it. Let him drink in peace and die in dignity."

Whatever.

The wild beast growled on. Cviic heard his own breathing grow heavy, his heart thumping in his ears. Against his will, he turned and checked on the very bad news.

Cviic couldn't believe what he saw. Their leader was cradling her head in his lap. His vampiric teeth were bared in an expression Cviic couldn't read, but knew wasn't good. It had been what? he thought, thirty minutes since they'd hightailed it out of the mall's lot? Ceasuvic hadn't uttered a word since. He just sat there, rocking her gently, snarling, sometimes rolling his head around his shoulders as if he were merely working out the kinks. It was an ugly, unseemly display all by itself. This was a man Cviic had seen put whole villages in Bosnia to the torch, line up every man, woman, child and dog over a mass grave and proceed to wipe out entire bloodlines in a matter of minutes. And now this man he had come to fear and respect like a god was actually dipping his fingers into the bloody puddle where a face had once

made men gape in lust. It was all Cviic could do next
to even dare consider reaching over the seat and slapping the colonel out of it. Ceasuvic began smearing
her blood over his skull. Running his hand over the
red ruins again, he daubed crimson splotches on his
cheeks. The colonel was out there in some psychotic
ozone, Cviic feared, oblivious to all and anything except for his bizarre ritual of blood painting. Who was
going to lead them if he didn't snap out of his grief?
And were they going to the Russians like this? Like
whipped mongrels, short of promised cash, their
feared leader lost in anguish like some lovesick
schoolkid, and wearing his lover's blood like a mask.
Who was going to explain? Who could?

"I see you, Vuk."

Cviic found Milenko watching him. He saw the
strange smile flicker over the wheelman's lips, the
eyes fired up by either laughter or hatred, Cviic
couldn't be sure. Then Milenko's cheek twitched, the
mouth slashed wide in a ghoulish grin. What the hell?
Cviic thought Milenko was about to burst out in
laughter.

In a low voice Cviic could barely hear above the
rain thudding off the roof, Milenko said, "If the Russians give us any crap whatsoever, I fear worst for
them. No mistake."

Cviic watched the odd fearsome expression as Milenko looked in the rearview mirror, nodding as if he
approved of the psycho show in the back seat.

"I just remembered."

"What?" Cviic asked, finding himself on the edge

of the seat as he heard the sudden concern in Milenko's voice.

"If a policeman pull us over... Well, none of us has a driver's license."

Cviic slumped back, heard the air rasping from his mouth, as he watched the smile break over Milenko's face. Now Milenko was out there in psycholand. And if the others were over the edge like this?

This wasn't good, he thought, flinching at a peal of thunder and another round of snarling. Not good at all. They were all dead men. It was simply a question of when and where, and who would kill them first.

THE EXECUTIONER gave Radin a shove that sent the man stumbling into the darkness. Bolan followed Radin out of the rain, shut the door, then locked and chained it. He hit the light switch by the doorway. It was an efficiency-size motel room. Nothing fancy, but it would serve Bolan's purpose for interrogation, with comfort and privacy enough to raise Brognola and Stony Man Farm.

"You have quite the way with the ladies. Offer me money like that, I ask if you have more."

Bolan ignored Radin's wry grin, but told him, "Somehow, that doesn't surprise me."

"There are still some good souls left in the world, like that fat girl. Is that what you're implying? They say fat girls make very good lovers. They say fat girls have very generous hearts—"

"Shut your hole."

The soldier told Radin to take a seat by the nightstand. He pulled the curtain back and saw that the young woman in the Honda Civic was already gone. Bolan indulged a moment of gratitude. Karla had proved the proverbial gift horse. It had been a stroke of luck, all around, first finding the all-night convenience store just before the on-ramp for Interstate 79, walking in just as the rain came back with sudden and renewed fury.

At first, Karla had looked suspicious, two big men in black stepping in, no one else but the three of them in the store, Radin with a face so battered and swollen the Frankenstein monster would have looked handsome in comparison. Then she spotted the cuffs on Radin.

Bolan had flashed his Justice Department credentials, told Karla he needed her help, and that there was five hundred dollars in it for her. She refused the money, Bolan having read the simple Good Samaritan in her right away. She quickly handed over some food items, cigarettes and even unlocked the beer cooler when Bolan asked. The six-pack was for Radin, Bolan hoping a smoke and a few beers would help loosen the Serb's tongue. They were on foot and needed wheels and a motel room, Bolan told her. No problem, she was bored. No one was coming in because of the storm, so she'd lock up and drive them.

She didn't ask questions either, as Bolan had her drive north about forty miles to a place called Slippery Rock, the soldier needing to put as much distance from Pittsburgh as possible. Finally, when she dropped them off at the motel's office, Bolan thanked her, saying, "You never saw us." Karla nodded that she understood, and Bolan left the five hundred dollars on the seat anyway, closing the door on her before she could argue. The desk clerk had proved himself mercenary, but he had been another step in the right direction to get Bolan going again. The clerk had told Bolan he could, in fact, get him a car at that late hour, since his brother was looking to unload a '67 Ford Galaxy. Three grand. Bolan threw in an additional five hundred from his walking-around war funds and promised another two hundred if delivery happened within the next hour. Mr. Helpful would get right on it.

It was time now to get down to business.

Bolan unzipped his war bag and hauled out the briefcase with its satellite link.

"They pay Justice Department agents pretty good in America."

All right, Radin was in a talking mood, Bolan decided. At the moment, all the soldier really knew was that the Serb killing crew was heading for a farm, some safehouse east off I-80. The soldier settled the sat link on the dresser. He dialed the combination, then opened the aluminum case.

"How about one of those beers and a smoke?" Radin asked.

Bolan pinned the Serb with a grim look. "I'm about to put in a call. What you do or don't tell me in the next few minutes will determine whether you get your party."

Radin nodded. "The beer and smoke."

Bolan uncapped two beers, putting one down by the sat link for himself. He moved across the room, placing Radin's beer and the cigarette pack on the nightstand.

"The handcuffs?"

Bolan pulled out the Beretta. "Stand up."

"Is that necessary? What, am I going to attack you, beat you up?"

"Indulge me."

When Radin was uncuffed, back in his seat and working on the beer and cigarette, Bolan said, "Let's talk."

Radin winced, attempting to smoke and drink by working around the spots where Bolan had knocked out his teeth. He cursed the pain, drained his beer and asked for another. Bolan tossed him another bottle, then the Executioner sat in the chair by the dresser and placed the Beretta within easy reach. He sipped his beer.

Already Bolan was feeling some wear and tear, and he knew this campaign had only just begun. Now that the running battle with his enemies was on hold and he was forced to sit still, the soldier felt a bone-numbing weariness settling over him. He didn't need to languish through this hiatus any longer than necessary. Bolan needed to pick up the opposition's trail, hopefully right after he touched base with Brognola and the Farm and ran down the list of what he needed from intelligence and tracking, to restocking depleted firepower. He also needed to locate the nearest airport for delivery of the items he required, and he'd have Brognola fly in a blacksuit or two from the Farm to pick up Radin. He also wondered if Jack Grimaldi, Stony Man's ace pilot, was available. The soldier wanted one-hundred-percent preparation, logistics paved, just in case a trip overseas was on the agenda.

Radin glimpsed the Beretta, choked down another swallow of beer, then said, "Ask your questions."

"We'll start with your humble origins."

"My what?"

"How you and what I think are a bunch of war criminals managed to get out of Yugoslavia and land in America."

Radin chuckled. "Pretty much all we have become, we owe to the Russian Mafia. And, I understand, a few Americans who have—how do you say— 'clout'."

Bolan felt his guts tighten. It was often said that the truth could be ugly, that if a man didn't want to know the answers to a fearful or even repulsive revelation he shouldn't ask the questions.

In Bolan's world, he knew the truth was often a nightmare. And if his suspicion about what the Serb might reveal in the coming minutes panned out, he was sure the truth would prove downright sinister.

"Keep talking."

THE FARMHOUSE WAS large enough to accommodate an Amish family of twenty. It was planted in the middle of wooded rolling hills, with the closest neighbor about two miles in any direction. Plenty of room and privacy to spare. He'd originally bought the safehouse through a cutout with the express desire for spacious comfort inside while keeping a good distance from any curious neighbors who might question the presence of armed strangers showing up in their quiet farming community.

At the moment, Ivan Churybik knew he could kiss off any creature comforts, scratch any intentions of playing the gracious host. The truth was he could feel the walls closing in. Hell, he thought, he could have been in a fifty-room mansion, clear on the other side, and still feel the silent rage building around him.

Churybik paced the dining-room area. He looked at his watch for the sixth or maybe seventh time in the past thirty-two minutes. He walked to the bay window and stared out at the darkness, silently urging the Serbs to show up.

"They are late."

Churybik looked at Duklov, who sat at the head of the massive oak table. The Russian underboss felt all five pairs of eyes boring anger and impatience into him. The other two goons, he knew, had pulled sentry duty, ready to come running as soon as the Serbs rolled in. But when would that be? And if they didn't show soon, or even at all...? At least, he thought, the choppers had been refueled from the bins rolled out of the barn. Now what was he thinking? That he could excuse himself and just fly back to New Jersey, Duklov could take it from there? Dream on. Duklov looked set to send him on his way, all right, but only on permanent vacation from the barrel of his AK-47.

"They'll be here," Churybik said, feeling compelled to speak, his nerves tweaking even more at the sound of Duklov drumming his fingers on the table.

"They are late."

How many times did Duklov have to say that? Churybik shot a nervous look over their AK-47s. Duklov had his own assault rifle laid out on thè table in front of him, his goons with weapons slung around their shoulders. Churybik's fear and paranoia started getting the best of him, as he imagined they looked ready to cut loose with autofire his way if they had to wait another five minutes.

At least the rain, thunder and lightning had finally stopped, all the earlier noise from angry Mother Nature having wound Churybik's nerves even tighter. He grunted at the childish stupidity of such a thought.

The two sentries marched into the dining room.

"Vehicles approaching."

"Show them in," Duklov said.

Churybik felt himself relax a little. He decided it was necessary to play diplomat right then, smooth the way for the Serbs. Duklov and the goon squad were human time bombs, one wrong word or look away from blowing up.

Churybik cleared his throat. "All right, now let's everybody remember this is business. Business. Nobody's going to go off half-cocked on anybody. No scenes, no hysterics, so let's everyone get the chips off the shoulders, hear them out."

"They are late."

Churybik gritted his teeth. Screw it, what was the use? If it was going to hit the fan...

He watched the open door to the living room, listened as car doors slammed shut outside, the sound of boots crunching over gravel. He waited, his heart racing, his stomach churning. They came in two at a time. They carried large duffel bags, Churybik counting them off, six, seven bags and more. So far it looked good. Churybik knew those bags were stuffed with cash. They were toting compact subguns, though, their faces as grim as hell, a few of the Serbs even cut and scratched around the eyes and cheeks. Clearly, they'd been in a fight, and Churybik was already fearing the answer to his question on that score. Then a Serb with bloody rags wrapped around his arm staggered through the doorway, bleeding all over the carpet, lifting a nearly empty bottle of vodka to his mouth. The guy chuckled quietly to himself, all but telling Churybik he was drunk out of his mind. And where was the colonel?

Duklov didn't look up as they filed into the dining room. Churybik felt the heat rise a few more degrees as the Serbs began to dump the duffel bags on the table. No hellos, no apologies for being late. Duklov maintained his statue presence, but Churybik was busy reading the Serbs, who acted as if the man from Moscow was nothing more than garbage that someone else needed to take out.

"Where's the colonel?" Churybik asked.

The Serbs didn't answer; instead just fanned out by the bay window. Churybik's head buzzed with questions as he broke their angry stares, then his heart lurched as he saw two of the Russians drape their hands around their AK-47s. The fuse to human dynamite was fast sizzling down.

Churybik then smelled the air as the Serbs crowded around him. They reeked of dried sweat, rain-mildewed clothing and blood. The knot tightened in Churybik's gut. Something smelled, for damn sure, but it wasn't their ripe bodies, he knew. Something was seriously messed up.

Churybik waited a full half minute, impulsively checking his watch, Duklov continued drumming, but his fingers were hitting the tabletop with a sudden furious rap. The underboss felt the heat rising around him.

Then Churybik saw the big shadow step through the door. He blinked, not sure what he was seeing, uncertain at first if the figure coming his way was even the colonel. A harder search beyond the white orbs staring back at him, and Churybik knew the face covered in some shiny substance belonged to Ceasuvic. Churybik's confusion and growing horror didn't stop there. He saw the colonel was carrying a blood-soaked body in his arms, a mane of crimson-streaked blond hair flowing from a face. Churybik felt the lump stick in his throat. The dead woman, he knew, was the colonel's lover, Karina. She was the only female "immigrant" under Moscow's original export, the rumor being Ceasuvic wouldn't even come to America without her.

Churybik felt sick. He caught a strong whiff of the

coppery stink as Ceasuvic entered the dining room, and Churybik knew that was blood all over the colonel's face. Blood? The colonel's blood, or her blood? He couldn't find his legs or his voice as his mind tried to fathom this horror show. In disbelief and shock he watched as this vision from hell laid the woman's body on top of the duffel bags.

To his credit, Duklov didn't blow up. "What is the meaning of this?"

"Shovel."

Churybik saw Duklov bare his teeth, his shoulders trembling with rage. "What?"

"You have shit in your ears, you asshole?" Ceasuvic snarled. "I want a shovel and a blanket, and I want it now!"

"Why, you insolent Serb piece of—"

Churybik saw it coming, somehow found his voice as Duklov snapped up his assault rifle, the Russians and the Serbs filling their hands with weapons at the same instant.

He might as well have been screaming from Mars. But Churybik had to try, as he threw himself between all the tracking muzzles of AK-47s and subguns and roared, "No! Wait!"

CHAPTER NINE

The promised callback came fifty minutes after Bolan touched base with Brognola, and he quickly brought the big Fed up to speed along with his list of needs, then signed off to ride out yet another hiatus. The soldier had roused Brognola from bed at his suburban home, and the big Fed still sounded tired and cranky. Bolan knew his friend was a staunch patriot, a work-aholic, a man dedicated to the tireless and never-ending pursuit of justice. Stress and interrupted sleep came with the job description. Whatever grumbling Bolan heard, he could be sure Brognola was suffering from a bad case of raw anger over the terrorist attacks that could now be linked to Serbian war criminals.

The Executioner slipped on the headset with throat mike.

"Sorry it took so long, Striker."

"No sweat. I'm waiting on wheels anyway."

"You sound maximum stressed."

"Stress keeps me running."

"Sounds like this time out you'll need all the angry fuel you can throw on the fire."

"Whatever it takes."

"Okay, down to business. Grimaldi was on R and R in Miami Beach. Kurtzman raised Jack on his secure cellular at some strip joint."

Bolan cracked a rare warm grin. "Everybody's having a party these days."

"Maybe it's the booming economy. What can I say?"

"I'm sure I'll hear all about it from Jack."

"I'm sure you will. Anyway, Aaron told him to put down the piña coladas and get his gear together."

"Jack's a trooper. I'll buy him a night on the town if we see this through to the other side."

"He'll appreciate that. All right, I scrambled a DEA jet through a source of mine down there. Jack should be pulling into MIA as we speak. The other items you want are en route. A Gulfstream has left the Farm, two blacksuits to pick up our friend. So the baby-sitting detail will be over shortly. I know, you'll be real sorry to see that Serb sweetheart dumped in my lap."

As if he knew he was being talked about, Bolan saw Radin waving his arms. The Serb was working on his fourth beer and it was starting to show, his eyes going mean, his attitude surly.

"Our friend wants to know about his own party," Bolan told Brognola.

Brognola grunted. "Why don't we just drop him off at the Playboy Mansion with a free grab-ass pass, Hef's special guest of honor. Tell him I'm working on it, but I'm not making any promises."

Bolan relayed the message to Radin who ripped off a short but savage burst of American-style cursing.

"I heard that," Brognola said. "I tell you what, considering what his comrades have done, he gets here and gives me any crap I'll jump up and down on his nuts so hard they'll hear him scream all the way to Serbia."

Bolan decided to skip relaying that particular message. Radin was starting to irritate Bolan anyway. The last thing he needed was the Serb squawking and stonewalling when they still needed to pick his brains. If they had to tell Radin a lie or two along the way to keep him talking, so be it.

Brognola informed Bolan of a small airport Kurtzman had located. It was off I-80 in the direction the soldier would head next.

"I'll find it."

"Aaron will keep up with his usual sorcery, tapping into databases, adding two and two. He'll be faxing whatever sat pics he can come up with of the general area in question. The Gulfstream has state-of-the-art surveillance and tracking packages onboard. They'll do a flyover and try to pin down this farmhouse. Layout, numbers, the works. They'll also break into all police frequencies, local and state, find out if any friendlies are headed your way. I have to tell you, I'm getting a headache just thinking about having to make the call to the FBI in Pittsburgh. The kind of wreckage you left behind, the FBI SAC will light a blowtorch in my ear."

"No civilian casualties."

"Right, a positive upshot. They just burned down a black drug dealing crew the DEA had a nine-month ongoing surveillance against, then slammed the door on the newer, kinder and gentler version of the Italian Mafia there before wiping out a major Iranian weapons export ring."

"What can I say? They're equal opportunity killers."

"Yeah, and they're politically correct, too. I'm sure the FBI will appreciate these Serbs taking a big bite out of crime in Pittsburgh. Okay, while we're on the Serbs, Aaron tapped into both NATO and UN databases. In case you didn't know, they both keep extensive files on war criminals, dictators, the whole range of international thugs who might see fit to do some rape and pillage on any Red Cross outfit sent to a country considered hostile. Well, Yugoslavia and its former provinces are at the top of the list. Our Count Dracula is, indeed, one Colonel Vidan Ceasuvic. He was known as Vidan the Impaler, ran his own death squads of paramilitary types, corrupt police with bones to pick with the locals shoved in his pocket, you know the type."

"I've seen enough of the man's work to get the picture."

"I'll bet you have. But the read we've got on this guy from our end, well, you can spell ruthless and insane in caps. Hell, the word on him is he even had two prisons in Serbia emptied out of its worst animals and cut them loose on the Muslim population of Bosnia like the proverbial mad dogs. They're still, I understand, digging up mass graves over there, and I'm talking five, six, seven hundred bodies. Now get this. What was somehow kept out of the world press was that this guy would sometimes have his intended victims whittle large stakes to a sharp point, grease up the tips with pig fat—"

"And impale them."

"I guess he has some sick fascination with the Romanian tyrant, Vlad, of the original Dracula fame, or whatever."

"It fits his style."

"Moving on, Aaron did a computer workup, comparing Roman Kowalski to Ceasuvic. He says whoever did the plastic surgery was a real butcher. I'll skip the rest on that medical score, but it's our Count Dracula. Working my own sources at Langley and the Pentagon, both myself and Aaron confirm that at least sixty wanted Serb war criminals somehow disappeared from Yugoslavia to parts unknown, and as recently as Kosovo. Not even the CIA has a line on them. Something may be a little hinky out there in spookland. Knowing your history with the CIA, I'll do my damnedest to try and steer you clear of any cutouts along the way. No promises."

"I understand. I'll take what I can get."

"Now you tell me there's a Russian Mafia connection."

"Viktor Tokinov."

"Aaron's also working up the background on the Tokinov family. Keep your sat link as close by as possible. I have the feeling you'll be getting reams of data. As for this alleged political connection in our own backyard, that'll take some detective work on our end.''

''It has to fit somehow. If what I'm hearing from our friend here is right, they've been in this country for almost three years, doing whatever it is they've been doing.''

''Right, the mysterious manila envelope stuffed with cash for unknown powers-that-be to lend a helping hand. Our Serb hinting the Russian Mafia is looking to buy influence on the U.S. political front.''

''You think we're getting our chains jerked?''

''After what the Chinese did during the last Administration, Striker, I believe anything is possible—hell, 'everything' is possible. I'm going to light some fires over at the White House, the Pentagon, a few other places. Any rumors, scuttlebutt, recent scandals I'll rake over with a chain saw. If there's a traitor here in town, I will have a name or names for you.''

''Amaze me, and as soon as possible.''

''I have to tell you, Striker, this one especially pisses me off. I keep thinking about those students. Those killers were Serbs.''

''Confirmed?''

''I was told they had a double-headed eagle tattoo. That's enough, given what we now know. Another problem of mine is worrying if they have more such massacres on tap.''

''The cells in Cleveland and Detroit we know about. Then there's one overseas.''

''According to our boy again. My guess is the team

that hit the NATO compound skipped Italy. They could be anywhere, maybe Serbia for all we know, but again I've got my own feelers out. They will be found or I'll pack my office.''

"I want first crack."

"You'll be the first to know as soon as I turn up anything. For right now I can have surveillance teams working the cells in Cleveland and Detroit. I'm considering either having them picked up or if they move your way—"

"That's your call. If you go in on them you might consider taking along everything short of an M-2 Bradley tank."

"I'll give it some serious thought. You and Jack watch your backs."

"I'll stay in touch," Bolan said, and signed off.

Radin suddenly stood. Bolan palmed his Beretta just as the room phone rang.

"Mind if I use the toilet?" Radin growled.

"Leave the door open. You've got thirty seconds."

Bolan kept the Beretta trained on the Serb as he moved past and into the bathroom. He picked up the phone. The desk clerk said the car was on the way, expected in twenty minutes.

"Bring it to my door."

The soldier hung up as he heard the bleating about a little extra something else for prompt delivery. Well, the ride on his gravy train was over for all concerned. In a short while the warrior would hopefully pick up the trail to the Serb killing crew. And the only train rolling into the depot from there on would be rampaging, and runaway.

THE BLINDING FOG of his grief had lifted, but he felt the rage roar on, his ears thumping with the hammering of his heart. Somehow he kept himself from triggering the mini-Uzi on the big Russian with the flattop block-head. He held his ground, just the same, heard "Brighton Beach" screaming at the top of his lungs, wading into a dangerous point directly between both sides.

"Put the goddamn guns down! All of you!" Churybik screamed.

"Your comrades first," Ceasuvic said.

"You first," the Russian rasped.

"Is the money in the bags, Colonel?"

Ceasuvic nearly turned his weapon on Churybik and opened up. Brighton Beach was only concerned about Moscow's money.

"All of it, and then some. Now, what about what I want?"

"I will have to call Moscow for confirmation and further orders," Churybik said. "Now, the guns! All right, how about everybody just lower the muzzles, inches at a time." No one budged. "I'm not taking this macho bullshit! This is business."

"My business. You call Viktor," Ceasuvic said.

"I will! First put the guns down!"

Ceasuvic saw the big Russian lower his AK-47. Maybe it was the impending call to Moscow, the Russians awaiting whatever the further orders might be from their boss. He didn't trust the moment, but the colonel gave the order in his native tongue for his men to turn their weapons slowly off the Russians. They did.

Then he glimpsed a body collapse in a heap on the floor. Out of the corner of his eye he saw Cviic standing over Pitritic. Cviic put a finger to the man's jugular, looked up and shook his head at the colonel.

"What the hell is going on with you, Colonel?" Churybik asked. "No answer, huh? I'll call Viktor, but you better understand you've got a lot of questions to answer."

"My shovel and blanket. I bury my woman first, then we talk. While I dig, you call Viktor. I trust that is agreeable with everyone."

"You better hope Viktor is in a gracious and understanding mood."

Ceasuvic bared his teeth at the big Russian. "Is that a threat? Are you threatening me? What is your name?"

"His name is Duklov, and nobody's making any threats!" Churybik answered.

"Duklov," the colonel grunted. "Do you come to collect their money or to kill us?"

"It's strictly business."

"You keep saying that," Ceasuvic growled at Churybik. "Answer my question."

"Nobody's going to kill anybody, Colonel. But maybe you can tell me why you people look like you've been in a frigging war. Is there something I need to know?"

"Lots," Ceasuvic said.

Duklov addressed Churybik in Russian. "I do not like this."

"I understand Russian," Ceasuvic snarled.

"You," Duklov barked at Churybik in English. "I suggest you find some clearing to hide the choppers. Looking at this one, my gut tells me trouble is on the way. If we need to fly out unmolested and fast..."

"My shovel and blanket."

"In the barn," Churybik said. "I'll get a blanket."

In Serbo-Croatian, Ceasuvic told his men to watch his back as he lifted Karina's body off the duffel bags, his mini-Uzi held in an awkward one-handed grip beneath her limp frame. The colonel backed out of the dining room.

"Bring Pitritic," he told no one in particular.

The colonel heard Brighton Beach heave a sigh of relief as he backpedaled across the living room. For now it was a stalemate. Fine. What was another hour or so either way? But when he finished burying Karina, Ceasuvic would have no problem tipping any standoff his way. Karina may be dead, with no promise of the night ending in pleasure, but if he didn't get what he demanded from the Russians, Ceasuvic would take great and perhaps final joy in killing them all. With luck and daring, he might even find himself left standing when the smoke cleared, able to take off for parts unknown with every last bag of loot. If it didn't work out that way, well, then he didn't care if he went down under a hail of bullets.

If nothing else, he would be with Karina.

THE EXECUTIONER was locked and loaded, and swiftly closing on the target area.

So far, everything from delivery of firepower to the pickup of Radin, to his present advance on the farmhouse had gone off without a hitch.

In a few short minutes that would change. The soldier was prepared to roll the dice of battle and take on any and all comers.

Getting in place to resume the hunt had been no fast chore by itself. The whole time frame—from the motel to this point of battle-readiness—had chewed up almost four hours. The good news was that sat pics from Stony Man had nailed down the precise location of the farmhouse, complete with images of armed men on the premises. Four vehicles and two choppers had been detected from Kurtzman's hacking into database imagery of whatever eye-in-the-sky flyover was available. The Gulfstream's own recon had turned up at least twenty images in and around the farmhouse on the thermal infrared tracking. Twenty to one odds was stretching it, but Bolan had faced down far greater enemy numbers before, and come out the other side.

The bad news was Bolan was forced to wait on Grimaldi's impending arrival. Stony Man's ace pilot was still en route, leaving Bolan momentarily with the Ford Galaxy as his only means of evac. The vehicle was parked in brush, a quarter mile back down a dirt road. A pager set for vibrating signal would alert Bolan that Grimaldi had claimed the jet left behind by the blacksuits, who would fly back under other arrangements made by Brognola. If and when he could, Bolan would contact Grimaldi, the soldier's headset with mini–throat mike in place.

It struck Bolan as curious that the Serbs were still hunkered down at an obvious safehouse, considering the amount of killing they'd left behind, the attention they had drawn to themselves. On that matter, the blacksuits had tapped into police bans. It appeared as if both the Serbs and Bolan had managed to put Pittsburgh behind with no one the wiser about suspect or vehicle descriptions. Between the thunderstorm, very few eyewitness accounts, the fact the running and gunning was surging away from crime scenes, and maybe just plain old good fortune...

There were times Bolan knew better than to question a stroke of luck delivered to him during a campaign.

Still, Bolan was puzzled. It stood to reason the Serbs would want to put as much distance to the state—even the country—behind them as possible. Then again there were the executive choppers. So, factor in three separate rip-offs, the duffel bags stuffed with loot, plus their own savage brazenness to confront opposition, and Bolan's guess was someone had flown in to meet with the Serbs.

He could venture another educated guess. And if the Serbian visitors at the farmhouse were Russian Mafia, then Bolan intended to go in for a clean sweep.

Suppose he even struck them all down here, the soldier knew it was merely another step forward on this campaign. There were dilemmas beyond this strike, questions hanging, shadow players involved somewhere beyond the wooded rolling hills of western Pennsylvania. In time, the warrior told himself, any treason beyond here would be rooted out by either Brognola, the Farm or both. Traitors, whether on the U.S. military or political front, were on hold.

Right then, the soldier knew he had his hands full.

Bolan tightened his grip on the HK-33 assault rifle with telescopic sight, then snugged the Uzi subgun higher up his shoulder, the nylon satchel with spare flash-stun, incendiary and fragmentation grenades hanging from the other side, settling tight between the shoulder blades. With his combat harness fixed with spare clips and still more magazines in the satchel, this time Bolan felt one-hundred-percent confident he would drop the hammer on whatever enemy numbers he found ahead. John "Cowboy" Kissinger, Stony Man's resident armorer, had sent along an M-203 grenade launcher, modified to be fixed to the HK-33.

Togged in combat blacksuit, the Executioner made swift progress up the wooded hillside, searching all points of the compass through his NVD goggles. There was no sign of sentries, trip wires or surveillance cameras, but he kept his senses tuned to the slightest disturbance around him. By the time he reached the end of his run uphill, he figured the first streaks of dawn were less than thirty minutes from breaking over the sleeping Amish countryside.

The Executioner topped the rise. He chose a fire point beside a fat oak tree, cover enough if they pinned down his position to throw back return fire.

Looking down, he took in the two-story farmhouse. It was a big place, he decided, capable of holding a small army. Searching, he took in the massive barn, forty yards from the farmhouse. There was a windmill, a stone water well, but he didn't spot the two choppers. He briefly wondered if the Serbs' guests had flown on, but he found the motor pool was consistent with his intel. Four vehicles were parked near the front porch, enough to transport whatever Serbs had fled the minimall.

The soldier stripped off his night vision goggles, then slipped the satchel and Uzi off his shoulders. He dropped to a knee and loaded the M-203's breech with a 40 mm grenade. The bay window facing him revealed three figures, the trio clearly outlined in white light. Another long surveillance of the perimeter, and he spotted two shadows on the front porch. Both of them had assault rifles slung across their shoulders.

The Executioner weighed two options. He could thread a sound suppressor to the muzzle of his HK-33 and take out the sentries first, then readjust his aim before they dropped and pick off the trio inside the window before all hell broke loose. Or he could just start pumping 40 mm rounds through the bay window, bring the whole damn house down on their heads and start picking off whatever hardmen scrambled out of the rubble.

Bolan lifted the HK-33, figured the range to the

bay window was sixty meters or so, on a downhill trajectory. The Executioner picked option number two. There was going to be plenty of noise anyway, so why bother with any kinder, gentler touch?

CHAPTER TEN

It took more than two hours and seven overseas calls before Churybik finally tracked down the boss at his dacha in Kiev.

"Viktor, it is me."

"Yes, it is you. You best bring me good news?"

Churybik felt his heart lurch for his throat. The underboss then started to pace the front porch, his nerves even more jangled now that the moment of truth had arrived. While he gathered his composure and searched for the right words, any plausible concoction of a story for the outrageous scenario the colonel had dumped in his lap, he was forced to listen to Viktor's bellyaching. The sudden burst of angry rambling struck Churybik as extremely odd for a man who had been burning his ear for weeks on end about his money and his business in America. But when Viktor Tokinov spoke, people listened or they died.

The boss again told Churybik how annoyed he was at the interruption. He told Churybik he was right then sitting in his whirlpool, two naked Ukrainian beauties by his side, the vodka flowing. While Tokinov groused on about his ungrateful children, how they were forcing him out of Moscow with all their scheming and petty demands—mostly about money—Churybik began to think Duklov was right about the most powerful gangster in Russia. What was he hearing on the other end anyway? Whining? A drunken diatribe? Self-pity and petulance? Or a soul gone soft, the mind tweaked from massive self-indulgence?

Churybik looked through the front door. Incredible as he found it, there appeared more sanity right then here among this savage rabble. The Serbs were scattered around the living room, the colonel in an easy chair with remote in hand, flicking through the channels. After the woman was buried, the Serbs had emptied their vehicles of all weapons, including four RPG-7 rocket launchers now canted against the living room wall. Two of Duklov's gunmen growled an excuse as they shouldered past Churybik. At least, Churybik thought, the last of the duffel bags were now being marched for the choppers, which were hidden in a clearing on the other side of the east hills. Duklov and the rest of his crew chose to isolate themselves in the dining room, all eyes focused out the bay window, the Moscow bunch clearly lost in their own angry thoughts.

"But enough about my problems, comrade. Talk to me, tell me all about your good news."

Churybik felt his Adam's apple bobbing as he swallowed, wishing he had a bellyful of vodka. There was no other way, he decided, than to tell the boss the whole ugly truth. In this instance the messenger could damn well be killed.

"I do not think you are going to like this, Viktor."

Tokinov boomed, "I already do not like it! Stop sniveling and report."

Churybik reported how the Serbs had gone on a killing rampage, slaughtering all parties in the three major outlets for their merchandise, effectively shutting down their pipeline that linked them to other western distribution points. He told the boss the Serbs had stolen back the product, meant to be resold—according to their crazy scheme—while they had seized the appropriate amount of cash from their now very dead black and Italian distributors.

"Doubling the profit."

Churybik wasn't sure he'd heard right. "Pardon me?"

"They just doubled the profit, idiot. Took the money and held on to the drugs. What about the load of weapons for the Iranians?"

Churybik winced. The line was supposedly secure with Tokinov's KGB Olympic scrambler. Even still, Churybik didn't trust speaking so openly about drugs, guns and dead men on a line that could be cut into by any number of sophisticated eavesdropping devices their enemies used. He was more suspicious now that Duklov had correctly nailed the boss as close to the edge of staring into the abyss of his own madness.

"Continue, please. No, not now, Sylvlinka, but I can use more vodka and caviar, and bring me a chunk of the stuffed veal. Go, I need to see you right this second in all your Ukrainian glory. Ah, yes, nice, nice.''

"Viktor?"

"I hear you, goddammit. Speak!"

Churybik moved out onto the porch, away from the colonel's two sentries, and sucked in a deep breath. He told his boss the half-million-dollar load of weapons was still in a truck, sitting in one of their warehouses in Pittsburgh. No reply from the boss, Churybik believing Tokinov was simply chalking that up to more profit margin. Then he told him the Serbs had lost the money at their last hit, some lone gunman— whoever the hell he was, by the way—dogging them wherever they went, something about a grenade blowing up the Iranian briefcase, but who could believe anything they said now? Couldn't Viktor see everything was spiraling out of control? And lost money was lost money.

In no uncertain terms, Churybik stated his anger and suspicion and fear about the mess they had left behind in Pittsburgh, how they had placed the entire organization in jeopardy with their Wild West Show. The silence on Tokinov's end became deafening, knotting his guts even more as Churybik went on spelling out his own fears. Because of the crazy Serbs there was little doubt in Churybik's mind the FBI and the Justice Department would link all the bodies left behind to their ongoing operations, maybe even track it all back to New York, from there even to the Motherland. No response.

"Viktor, are you there?"

"Of course. I'm listening, idiot."

Churybik choked down his growing anger over all the insults he was enduring. Another deep draw of breath, and he stated the Serbs had obviously planned this butcher run and rip-off all along. From the beginning the colonel had obviously simply allowed himself to become part of the organization, but only to acquire his own nest egg, which appeared sizable, by the way, since the colonel had handed over another half million he had stashed away at the farmhouse, as if that made up for the Iranian debacle. The colonel insisted his own war chest could now purchase what he had wanted all along, and he was insisting on immediate delivery, all arrogance and indifference to the havoc he had wreaked on their business. So, it had all been an act by the Serbs, and Churybik felt duped and betrayed. He didn't think the organization could ever recover from this treacherous Serbian blow on the American front. If it did, it would take years to rebuild what the crazy Serbs had destroyed in a few short hours.

"How much did they bring you?"

Churybik reported between the product, the cash and the truck with its weapons he figured it was all somewhere in the neighborhood of twenty million, that was if he counted on reselling the product. But who would buy from them now? Who would trust them?

"What should I do, Viktor?"

Churybik waited for the man to answer. The pause

was so long he began to think Viktor wasn't there. Then he heard chomping and slobbering on the other end, Tokinov no doubt inhaling his stuffed veal. A swallow, a belch, and Tokinov erupted in a burst of uncontrolled laughter.

When he stopped laughing, Tokinov said, "Oh, the beauty, the insane genius of what they did. I love them, I will kiss them when I see them. Oh, those Serbs have King Kong balls. If only I had more soldiers like them."

"What are you saying?"

"I am saying you could take lessons from them in what it is to be a man. I knew what the colonel wanted. I read right through him from the start, idiot. Listen to me. They made all of us a lot of money. That was my intent, but only one of the reasons why I had them pulled out of their country and brought to me. I made a promise to the colonel from the beginning, and I am prepared to deliver."

"So, we just shrug this all off as the cost of doing business?"

"Comrade Churybik, what you do not understand is that I knew they wanted retribution against NATO. They needed to take their pound of flesh from America the beautiful and pompous. I despise this NATO, and I hate America even more. I see America out there, flying her jets and B-52s and whatever else over sovereign nations, bombing away indiscriminately, killing women and children and old men, blowing up embassies and hospitals in the name of what they call democracy and freedom for all. Fuck them! I also hate what our own country has become. We have become weak and as corrupt as the West ever since we turned so-called democratic. It is all a sadistic joke America has played on Russia. They bomb whoever they feel is a threat to them, and we are supposed to sit by with our fingers up our butts because they give Russia so much money every year, which, need I inform you, only falls into the hands of corrupt politicians.

"Hear me. I no longer believe in much; the world, it breaks my heart more every day. I am too old, too privileged, too pampered, too rich. I am bored and I am restless and I am angry. I need fire in my soul again. The Serbs were meant to give me that feeling of being alive again. They march unflinching into the eye of the storm. They kick ass and do not look back or question what they are all about. They take what they want and they stick a middle finger in the eye of anybody they don't like or who has the audacity to disagree with them. Am I making myself clear to you?"

He wasn't, but Churybik lied, "Yes, I think so."

"You think so. I am sick and tired of all my people thinking so, thinking only about their bank accounts, racing around in some vain attempt to secure a future of comfort and pleasure, their own little nirvana fiefdom, as if they will live forever. Do you not see? It is all here today, gone tomorrow. The party, comrade, always ends. Loved ones disappoint, your comrades run around behind your back, jealous of all you have rightfully earned by blood, guts and raw talent, while wishing only to take what you have. It would be easier and far more simple if we could all live like some Tolstoy or van Gogh or Fyodor, but I did not create man in all his impurity and self-serving way. Your middle finger is your god. You ask and you want nothing from the world. Your balls are like pistons, forever pumping, juiced like U-235 radiation. My Serbs are my dream come true, they are my pistons, they are the King Kong balls of my empire.''

Churybik felt himself reeling but forged ahead. ''I am not so sure the ones you sent share your opinions.''

''Is that right? Put Duklov on this instant.''

Churybik marched across the living room and held out the cell phone. ''He wishes to speak to you.''

Without acknowledging Churybik's presence, Duklov plucked the phone out of his hand.

Churybik stood beside Duklov and felt the grin dying to cut his lips. He wished he could hear the dressing-down the boss was putting to his hotshot. To his credit, Duklov never changed expression, though, grunting and nodding and telling Tokinov he understood for the full minute he was forced to sit there and take it. Finally, Duklov held the cell phone out.

''He wants to talk to the Serb.''

Churybik enjoyed the way he snatched back the cellular, wanted to chuckle at the scowl carving that ugly face as he wheeled and marched straight for Ceasuvic.

''Colonel, Viktor wishes a word with you.''

Ceasuvic made him wait, then finally took the cellular phone. More grunting, another long minute passing, then the colonel said, "They are in Greece. Yes, that is good. Thank you. Yes...I can accept delivery of only two of them...I understand that I have caused grief. I regret what has happened, but I appreciate your understanding. Yes, I believe that, too."

Churybik felt his paranoia flaring up still more as Ceasuvic held the cellular phone over his shoulder. Believed what? As he took the phone back, he heard the colonel say, "You seem to keep thinking I do not understand Russian. I do not appreciate being called crazy Serb. And repeatedly."

Angrily, Churybik marched off. From top to bottom everyone was hell-bent on treating him like some lackey. He had just about had enough. But what was he going to do? Grab an AK-47 and blaze away? Viktor started barking in his ear.

"I am tired of sitting still in Russia. I need a vacation. Greece sounds good. I need to get back out there, refind myself as man and warrior anyway. Here it is. I told the colonel it will take perhaps another twelve hours or so to round up what he wants, hammer out the finer details. You will take them to our casino in Atlantic City."

"The Olympus?"

"Idiot, it is the only one we have there."

"I understand that, but—"

"But what? Get them a suite. They have a free ride, everything on the house, that includes Duklov, if he can get his head out of his bigoted ass. If anything happens to the colonel, I will hold you personally responsible. When you get there, call me."

That was that. Churybik looked around, incredulous. For what seemed like an hour he felt as if he were standing alone, on another planet. He was shaking his head, wondering what insanity would strike him next when something shattered the bay window.

The next thing Churybik knew he was eating the floor, glimpsing the fireball burning out of the dining room, hurling figures and whole slabs of debris his way, the entire building shaking with seismic force.

Ivan Churybik heard his own bitter chuckle as he watched Duklov haul himself out of the rubble, the big Russian cursing, pulling a shard of glass out of his thigh. No matter what happened next, Churybik found the bloody stumbling bulk of Moscow's killing finest a beautiful sight to behold. Somebody out there must have borrowed a page from the Duklov textbook on real power, Churybik thought.

That somebody was making things happen, all right, but it sure as hell wasn't Duklov, or anyone else close by for that matter.

NO SOONER WAS Bolan's first 40 mm grenade lighting up the dining room and blowing the trio by the window all to hell than the Executioner had the M-203's breech fed with another frag bomb. He pumped one more 40 mm round through the smoky maw, then reloaded the M-203 with an incendiary round. He chose a window on the first floor, near what he figured was the front doorway leading to the living room.

Bolan tapped the M-203's trigger, rode out the recoil and watched the grenade streak forward.

He had his fire started a moment later, then hit them with a flash-stun round as they started bulling out the front door. The blinding light show sent them staggering this way and that, tumbling off the porch between fits of coughing.

The Executioner held back the trigger of his HK-33, sweeping a long burst of 5.56 mm doom over the hardforce. By the time he burned out the clip, he nailed three shadows, dropping them in limp sprawls across the porch.

By now they were shouting at one another, hands flapping in his general direction. Return fire opened up from the porch, but the lead snapping off tree bark became the least of Bolan's concerns in the next moment.

The soldier recognized the cone-shaped warhead fixed to an RPG-7 rocket launcher as flames leaped out the windows fronting the porch. Another rocket man joined his comrade as they pegged the area of his muzzle-flash.

Bolan was up and running, HK-33 in hand, his legs pumping like pistons. He was charging down the hill, throwing himself into a headfirst dive for thick brush when twin deafening peals of thunder shattered his senses.

CHAPTER ELEVEN

Ceasuvic chucked away the spent RPG-7. If he and Milenko had accurately pinned down the enemy's position, then unloaded their warheads in time, their mystery hunter was burned human toast up on the ridge.

There was no doubt in his mind who had brought the house down on their heads. Sure, he would have preferred killing the bastard up close, tasting bittersweet revenge for Karina's death while staring this nameless adversary in the eye, but he would take whatever he got right then. Dead was dead.

The colonel breathed in the stink of cooking flesh, glanced at the jagged teeth where the front wall had stood, heard Brighton Beach on his handheld radio barking for his pilots to fire up the choppers. He took a time-out to consider his luck, if he could even call it that.

The bastard's initial hammering actually saved his life, Ceasuvic reflected. He was running across the living room when the second blast bulldozed slabs of rubble up his backside, flinging him down a hallway that provided relative safety from the next two explosions. It most certainly kept him from being temporarily blinded by the flash-stun grenade. Together with Milenko, he crawled out of the rubble, saw them out there on the porch, grabbing their eyes, then trying in vain to return fire, deaf, dumb and blind men dying where they reeled. Another of Duklov's cronies was killed on the spot, while still two more of his own soldiers died under a hail of bullets. Somehow, on the way out the door, Ceasuvic and Milenko had spotted two RPG-7 rocket launchers, the weapons miraculously undamaged.

Ceasuvic counted heads. Brighton Beach was already running like hell away from the bonfire. The last of Duklov's goons were charging across open ground, weapons poised as they intercepted the Russian underboss, both of the bagmen way too late to be of any use now. And Ceasuvic discovered the entire force he had begun the night of killing with was down to Milenko and Cviic.

Unbelievable. One man. Ceasuvic felt sick to his stomach. He quickly convinced himself none of his people had died in vain that night. Oh, yes, there would be an accounting, and soon, or he wasn't worthy to be called Serb. At least reinforcements were on the way, which meant a quick call to order them to this Olympus casino in Atlantic City. He could make arrangements with Churybik to jet his men to New York. If he read Tokinov right, Ceasuvic believed he and his Serbs were viewed by the boss as some sort of twenty-first-century knights, crusaders in search of their own Holy Grail, riding to slay the modern-day dragon of NATO. In twelve hours or less, he hoped he would be en route overseas, picking up the packages, and on his way to living up to whatever fantasies about them Viktor Tokinov might have.

Originally, he had told Tokinov he wanted three of them. But the Russian boss had laid out the sticky problem of former KGB associates breaking into the Spetsnaz armory in Ilisk, just walking off with the items, even though everyone involved was bought and paid for by *mafiya* money, right down to the eighteen-year-old conscript guarding the gate. Tokinov explained the SVR—formerly the notorious KGB—was working in a loose-knit fashion with the American Justice Department and FBI, both sides trading off intelligence but only when it suited their own purposes. Black market selling of Russian hardware was always on the suspicious minds of the Americans, the colonel knew. Especially when it came down to what Ceasuvic would soon get his hands on.

Ceasuvic had little doubt the boss would deliver, even though Tokinov claimed he was seeing shadows everywhere these days, hinting he didn't even trust his own children. A man in his position could never be too careful or paranoid, Tokinov had said. All he had to do now was iron out the logistics. That was good enough for the colonel. If nothing else, he sensed the future was falling into place, and on his terms.

Again he heard the Russian underboss yelling back at them. Ceasuvic took a step away from the roaring flames when he spotted a figure slithering around a mound of debris just inside the burning tomb, rolling away from the fire in an awkward struggle that betrayed serious injuries. Now that another moment of danger had passed, he wondered what had happened to Duklov. Now he knew.

"Go, I will catch up," the colonel told Cviic and Milenko.

Ceasuvic braved the flames lapping for his face as he bulled through a narrow space between wood shards. He left the mini-Uzi slung across his shoulder, opting for the sound-suppressed Glock. He chuckled as he stood over the Russian. A part of him was angry that Viktor would deem it necessary to ship out a goon squad to collect the money, but he understood it was business, nothing personal. Ceasuvic could accept the Old Man's concern about the late deliveries of money on his end, but that didn't mean he had to suffer abuse from some lackey gunslinger.

Duklov hacked as black smoke wreathed the hatred in his face. The way Duklov dragged himself, Ceasuvic knew the Russian was in agony, suffering from either internal injuries or a broken bone or two. The colonel took pleasure in the Russian's pain. This goon had come to America to kick some Serb ass, throwing his weight around, trying to give the impression he was the toughest, most sadistic killer around. To Ceasuvic, the Russian tough guy now looked like a snake with broken vertebrae. Better still, Duklov had never even fired off a single shot in anger, the tough guy simply getting tossed around by the mystery gunman's fireballs like trash in the wind.

"You Serb bastard. You are responsible for this."

"Still playing tough guy, I see. My friend, you are no Charles Bronsonkov or Clint Eastwoodski."

Ceasuvic laughed, then coughed as smoke pinched into his nose. He felt sweat break from his forehead and his eyes stung as Karina's blood ran into them. It was nearly enough to blind him, but at the last instant he caught Duklov grabbing at his ankle, the dagger thrusting up. Ceasuvic fisted the knife hand, held the blade inches from his kidney.

"Anyone ever tell you, Comrade Duklov, you have a very bad attitude?"

Before Duklov could reply, the colonel put the muzzle of his Glock to the Russian's forehead and squeezed the trigger.

He was outside and running in the next moment. He wasn't sure if it was fear, rage or paranoia or a little of each, but he looked back over his shoulder. The pall of smoke was thinning up on the ridge. If he could spare the time, he would have hiked up there to confirm the kill. If the bastard had been anywhere close to ground zero...

He could only hope the relentless menace was a broken sack of dead bones. If not...

Ceasuvic shoved that fearful thought out of his mind. The future was now his for the taking, he knew. The entire barbaric hordes of NATO—and most certainly not one man—could stop him now.

It was nearly time to shove his vengeance in their faces.

He was not only Serbia's avenging angel, he thought, but soon he would be the instrument that might well push the entire world toward war.

BOLAN WASN'T SURE how long he'd been knocked out, but he feared enough critical time had passed for his enemies to either charge the hill or bolt the scene. He staggered to his feet, his ears chiming from the double blast. He was cut and nicked from scalp to jaw, but otherwise unharmed. It had been close, he knew, judging from the chunks gouged out of the ridgeline and the one blown out of the tree above. A few feet, here or there...

Why question his luck and fast feet?

Adrenaline pulled Bolan together as he found his HK-33 in the brush. Looking up the rise at the final drifting tendrils of smoke and dust, he searched the ridgeline, feeding the assault rifle a fresh clip. Locked and loaded, the Executioner moved off at an angle, away from his original fire point, watching for shadows creeping over the ridgeline. A band of firelight glowed beyond the rise, branding an unnatural daylight far sooner across this slice of quiet Amish paradise than he would have cared for.

When he hit the ridgeline, HK-33 ready to cut loose at any shadow he found, the Executioner saw only empty terrain waiting below. The way the farmhouse was raging into a firestorm, the soldier knew it wouldn't be long before that fiery beacon drew the local and state police.

Searching beyond the barn, he spotted a shadow at the last moment before the figure vanished into the first stand of trees at the bottom of the hill.

Going back to the car was no option at all. So far his luck had held as far as facing down cops, but this time felt different. With all the racket they'd made, someone had more than likely called in the cavalry.

Bolan ran down the hill, gathered speed as he hit level ground, then sprinted past the firestorm. They were going for the choppers. He had shaved still more enemy numbers, but if he lost them now there was no telling if and when he could pick up the hunt.

As he finally made the wooded eastern hills, the Executioner felt the frustration and anger boil up in his guts as he spotted two choppers rising up above distant treetops. He was loading his M-203, but he knew it was already too late. The distance to the choppers was roughly three hundred yards as it stood, and before he could even think about drawing target acquisition and attempt a lucky shot, the pilots had the birds dipped at the nose and streaking away at full pitch.

Bolan watched them vanish beyond the tree line. They were flying east, New York–bound, if he didn't miss his guess.

And where the hell was Grimaldi?

The Executioner decided he needed to put himself a quick distance from the slaughter zone. There was nothing he could do at the moment except wait, search for some open field long and smooth enough for Grimaldi to land the jet. Viewing the rolling wooded countryside, Bolan began to doubt he'd find any suitable stretch for Grimaldi to pick him up but at least the storm had passed, a few stars fading now to the rising sun.

The Executioner moved out, knowing he could only keep running and searching.

Keep hope alive, keep hunting.

PETER FRITCH FELT the full burdensome discomfort of his 250, five-eight frame that morning. Even the briefcase seemed like a bowling bag with ten-pin ball inside as he waddled for his Lincoln Towncar. He knew, though, it was neither body nor briefcase that saddled him with extra weight at the moment.

It felt as if life were holding a knife to his throat.

The past few years had seen him make an easy and swift climb up the political pecking order, a power player making all the right moves, saying all the right things, reaching out and touching all the right people at the right time. It had been so easy, gaining power, prestige and fattening several bank accounts.

Well, it had been too damn easy, and along the way he'd stepped in something he couldn't simply scrape off the bottom of his shoe. No, it was reaching critical mass, and right in his own backyard. And yes, something was about to go terribly wrong, if it wasn't already happening.

Out of nowhere he felt sorry for himself. He recalled his vacation in Kiev three years earlier; that trip he'd taken alone, and where he'd met his current dilemma. One Ukrainian beauty had changed his life forever. And the Russian Mafia had the pictures to prove it. There was no way he would ever allow his wife to discover his infidelity. The public scandal would be bad enough, but he loved his mansion, his cars, his vacation homes, his fat bank accounts. No way was he about to give up the good life over one indiscretion. No mistake, she would financially skin him alive, and worse. If that happened he would be broke, unemployed, scorned. After the last Administration, he knew the polls now reflected America's impatience and intolerance for their lawmakers' and leaders' tawdry little sex adventures. God forbid anyone would ever find out just who and what had him personally by the short hairs. He would be labeled a traitor, no doubt marched off to finish out his life behind bars for high treason.

Oh, God, he moaned to himself, why, how had this all happened?

The night had been long enough, jetting down to Virginia Beach, then back to Dulles after his brief meeting with the Gray Man. No sooner was he home in his Great Falls estate with a combo of lasagna, sleeping pill and two glasses of whiskey under his belt and ready to slide quietly under the covers next to his snoring wife, than the phone started to ring. It wasn't unusual for him to get phone calls at three or four o'clock in the morning. After all, he was the President's spokesman to the press, the messenger who trooped out there before the cameras, quelling the fears of John Q. Public, always wearing a brave face, while sometimes forced to smear the skeptics with sufficient bullshit propaganda to get them off the President's back about one thing or another. Between the media sharks, the President or the President's underlings, he was on call around-the-clock. There was always some crisis these days, but he knew they lived in a world one step away from anarchy.

The problem was that the three calls several hours earlier had no voice on the other end. Whoever called listened in silence as he bleated out his questions and irritation, then just hung up. And it was his own private line to the White House, no less. If "they" could discover that number, he shuddered to think what else they were capable of. Fritch might know what the hell was going on, but that didn't mean he had to like it, much less believe his nerves would stand up to their cloak-and-dagger intimidation. They were checking up on him, sure, letting him know he was being watched, that they had the power to play God, interrupt every area of his life.

He keyed open his door and settled his bulk behind the wheel. Depressed suddenly, he looked at his mansion, the brick-and-stone fortress having cost him a fortune. Now he wondered if all the motion and laser sensors, security cameras, silent alarms and not-so-silent pit bull would be enough to alert him if one of those strangers the Gray Man had mentioned decided to pay him an unexpected visit. Maybe he needed a gun. Maybe he simply needed a long vacation, to hide somewhere on a beach, riding it out, hoping that while he was away the sharks would devour one another. There was the condo in Florida, a villa on the French Riviera, slices of heaven where he could escape from the pressures of life. Of course, stress came with his position, and he enjoyed the power he wielded, wanting nothing else in life but to be crowned Secretary of Defense by his old friend, the President. More pressure, yes, but more power. The kind of stress he was now placed under could literally kill him.

And what if he was found out? And now he had shadows lurking around, maybe he was even right then being watched. Was that a shadow over there in the woods? No, it looked like a mere cloud passing beneath the sun. Or was it?

This was crazy, he told himself, even if it was all too terribly real. He knew if he ever came under any suspicion it would be easy enough for the FBI or the Justice Department to smell him out. There would be surveillance, phone taps, and his midnight meetings were easy enough to track if they thought him a traitor.

Forget it, he told himself. He was covered. He had to believe in the Gray Man's proven knack for spotting trouble and taking care of problems before they blew up in everyone's face.

He fired up the Lincoln, trying to convince himself it would all work out, to trust in the Gray Man, believe in his own destiny as an individual meant to achieve individual greatness, even immortality. It looked as if a cloudless day, bright with sunshine, would hang over Washington. Cheer up, he told himself, have faith—

What the hell was that?

He couldn't believe what he was seeing as he drove down the brick-paved drive. The tall man in black was standing by the wrought-iron gate, punching at the code box. The stranger was actually grinning at him through the windshield, the gates opening. No one but himself and his wife had the codes. His mind reeled with terror. If it was that easy for them to find out the codes to his front gate, tap into his private secure line to the White House, what was to keep them out of his home? He determined to buy a gun by day's end.

Fritch started to get out of his car, then he felt his stomach clutch as the smiling stranger reached into his trench coat. He felt the scream build in his lungs, wondered why he couldn't get his legs to move, fold himself down behind the wheel, reverse the car out of there. Three moves could put him in full retreat, but fear held him immobile.

But no gun emerged from within the trench coat. Instead, Fritch saw the fat manila envelope tossed on the hood.

"Who are you?"

The stranger chuckled, as if he had to ask, then stepped back and disappeared around the brick piling.

Fritch looked over his shoulder, hoping to God his wife was still asleep. If nothing else, she was sharp and suspicious as hell these days. If she was watching this bizarre encounter, she would hammer him with a slew of questions, flapping her hands and bouncing around, nagging him straight into a full bottle of whiskey.

Fritch heard himself suddenly wheezing as he squeezed out the door and snatched up the envelope. When he was safely back behind the wheel, he dropped the Lincoln into Drive, then eased past the gate. He searched the tight asphalt road that cut through the woods in both directions. The laughing man was nowhere in sight.

Fritch braked the Lincoln when he knew he was hidden from his home. He opened the envelope and pulled out the thick stacks of hundred-dollar bills. He figured there was at least two hundred grand this time. He was becoming an expert at judging how much money they sent him just by hefting the weight. There was something else, a sheet of paper, he saw, folded at the bottom. Fritch worked the paper out, yelping as the edge of a brand-new bill cut his finger. He was sucking a trickle of blood as he opened the sheet of paper.

Just like that, he saw the day would suddenly prove far from bright and sunny. In fact, he could read the thunderstorm on the way as he absorbed the enormity of what the note said:

Stay available for the possibility of an unexpected lunch date. Ivan comrades need a word with you. Enjoy the campaign contribution. We are hopeful for you.

Peter Fritch crumpled the note.

CHAPTER TWELVE

Three hours on the run brought good news and bad news to Bolan. The bad news was that two police helicopters were buzzing the skies like hungry insects a quarter mile or so behind the soldier, and bearing down his way. The sun was up, shafts of light dancing through the canopy around him. He strayed from the light, but if the choppers had spotted his dash across the cow pasture he knew they would drop on top of him, bullhorns announcing that they were cops. Turning, he saw they were hovering at some point to the west, the storm of leaves and brush blown up by rotor wash in a clearing stoking the soldier's fear that he had, indeed, been made as a suspect, and one that would be approached as armed and dangerous.

The good news was the pager on Bolan's hip had vibrated moments earlier, signaling him Grimaldi was in the game. Bolan hit the com-link button on his headset, then crouched beneath the lip of a gully that led to a creekbed. The bleat of rotors suddenly faded as Bolan saw the choppers lift off and peel away to turn their search north.

Alone now, the silence around Bolan was interrupted only by the pounding of his heart in his ears, his starved lungs sucking in long slow gulps of air. His stamina and strength were on a par with any champion athlete, but he had been running for more than twelve hours, with little food, no sleep and on his legs nonstop the past three hours. Factor in a constant roller-coaster ride of adrenaline in the face of combat, and he could feel the strain pushing his own endurance meter toward exhaustion. But in his world there was never a finish line—only brief time-outs to refuel the body with food and water, indulge in a few long hours of sleep, depending on the circumstances. He had been there many times before. When the going got tough, the way of the warrior was to dig deeper, push harder, suck it up.

"Striker to Flyboy, come in, Flyboy."

"Partyhawk here, Striker."

In different circumstances, Bolan would have been vaguely amused by Grimaldi's handle. "I hope you're airborne, Partyhawk."

"I've been in the air for thirty minutes, Sarge. Murphy's Law kept me from raising you before now. Blacksuits neglected to inform me my handheld link to you was stowed away in one of three very large war bags. Try flying this puppy on autopilot sometime, while you're digging for the handheld in the haystack. Oh, well, shit happens, right?"

"That's one way of putting it."

"Okay, let's sitrep. I did a flyover of what's left of the farmhouse the big man faxed as part of my recon pics. Forget the pics and grids, I could pin down the smoke from five miles away. There are enough squad cars and fire trucks on-site with lights flashing to light the place for the mother ship to land. You should know the police bands, state and local, are screaming for someone's head on a stake, but they have no description of any suspect. Seems they believe the mess back in Amish heaven is linked to three separate urban battlefields in Pittsburgh. But I guess you wouldn't know anything about that."

"I was only there to lend the bad guys a helping hand."

"The body count I'm hearing about over the police bands tells me you were quite the help. I only hope you've left me a little action after I pick you up."

"Lots of butcher work still left, Partyhawk, so keep the faith. Anyway, unwanted friendlies are already in my area. Choppers. I need evac, and five minutes ago. Thing is, I've been running up and down wooded hills for three hours. Anything remotely looking like a suitable field is just one big cow pasture. Deep tractor ruts…"

"And plenty of cowpies, I copy. I've seen the fields and I doubt I could even drop a chopper in any of them without going up to the belly in dung. I've got your position marked on the homer in your pager, Sarge. Now, I hatched a crazy little idea as soon as I saw I wouldn't be able to set this bird down anywhere in your area. You ready for this?"

"Let's have it, Partyhawk."

"You're a little over a half mile from the interstate.

Presently I'm five miles and closing on your position. After I spotted our gift from Lady Luck I flew over, then circled back. And what I'm looking at ahead makes both of us two very lucky SOBs.''

"I could use the break, Partyhawk."

"It comes on someone else's misfortune, but all I can do right now is say a prayer for whoever it is. A tractor trailer has jackknifed, presently burning up across all eastbound lanes. State police are on the scene, and no traffic, repeat no traffic is being let through to head east."

Bolan knew where Grimaldi was headed. "Sounds like a little R and R has you game as ever, Partyhawk."

"It's all in the hangover. Okay, if you stay running on your present southeast course, you're on an angle to come out on the interstate about three football fields beyond the barricade. Traffic in the westbound lanes has slowed, with everybody rubbernecking the action. A quick dash across, over the median, I'll have the door dropped with a quick flick of a switch...well, the rest is up to you."

"I'm headed out now, Partyhawk."

"Remember, it's in the timing. But if I fly over and you're not in position, stay put, we'll do it again."

"Roger, Partyhawk."

The Executioner splashed through the creek, scrambled up and out the other side, then began beating a hard run through the woods. A dog barked, a chain rattled from somewhere as Bolan palmed his compass, ignored the Private Property Trespassers

Will Be Shot On Sight, and squeezed through a loose tangle of barbed wire. The property owner, Bolan figured, obviously didn't belong to any peace-loving Amish clan.

Whatever, there was daylight ahead, as the soldier found the woodland and another stretch of barbed wire give way to a gently rolling slope. Beyond that rise, Bolan knew evac waited.

The Executioner cleared the woods and wire, again starting to pump his legs for all he was worth. By now the sweat was flowing freely, burning into his eyes, plastering blacksuit to hot skin. The nylon war bag and Uzi over his shoulders were added burdens, but the discomfort and the grim thought of getting scooped up by the cops only drove him harder.

The Executioner found his evac site just as Grimaldi laid it out. Westbound vehicles crawled at a snail's pace, traffic bumper-to-bumper with spectators gawking at the fireworks show dumped across the eastbound lanes. A half-mile run to this point put Bolan behind schedule as he scanned the skies and discovered Grimaldi already streaking overhead. Bolan raised Stony Man's ace pilot and confirmed round two.

He waited as Grimaldi banked to the south, swung wide in an arc to double back. The soldier was forced to descend a steep rock-littered embankment, and he had one shot only to scramble down and get in position on the east lanes. If he missed the first time around, the state police would scoop him up, end of show.

On the way down, the Executioner counted six state police vehicles, the lawmen fanning out, holding back a traffic jam that had no end in sight as far as Bolan could tell. A wailing siren rent the air, and he saw the paramedic crew burst onto the scene.

Figuring he had picked up another one-hundred-plus yards more than Grimaldi's original estimation to the barricade, Bolan bolted across the highway's shoulder. He weaved in and out of cars, a few horns blasting at him, someone shouting something about the weapons around his shoulders. He was across the grassy median divide, checking the sky to the west when Grimaldi patched back.

"Sarge, one of the smokys alerted their flyboys to get over here, suspicious aircraft in the area. That would be me."

"That would be you."

"I see you, I'm coming in."

And he found Grimaldi was, indeed, streaking low and fast, the sleek bird zipping over the traffic jam, wheels nearly dropping on top of car roofs, before the ace pilot blew over the stunned troopers. The jet's slipstream alone bowled several troopers off their feet as if they were sideshow acrobatic acts in some aerospace circus.

The Executioner hit the east lanes as he heard Grimaldi touch down with a screech of rubber from some point far behind his run. The jet was a lumbering blur in Bolan's sweat-teared vision, the aircraft shooting past the soldier, its turbofan Rolls-Royce Spey engines shrieking in his ears. Bolan hugged the slipstream and forged ahead. After running another hundred yards, Bolan found the jet slowing as Grimaldi put on the brakes, the Executioner cutting the gap inside a fifty-yard homestretch.

Bolan looked back at the sound of Klaxon wails. Flashing lights were breaking from the barricade, and three, then four cruisers started to barrel toward him. Twisting his head again, Bolan spotted the two police choppers soaring past the tree line beside the interstate, flying in on the flaming heap that had traffic stopped, but still a good mile out behind the barricade. It would shave it close, all around, but if the pilots in those choppers went into textbook defensive maneuvers to stop their evacuation, Bolan knew they would set down on the highway beyond the Gulfstream, preventing liftoff.

Bolan knocked the gap to freedom to fifteen feet to the tail fin and counting when he saw the port boarding door fold out and down at Grimaldi's electronic touch. Charging for the tapering fuselage, he was forced to haul himself beneath the wingtip, straying from the heat blasting from the turbofan engine. With one final surge of strength, Bolan dug deeper still for whatever was left, angled on the ladder. Lunging, Bolan grabbed the rail. His legs suddenly gave out, whiplashing him into a sideways arc that threatened to wrench his hands from metal, hurl him back and gone. Fueled by desperation, Bolan swung his legs back, heaved himself onto the boarding ladder and shouted into his throat mike, "Go!"

The Executioner rolled onto the cabin's carpeted

floor. He saw Grimaldi looking at him through the open cockpit door.

"Welcome aboard, Sarge."

The Executioner took a moment to catch his breath. "Glad you could make the show, Partyhawk."

"Always my pleasure. Wouldn't have missed this for all the strippers in North Beach."

Bolan felt the jet gather speed rapidly, saw the boarding door fold up to shut out the howling wind. He went to a cabin window. A cruiser was racing up on the port wing. The lead chopper was boring down like some carnivorous bird, zeroing in to soar past the fuselage and drop down beyond the jet's nose. Then the chopper was losing ground as Grimaldi fed the turbofans all the thrust they could stand. Bolan braced himself as the floor tilted, and he saw the sky rolling up beyond the cockpit glass. He struggled to wade uphill against the lift, then grabbed the edge of the doorway.

"Nice tan," Bolan told Grimaldi.

"Must be the Italian in me."

"So, how was Miami?"

Grimaldi grinned around his dark aviator sunglasses, glancing back at Bolan over his shoulder. "Hated every minute of it. You know, a guy like me can go rusty from too much sun and fun."

"Yeah. I saw your landing," Bolan cracked with a wry grin. "Nearly took the heads off a couple of those smokys."

"Just my way of saying hello, Sarge."

Atlantic City, New Jersey

CEASUVIC TOOK IN Las Vegas-by-the-ocean, staring out the cabin window as they choppered toward the Olympus casino-hotel from the west. Take away the water and white sandy beaches, strip away the gaudy glitz of the neon front, and Atlantic City didn't look like all that much to the colonel. A dozen casinos loomed over the boardwalk. There used to be eleven before the Russians erected their own gambling mecca, meant to clip the pocketbooks of Americans, of course, only the casino, he suspected, was a major money-laundering factory. Briefly he wondered how many bribes were paid out to legitimate business and casino owners, or how much Italian Mafia blood had been spilled in order for the Russians to stake their claim here.

It looked to Ceasuvic as if the Russians had managed to squeeze themselves onto a lot in the deepest corner at the north end of the boardwalk, between the Absecon Lighthouse and the Showboat Casino. Below, the colonel took in the jammed maze of cottages, while other seedy-looking tenement dwellings were woven around the jumble of traffic and herds of pedestrians, with shops and all manner of businesses catering to the beach crowd and tourists.

Ceasuvic looked away. At night he imagined the glittering skyline screamed hope and salvation through the roll of the dice, the winning card, the lucky pull on the slot handle. By day, he could see pockets of obvious poverty and misery, right in the backyard of the rich, the powerful and the privileged.

He was fast growing more sick of America in all of its hypocrisy. They often said the rich were superior. That concept, he believed, was false. The rich only felt superior. If every man and woman one day woke up rich, down to the lowliest bum on the street, then being wealthy would no longer mean anything, since Everyman was on the same playing field. The rich, he concluded, needed the poor to stay right where they were, to serve them, to envy what they could never have, to grovel for the scraps or devour one another in their lives of loud desperation. Ceasuvic was quite pleased with himself for seeing it all for what it was, for being smarter than the world. The rich killed by simply existing. And he was the war criminal?

It had been a long flight, the Russian underboss and the two survivors of the late Duklov's crew sitting in silence for the most part. Ceasuvic was looking forward to getting off the chopper, settling down with some food and drink, maybe taking a stroll through the casino. Milenko and Cviic sat across the aisle, both of them having ridden out the flight in stony quiet, deep in their own grim thoughts and worries, the colonel suspected. The Russians kept their AK-47s canted between their legs, Cviic and Milenko with their subguns in their laps. The cell phone appeared to be Brighton Beach's only weapon.

The bottom line was, Ceasuvic wasn't coming to Atlantic City to gamble or take in the sights. It was a layover, where he could regroup, clean up, wait to hear good news from Viktor. His reinforcements were on the way. They were twenty strong from the Cleveland cell, riding in five separate vehicles. As a pledge of continued cooperation, Ceasuvic had agreed— when asked by Viktor—to leave his Detroit people in place, for whatever they were now worth. Earlier, Ceasuvic had argued briefly with Churybik about having his Cleveland crew flown to the New Jersey shore. The Russian underboss said they were already on the road and that the closest major airport was in Pittsburgh; why risk trying to board twenty grim-faced Serbs on some flight, if he even could make the arrangements? Ceasuvic let it go with a shrug.

The colonel again felt the Russians staring at him. He had already answered their original question about Duklov, but he sensed they weren't satisfied with his one-word response of "Dead." If they insisted on some attempt to interrogate him...

"Uh, Colonel, a moment before we land."

Ceasuvic looked beyond the two Russians, reading the fear and worry all over Brighton Beach's face. "I am listening."

"I've ordered up a veritable feast to our penthouse. You have a wet bar, stocked with plenty of chilled vodka as you requested. I'm saying it will be several hours before I'm able to reach Viktor again."

"The jets are fueled back at your airport and prepared to fly out at a moment's notice?"

"Yes, but forget that for a minute." Churybik gave the Serbs a frown, wrinkling his nose. "If you go down to the casino, uh, would you mind taking a shower first. You three are a little ripe, if you don't mind my saying so. I've already seen to getting the three of you a change of clothes.''

Ceasuvic felt an uncontrollable rage burning in his gut. He smiled in the face of insolence. "Of course, I understand. A shower and a drink would be most welcome.''

"And food. I don't know when we'll get the chance to eat again once we're back in the air.''

"Of course. Food." He saw Churybik's gaze narrow. "Something else?''

"Yes, there is. For now, I'm going to neglect mentioning our problem back in Pennsylvania next time I speak with Viktor.''

"I believe that would be the wise thing to do. Why burden Viktor with any more grief?''

"Comrade Tokinov will hear it from me.''

"And what exactly will that be, comrade?" Ceasuvic asked.

The crew-cut Russian said, "You never fully answered my question.''

"I told you.''

"What happened to Igor?''

"Dead.''

"I saw you go back into the house.''

"If you will excuse me, comrades," Ceasuvic said, standing, "I feel the sudden urge to relieve myself.''

As he took a step toward the bathroom, he told his men in Serbo-Croatian, "Back my play.''

"What was that?''

Ceasuvic stopped, his hand drifting inside his coat. They weren't going to let it go. Over his shoulder he told the Russians, "What I meant is that I thought he was dead, but as I went back inside I found he wasn't. I gave him a final lesson in attitude adjustment."

They were reaching for their AK-47s, halfway on their feet, Brighton Beach standing and screaming, when the colonel wheeled. The sound-suppressed Glock 17 chugged two quick rounds, Ceasuvic boring a dark hole, one each between the eyes. The last of Duklov's crew crashed into their seats, AK-47s tumbling to the carpet. The bullets had blasted out the backs of their skulls, stuffing now floating above their shattered heads where the seats had absorbed the rounds.

Before Churybik began to squawk, Ceasuvic leathered his Glock and asked, "Now, what were we having for lunch?"

CHOOSING ONE of seven lunch specials at his favorite Capitol Hill restaurant was sometimes the hardest part of his day. They were running Italian cuisine today, and the choices were especially agonizing.

Peter Fritch sat in his reserved booth, a gin martini in hand, his nose pressed in the menu. He dropped the menu, knowing it was pointless to select something other than one of the specials, even though he was leaning toward the London Broil Béarnaise. He scanned the dining-room floor beyond his private enclave, then checked his watch. He had a few minutes before the President's men arrived to groom him for the announcement his friend would make later that afternoon when they cut into the soap operas for a special report.

The place was packed with the Hill crowd, the air electric with the buzz of important men and women who passed the country's laws, who made life-or-death decisions, which sometimes even concerned the destiny of entire foreign nations. Fritch smiled and waved at the junior senator from Florida, who was dining alone with his twenty-something blond secretary.

He was sipping his martini, about to distract himself by scanning the celebrity wall—where the owner was photoed with all the right and beautiful people—wondering when his plaque would go up on that wall of honor, when he glanced beyond the bar—

And damn near choked on his olive.

Before Fritch could heave his bulk out of the booth and intercept him, the Gray Man had slid in right beside him, wedging him in the corner.

"Are you completely insane?" he snarled. "There are people here."

"Stop whining," the Gray Man growled. "These assholes can't see anything more than the tits on some babe."

"Something you should know about."

"I paid my dues, friend. I earned this attitude to be able to throw my stones around."

"You flew all the way up here to talk about your balls?"

"I'm here to discuss your future. I'm here to talk about life or death."

"Didn't we dance to this tired number last night?"

"Things have changed."

Fritch read between the lines, couldn't find his voice as the Gray Man dumped a shaving kit on the table.

"Take a peek."

He saw the waitress suddenly standing beside him. He started to bleat, "My friend won't be—"

"Double Dewar's, neat. You can put it on my friend's check."

Fritch looked around the dining room, hoping to God no one was watching.

"Stop that or I'll reach over and slap your face."

"Why you…"

"Look inside, this instant."

As if it were some obscene object, Fritch hesitated, then zipped open the kit. He blanched when he saw what was inside.

"You were busy this morning making calls to some of your Pentagon cronies. You sell yourself pretty good, I'll grant you that. But I've always maintained most people are stupid."

Fritch zipped up the bag and put it on the seat next to him as fast as he could make his trembling arms move. "You've got my phones tapped."

"Hey, I'm only trying to help. You said you wanted a gun, now you have one. Serial number's filed off," the Gray Man forged ahead, even as Fritch started flapping his hands for silence. "Can't be traced. You're that sick of your wife, there's your ticket to freedom. Only we both know your problems are far greater than what goes on under your own roof.''

"You bastard, this has gone too far.''

"No, you're wrong. It hasn't gone far enough. Hard truth is, it's only just begun. Hey, congratulations are now in order. Yes, I've still got a few friends close to the President. I hear the announcement will be made this afternoon. Why is it you pricks always see fit to cut in on my soap?''

Fritch put on a plastic smile for the waitress as she came back, placed the Gray Man's drink on the table, asked if they wanted anything else right then.

"Give us some time before I—we order,'' Fritch told her. When she marched off, he pinned the Gray Man with an angry stare. "I saw your goon this morning.''

"Not one of mine. You can be sure he's Ivan, though. Look, you need to wake up and smell the yuppie stink, friend. This town is crawling with Russians these days. They want influence and they will buy it, believe me. Many suits are up for sale in this town or have gotten caught with their little Oscar Meyers hanging out where they shouldn't—and believe me there could be film at eleven. Listen up, because I'm telling you for the last time they want their man in the White House come next election. Now, do you want to stay on the gravy train, or would you like for either myself or one of our Russian associates to drop you off at the next stop? Someplace maybe called Dead Man's Gulch, or horror of horrors for you, a town named Cell Block Bubba. Oh, by the way, if you need help with what I brought you, I can give you a few quick lessons."

"Thanks, but I'll figure it out myself."

"Well, figure this. Our friends in Russia have gone ahead and advanced a purchase order to our...well, I know how paranoid you are, so we'll call them the Double Eagle Crowd."

Fritch hung his head in disbelief.

"Drink up. This is your day. You're going to be SecDef. Your responsibilities to the world at large and especially to our friends have just jumped to new and wonderful heights."

Fritch looked at his watch, scanned the lobby.

"Don't worry. As soon as they show up, I'll make myself scarce. Hey, fat man, I want your undivided fucking attention."

Fritch shot a scowl at the Gray Man, his double chin quivering from rage.

"Something is going to happen in the next day or so in that part of the world. And it involves a mushroom cloud or two."

"What?"

"You heard me. Now, you will be contacted with instructions on how to proceed. As it will stand, you will become the frontline negotiator, the man of the hour."

"Do you understand that the President hasn't the first hint about what is going on around him?"

"I'm aware he's in the dark."

"He's innocent!"

"No man is innocent."

Fritch saw them filing through the doorway. "You've got to leave this second."

"Sure. I wouldn't want you to soil your fancy pants right before you went up before the nation."

Fritch felt his horror mounting, as the Gray Man took his sweet time, killing his drink in two long, slow gulps.

"I'll be in touch. Hope I didn't spoil your appetite."

Fritch sucked in a deep breath, trying to wash out the queasy feeling in his gut. This was a nightmare. How had this happened? What would he do? What could he do?

Fritch watched as the Gray Man just strolled away, as cool as a fall breeze, even excusing himself as he brushed past the President's aides on his way out the door. What was that look on Balton's face? he wondered. Confusion? The man slated to be the next press secretary was turning his head, watching the Gray Man go. Oh, God, did he recognize the Gray Man? If he did, what bullshit cover story could he lay on Balton?

Somehow, Peter Fritch found his legs, hefted himself out of the booth and put on his best winning smile, his hand out to start pumping the right people.

Show time.

The world was still his for the taking, and by God

he intended to take the ride all the way to the top. No Gray Man, no murderous Serbs, no Russian gangsters would deny him his page in the history books.

No way.

CHAPTER THIRTEEN

Showered, their bellies comforted by a smorgasbord of various ethnic cuisines, their heads buzzing with the right amount of alcohol, Ceasuvic, Cviic and Milenko exited the elevator.

The casino was massive, and the colonel found himself walking into a frenzied beehive of gambling and drinking, as if there were no tomorrow. Other than the gold-and-brass trimmings, the decor was pretty much Roman-Greco, none of it apparently meant to betray the roots of its owners. Coliseum-type pillars rose from white marble floor to glass ceiling, encircling the vast arena of gaming pits. A statue of Hercules holding two chained lions stood at the far end of the foyer, with various goddesses in different states of undress smattered around. There were gladiators with swords and nets standing guard at the edge of the bars, which faced each other from opposite sides of the gaming arena, both watering holes looking to run two hundred feet or more. Then Ceasuvic found everything dwarfed by the Godzilla-size statue of Thor with his hammer, which loomed from the center of the baccarat pit.

The colonel took the scenic route through the lake of blackjack and craps tables, finally strolling past the line of roulette wheels. Security detail was easy enough to pick out. Big and grim, with earpieces in place, they wore black suits and matching slacks, all of them showing a bulge of shouldered hardware beneath the coats. Ceasuvic counted six, but he knew there had to be more Russians roaming the premises.

The crowd itself was well-dressed for the most part. Ceasuvic noted a lot of well-heeled women, men in dinner jackets, a tux, here and there. There weren't too many shorts or sandals, certainly no tacky undershirts advertising this or that Atlantic City hot spot.

Class.

The colonel was dressed in a loose-fitting Armani jacket, his mini-Uzi in web strap rigging and shoulder-holstered sound-suppressed Glock easily accessible, Milenko and Cviic likewise dressed in silk and armed with compact SMGs and side arms. The slacks were Italian silk, too, and for the first time he could remember Ceasuvic felt good in clothes, even indulged a moment to take a whiff of the Brut aftershave he'd splashed on. If it weren't for the combat boots, they could have passed themselves off as foreign tourists.

He was leading his men to the bar, when he spotted the problem on the stool. Eye contact was brief, but it was long enough for Ceasuvic to read the situation. The guy was too squeaky clean, dressed too cheaply and looking too wary, the colonel suspected, to be anything other than an FBI or Justice Department agent. The final tip was the bulge of a weapon beneath the jacket.

Ceasuvic wondered if the casino itself was under surveillance as a link in the Russian Mafia chain, or whether the three of them were about to be arrested. If Churybik suspected the casino was under FBI surveillance, then Ceasuvic should have been informed. The colonel decided not to go back up to the penthouse to raise a stink. Besides, Brighton Beach was too busy right then playing with his cell phone.

He decided to go with whatever play was showed them. In Serbo-Croatian he told his men what to do, then strolled away to smell out any more cheap suits.

Joe Danko hated stakeout detail. Pulling surveillance duty every time out of the office was no way to advance a career, especially one that was already on the ropes.

Waiting for something to happen was always bad, since more often than not the suspects knew they were being watched and never did what they were supposed to do to get caught in the act of a crime. Six years on the FBI's Special Task Force on Organized Crime in New Jersey, and he'd only managed three arrests, all of them midlevel drug dealers, white-collar types who ended up rolling over any- and everybody to get a reduced sentence. But by the time Danko was ready to make more arrests the big fish had wiggled out of the FBI's net. The proverbial shit did roll downhill, so he found his superiors criticizing him to hell and back for shabby detective work, his lack of foresight, which allowed the bigger game to flee the country for parts unknown.

All too often these days Danko would look around at his fellow agents and find the other guy grabbing the glory, getting the promotion, stealing thunder that should have been his. Maybe it was his baby face, he thought, the thinning blond hair of a guy going bald, and he wasn't even thirty. Hell, a few of the senior-ranking agents still called him "Joey." Not Joe, or Joseph or Agent Danko. Joey.

Well, Joey this, he thought.

Tapping into phones, computer hacking into bank records, paperwork and stakeouts were all part of the job description, but Joe Danko wanted respect, needed to redeem himself for past failures. To get that he knew he had to do something important, something big that would make the upper echelons turn their heads and view him in a new light.

Part of the problem, he figured, was that he had never fired a shot in anger, never even been the first one through the door on a raid. Did he even have the right stuff to perform under fire? Whatever, insecurity was eating him alive. No combat, and with no major busts on his record, he began to feel the whole world was smirking at him.

All right, maybe the solution was wetting his hands with some bad guy's blood, carve a notch in his belt for the Special Agent in Charge on this gig to take notice that he was a stand-up lawman, not some office flunky fit only to shuffle paper. Damn straight, it was time to find the gladiator inside himself, he thought, as he raked a gaze over all the statues of warriors and gods of thunder and whatever other fighting men loomed around him.

Fat chance of kicking some butt today, he brooded, as he strolled the banks of slot machines, noting all manner of tourists, homegrown and foreign, pulling on the handles, the air electric around him with a frenzied hope quickly deflated by angry frustration, as if the machines themselves were screwing them over, taunting them. Everyone crying to make it big, he thought, a one-shot deal that would land them on easy street. Not too unlike himself, he had to admit.

He adjusted his dark sunglasses, shuffled his tired, agitated, skinny frame, again impulsively touching the bulge of the shoulder-holstered Glock beneath his dark jacket. This detail wouldn't put him over the top, unless, of course, something did happen, and he was right there in the thick of it. For one thing, the Justice Department had stepped in, playing God, as if the FBI weren't good enough to go up against a bunch of Ivan gangsters and needed their hands held on this one. Now they were ordered to wait for some Justice Department special agent hotshot—Ballard or Baldwin or something like that—to show up at the Olympus and take charge. The standing order was to watch any suspects who might turn up in the casino, and not to approach. And the suspects were Serbs, of all damn things, alleged to be somehow responsible for the two terrorist attacks on American soil, the killing of

NATO bigwigs over in Italy. Somehow the Justice Department had linked up with the FBI on the Serb angle, everyone exchanging intelligence on the fly.

Earlier his boss, SAC Williams, had briefed the six-man FBI detail. Danko had perused the surveillance photos, the report from the FBI and Army Military Intelligence on these Serb bad guys. Other than being mean and determined in the eyes—most of them scruffy around the edges but all of them clearly looking like lifelong felons—Danko had told himself he wasn't impressed. Foreign riffraff gone wild on U.S. soil, big deal. And the head honcho looked more like something out of a circus freak show than the most wanted war criminal to come down the pike since a few Nazis fled to South America. At least this Ceasuvic would be easy enough to spot in the crowd. If he showed at all.

The handheld radio crackled on his belt.

Danko weaved between the slot players, found a pocket of privacy beyond the fountain and palmed the radio.

"They're here, Danko, three of them. The colonel is headed your way. Remember, keep a low profile," Williams told him. "Our three Justice friends are slowly moving in your direction."

"Is their special agent here yet?"

"What's with the attitude, Danko?"

Danko decided he had better moderate his tone, or he knew Williams would yank him out of the game. "Feeling my nerves a little, that's all, sir. These guys are supposed to be the worst killers since John Dillinger, and we're ordered to stand around and just watch the suspects play craps, or whatever."

"Special Agent Ballard is en route, five minutes away. He just raised me. When he gets here we'll make our move. I don't need any cowboys. You copy that, Joey?"

Danko gritted his teeth. "Yes, sir, loud and clear."

Williams signed off. As Danko turned, moving away from the fountain, he spotted the Serb colonel. The man was larger than life, towering over the milling crowds near the craps table, uglier than sin, too. He looked weird, freakish to Danko, not someone who was supposed to be in charge of a runaway killing machine. What was that? he wondered. Had Ceasuvic just glanced his way?

Danko sucked in a deep breath and made the decision that would either cost him his job or crown him with long overdue glory. Besides, five minutes was a lifetime to hang back and wait for some Justice Department issue to roll in and get the show started. The order was to monitor this war criminal, make no moves—or maybe Danko simply hadn't understood, sir, already thinking ahead to make sure he was covered from any fallout for his blatant disobedience of a direct order. Well, things happened, Danko thought, when a bad guy was in your face. Maybe he just needed to light a fire at the right moment, make things happen, his way.

Maybe this was his day to shine, after all, Danko decided, as he followed the war criminal into the arcade. Again he touched the bulge of his weapon.

The time had come to show all concerned, whether friendly or hostile, that he was no one's flunky.

No more "Joey" after he made his next statement.

THE SKINNY GUY with the sunglasses was easy enough to nail as a Fed, his intent even more clear to Ceasuvic.

The baby-faced badge wanted to prove himself a tough guy, claim one big shaved-head Serb as his trophy.

Not this day, son, Ceasuvic thought, nor the following, not ever. Babyface was a done deal, only he didn't know it yet.

The colonel couldn't help but wonder if the Feds were stupid, careless, or if their brazenness was backed by an army of badges ready to tear through the place.

Not that it mattered to him. They were about to force his hand, leave him no option but to shoot his way out.

No problem. He could accommodate their death wish.

So far he had tallied six cheap suits, but there could be more scattered around the sprawling casino with its off-shooting restaurants, the gym and arcades. Ceasuvic wished he could indulge a long hard laugh at the obviousness of what they were. Same suits, same haircuts, all of them acting as if they were in charge of the moment, even though he could feel their nerves, these tough guys probably unsure of themselves in the long run. Which, he knew, could make them doubly dangerous if they felt the urge to advance limp careers at his expense, or prove themselves macho lawmen in their own eyes or to their peers.

Like the measure he took of Mr. Sunglasses, his instinct warning him the guy was looking to be some kind of hero.

Ceasuvic had even seen the skinny guy gape at him, talking on the radio, all agitation and anger, a moment before he strolled for the arcade's archway entrance.

If it went to hell, as he suspected it would, then Cviic and Milenko had the suit at the bar covered. Beyond that, Ceasuvic would use any means at his disposal to clear the casino, get the hell away from the Olympus.

One gesture of hospitality might or might not work to their advantage, he knew. Churybik had already called down to tell the security detail that the Serb trio was to be treated with the utmost respect, given anything they wanted on the house. That, Churybik had told the head of security, came straight from Viktor Tokinov. Of course, he didn't think the security detail would take kindly to the guests of honor shooting up the boss's casino. If the Russians turned ugly, well, accidents happened in combat.

He needed only the right moment to launch his attack. Beyond that it was anyone's guess if the three of them could make the elevators, ride to the penthouse, get Churybik in gear and fly away. A sick feeling of angry desperation hit Ceasuvic in the gut like a punishing body blow. If it was all going to end here, then he would finish it on his terms. And more than a few Feds would get killed in the process. Someone else from the other cells would have to carry the torch from there.

Ceasuvic played it cool, wandered into the arcade, just another tourist. Some uncanny sixth sense was working overtime now, and he could feel Mr. Sunglasses closing in on his general vicinity without having to look back.

Strolling through the mixed throng of adults and teenagers, Ceasuvic discovered right away what all the fuss here was about. First he saw the flashing neon sign hanging from the ceiling, which promised a million-dollar jackpot for any winner in the arcade. Next he found the banks of video games, all oriented to full-scale, graphic blood-and-guts combat. Folding his hands behind his back, Ceasuvic watched, amused, as the players triggered plastic pistols and machine guns with grim intent, hollering in angry glee when they scored hits, cursing when the caricatures killed them. There were SWAT games detailing raids on criminal hideouts.

It looked as if the younger crowd would simply leave the wounded where they fell, all the racket of men in pain seeming to urge the kids to dig deeper, shoot harder, kill and maim with even more heightened rage. The machines constantly pounded out the audio simulation of all manner of weapons fire.

Ceasuvic had to smile at what he saw. Some of the kids showed the definite potential of stone-cold killers in their eyes. He fought the urge to lecture them about how it was very different when the bullets and the blood were real. Just the same, he clearly picked up the vibes of primal animal aggression, kid or adult, male or female.

Welcome, he thought, to Viktor Tokinov's contribution to American culture.

"Hey, mister, I need a partner. You want to play?"

Ceasuvic stopped, looking down at the cherubic face of a boy he figured was no more than twelve. The kid was wild-eyed, breaking a sweat, as he gestured at the unmanned machine gun beside him.

The colonel shook his head. "I am sorry. I am afraid violence makes me very nervous."

The kid frowned, looking at Ceasuvic as if he'd just arrived from another planet. "It's only a game, mister."

"Indeed. I am sorry. I have no stomach for even simulated killing."

Ceasuvic left the kid to it.

Glancing around, he caught Mr. Sunglasses putting on the same spectator act. Ceasuvic decided it was time to cut the charade.

After a complete circle of the arcade, the colonel walked beyond the last bank of video games, hastened his pace, hoping Mr. Sunglasses would get nervous, realize he'd been made and put some urgency to his sorry tail job.

Ceasuvic rounded the archway and took two steps down a hallway that led to the rest rooms. Luckily, the hallway was free of traffic. In a few short moments, it wouldn't matter who was there.

The colonel pulled out his Glock, then mentally walked the distance it would take Mr. Sunglasses to come through the archway. He was off by a step or two, but by the time the guy showed, Ceasuvic was ready, and he exploded into action. A look of shock and horror carved Mr. Sunglasses's face a heartbeat before Ceasuvic fisted his jacket and flung him across the hall. The man bounced off the wall, digging in vain for his weapon, fingers fumbling inside his jacket, when Ceasuvic shoved the sound-suppressed muzzle between his eyes.

"I am afraid I will not make your day," the colonel growled, and squeezed the trigger.

A scream ripped into his ears from close by. Wheeling, he found a cocktail waitress release a tray of drinks, her hands flying up to her mouth. Ceasuvic stowed the Glock and worked the mini-Uzi free of its webbing. He needed a hostage and decided to charge the waitress when a young face appeared in the corner of his vision.

It was the lonely cherub.

CHAPTER FOURTEEN

"Ballard, come in, goddammit!"

Bolan plucked the handheld radio from his belt. He was angling off the boardwalk, bearing down on the row of dark-tinted glass doors that led inside to the Olympus when he saw the human stampede burst from the casino. They were screaming and slamming into one another, a few bodies wedging into doorways before they were bulldozed outside by panicked runners from behind, only to be trampled underfoot or the falling angry weight of terrified civilians, shoved this way and that.

Given the circumstances, Bolan didn't want to make some sweeping judgment, but what he saw rushing his way was a display of human nature at its worst. It was every man, woman and child for themselves, all concerned hell-bent only on saving their own necks. Bolan braced himself to somehow forge through the rush of humanity without getting bowled down, bones snapped like matchsticks.

A quick sideways glance, and Bolan found that Grimaldi looked equally grim in his determination to find some way through and beyond the tidal wave of descending flesh and bone. Shoulders squared, chin tucked in, Grimaldi charged beside the Executioner, both men hauling out mini-Uzi submachine guns from special shoulder rigging, the warriors bulling into the stampede. Using their weapons to wave some of the runners out of the way, more of the panicked crowd vented screams of terror at the sight of still more armed men. In other pockets of human missiles streaming at them, the warriors were forced to elbow, chop, slash or lower their shoulders like fullbacks hitting the line, one yard out from six points. It was ugly, rude to the point of reckless and borderline inhumane, but Bolan knew there was no other way to break through the madness and get inside the casino. If he had to whack a few civilians out of his path to get inside and save some lives, so be it.

Life was tough all over, thanks to a few murderous Serbs.

Bolan had his standard side arms holstered beneath his loose-fitting windbreaker, with Grimaldi backed up by a Beretta 93-R, spare clips in their pockets, but once again the Executioner feared it was all too little too late. As FBI Special Agent Williams barked his distress again, Bolan caught the sound of autofire on the agent's end. All hell had broken loose inside. There was little doubt in Bolan's mind that it was Ceasuvic who had started the fireworks. Silently the soldier cursed the timing. The colonel seemed blessed by some eerie or quirky fate that allowed him to jump the gun and beat a savage withdrawal just before Bolan could drop the noose over his head.

The soldier felt his frustration and anger reach new heights, wondering briefly what had gone wrong when the orders were crystal clear not to approach the suspects.

Whatever, it was time to torque it up, bull ahead into another hellstorm. Forget that Grimaldi had tracked the Russian choppers to their refueling site at Tokinov's Jersey airfield. Never mind that Brognola had scrambled this operation between the FBI and the Justice Department, all hunches figuring the Tokinov casino in Atlantic City was the temporary hole-up site for the enemy, especially after the choppers were tracked again by the jet's long-range radar, headed in this general direction. Sure enough, a Justice Department agent was on hand with a sedan, when Grimaldi had picked a field to set down in, twenty miles or so west of Atlantic City, the agent scrambled for their touchdown at the last possible half hour. Apparently, the Olympus had been under FBI surveillance for six months, the casino suspected of being a transshipment point for hefty sums of cash destined for Moscow. The Olympus had been slated to go down before Brognola had stepped in and inserted Bolan into the FBI's scheme, everything about this operation seat of the pants, to be sure, but the big Fed had worked some last-minute magic, just the same. The way had been paved for Bolan and Grimaldi to get there, with Special Agent Ballard placed in charge of the joint venture, but the soldier knew another road to hell waited on the other side of the front doors.

Bolan slowed his pace, shouldering through runners, reaching the doors. "Ballard here, Williams. Sitrep!"

"I got three suspects, Ballard. The Serbs, positive ID, this whacked-out Ceasuvic right in front of me, too. I got three agents down already, along with a half dozen or so civilians, some dead, some wounded. These bastards just started shooting up the place, Ballard. They've got a hostage, a kid, and they're moving for the elevator lobby. Not only that, but the goddamn Russian security force is now taking potshots at us, figuring this is a major bust! In short, we're pinned in a standoff!"

"Myself and Agent Griswald are coming through the front door now."

"Well, the cavalry's a few minutes late, Ballard."

Bolan understood the man's rage, but this was no time to point fingers. "Don't fire on the Serbs as long as they have a hostage. You copy?"

"Best you can do, I guess I gotta take it. Yeah, I frigging copy that!"

The Executioner hit the foyer running, took in the action on the fly, weaving and bobbing through the stragglers fleeing the hell zone. In all directions beyond the entrance, the sprawling casino was a hornet's nest of pandemonium. Bodies were dropping near the baccarat tables, a tuxedo chopped to crimson ribbons in that direction; bullets finally hammering off the base of the statue of Thor. Players and tourists were sailing over craps tables, diving for cover. Other bodies were drilling into one another, a few runners slamming one another off slot machines.

At some point about fifty yards ahead, Bolan spotted the FBI-Justice team. They were hunkered down in the baccarat pit, weapons aimed toward the bar on the north side.

And Bolan found the unmistakable ghoulish visage of the Serb colonel. Sure enough, it was a stalemate at the moment, and Bolan read the Serbs' defensive evac tactic for what it was.

The colonel had an arm locked around the throat of the teenaged boy, the trio backpedaling down the front of the bar for the short flight of steps that led to the hallway with its bank of elevators. Flanking the hostage, two other Serbs had the muzzles of their stubby SMGs jammed into the boy's ears.

They had created a perfect human shield.

Normally, Bolan could have shot out a leg, an elbow, something that would jolt the hostage-taker with an instant of agony before the Executioner put out his lights with one between the eyes.

Not so here.

It didn't matter if he killed one of the trio. The other two would still have enough time to shoot the boy before they went down in a hail of bullets.

The Serbs were game to commit suicide at the moment.

Bolan couldn't recall in recent memory having gone up against such tenacious opposition. Their will to go down, even if it meant dying here, flared Bolan's suspicion that something far more sinister was on the Serb back burner than runaway slaughter on U.S. soil.

The Executioner and Grimaldi bounded down the steps into the gaming arena. Ceasuvic had gained the upper hand for the time being, but Bolan had to hold on to hope, fleeting as it might be, that he could find a chink in their armor.

Something, anything to cut this madman down, once and for all.

CEASUVIC DRANK in their fear, horror and uncertainty like chilled vodka. He backed up, the boy surrounded by the three of them in what the colonel called the Talon Tactic. It was a ploy he had used in the killing fields of Bosnia. If they needed to evac a building that was under sniper fire, three men would snatch the closest available hostage, create a ring around their catch, usually a child. It always struck Ceasuvic as amazing, even pathetic, that the opposition would hold their fire, not risk a hero's shot to free the hostage. Of course, if the opposition opened fire, the hostage was dead anyway, and the hostage-takers were left with no option but to go down fighting like lions, dying on their feet. It was a gamble Ceasuvic was always willing to take, preying on the compassionate side of the opposition.

So far, the Talon Tactic was working just like it had in Bosnia.

The surviving agents were huddled in the baccarat pit. At least two of them had gone down in the opening rounds, Cviic and Milenko catching the Fed at the bar in a scissoring cross fire of bullets, knocking him off his stool.

Ceasuvic had gone to work right away, jacking the kid along, spraying the crowd, creating the necessary chaos to get him to the point where he was now close to the steps that led to the elevator lobby. He had just loosed another short burst of subgun fire into the gaming pit, nailing a few tourist runners, making sure the Feds understood he was prepared to die standing. The kid was still wailing in his armlock from the sudden roar of autofire in his ear. He squeezed the kid's throat, cutting off his air until he got the message to be quiet.

"Let the kid go! You'll never make it out of here!"

Ceasuvic pinned the booming voice to a statue of some goddess at ten o'clock in the baccarat pit. The black guy had come out of nowhere, and the colonel had heard him bellowing out the orders, Feds taking up cover, leapfrogging around, trying to close in.

"You a tough guy?" Ceasuvic laughed down at the angry black face. "Why don't you come up here and get him yourself?"

"Give it up!"

"I see, you are true hero," the colonel taunted, carefully backing up the steps. "Sounds to me like you and your boyfriends, especially the skinny blonde I shot, could have used a week in Kosovo. Imagine yourselves getting passed around by sex-starved Serb soldiers. Toughen you up some."

"Why, you son of a—"

"Your boy wanted to be a hero, some kind of Dirty Harry he was. Go back to the arcade and see where that got him. He wanted me as a trophy, only now he squats like a girl on the mantelpiece of the Devil."

"You mother—"

A handheld radio suddenly crackled with the familiar voice of Churybik. Swiveling, Ceasuvic spotted the instrument snarling out Brighton Beach's voice near the outstretched hand of one of the Russian pit bosses who had been killed when he had opened fire on the Feds.

"Milenko, quickly. Grab that!" Ceasuvic ordered in Serbo-Croatian.

A short dart to the fallen Russian, Ceasuvic fanning their positions with his mini-Uzi, and Milenko came back with the handheld radio, reclaiming his part of the ring.

"Hold the boy tight!" Ceasuvic released his own hold on the hostage and hit the transmit button.

In Russian he said, "Churybik, you neglected to tell me your casino was crawling with FBI!"

"What the hell is going on down there, Colonel?"

"Get the choppers going now! We are coming up!"

"Colonel—"

"Shut up, idiot! Just do it or we will all be killed, or worse, arrested!"

"Viktor will hear about this!"

"Viktor will hear you are an idiot for not knowing the FBI was right here in your face!"

He heard Churybik curse, but he was already tossing away the radio. Slowly they backed toward the elevators in the lobby, Ceasuvic glancing back and forth, seeing the crouched shadows trying to close on the steps ahead.

"Any closer, the kid dies!" the colonel bellowed. "We die, too. I do not care!"

They froze, and Milenko hit the button on the closest elevator. Ceasuvic was wondering what to do next, when suddenly Milenko volunteered to die like a lion.

"Colonel, you have told me what this is all about. It will be worth sacrificing my own life. Go," Milenko said, then reached into his coat pocket and pulled out three Russian frag grenades. "My gift, sir, to you. Just remember me when you are victorious."

Ceasuvic showed this worthy Serb a smile. "Keep one for yourself. Use it as soon as we are in the elevator. That way, if you can…"

Milenko shook his head. "Just get out of this country. It will be enough if you succeed."

"I will succeed. Serbia will prevail, or we die as one people."

"Then my death will not be in vain, sir."

The elevator bell chimed as the door opened, beckoning the final leg to immediate freedom. If he could have spared the moment, Ceasuvic would have embraced Milenko. It was all too rare these days to find a soldier who believed in the greater good of those he fought for, much less was willing to die for it.

Ceasuvic gave Milenko a nod, held the brave soldier's stare for a long dangerous moment. Along with Cviic, he hauled the kid into the elevator. He took the key from his pants pocket, slipped it into the slot above number fifteen and keyed them in for the penthouse floor.

The doors closed, drowning out some of Milenko's ferocious battle cry, the rattle of his automatic weapons fire. Ceasuvic couldn't help but admire that sort of loyalty, commend the man for his unflinching bravery. Ceasuvic silently, feverishly wished Milenko luck, hoping the man at least managed a few federal kills, a tourist or two at worst, before a cheap suit scored a fatal shot.

THE SERB OPPOSITION had clearly crossed over to a point of no return. Up until then they seemed driven by a sense of direction and purpose, misguided and wrong as it was. And so far, Bolan still didn't have any idea what their ultimate goal or destination was, but his adversaries all of a sudden appeared as if they didn't care if their master plan went down with the ship, as long as they made sure a whole lot of people sank right along with them. Bolan had seen this sort of mindless savagery many times before, when the enemy knew the end was upon them. Yes, the Serbs were now feeding their sense of mounting desperation and impending doom with indiscriminate slaughter, which included taking innocent lives. If they couldn't live, no one else should either.

Bolan scanned the elevator lobby, running past the roulette wheels.

One of the Serbs had lagged behind to hold back any advance on the elevators. The hardman was wheeling around the corner, his Ingram MAC-10 blazing away, the Serb hollering at the top of his lungs, when Bolan came under sudden fire. The Executioner was leaping over the dead and the wounded, Grimaldi peeling off his flank, when he spotted what he strongly suspected was part of the Russian Mafia's security detail. The big goon stood on the landing near the entrance to a restaurant, triggering a .44 Magnum pistol as fast as he could squeeze the trigger. Bolan slashed his charge between a row of slot machines. Even with the combined racket of shouting and autofire, Bolan's ears took the full spiking of the hand cannon's peals as slugs shattered glass, sparks taking to the air like pinwheeling firecrackers above the Executioner's head. He cut another dangerous charge between the next row of slot machines, and glimpsed the Russian hardman digging a speed-loader out of his jacket. The Russian caught sight of Bolan bringing up his mini-Uzi, started to beat a run to his left when the Executioner held down the subgun's trigger, gave the guy some lead and kicked him off his feet with a 9 mm stitching up the ribs.

The soldier found the home team trading shots with the Serb. Then he spotted another Russian goon creeping up on the backside of the Justice-FBI men, his hand cannon poised. The Executioner blew him off his feet with a 3-round burst of 9 mm Parabellum shockers.

On the move toward the bar leading to the elevator banks, Bolan assessed the situation. The Serb was holding back any charge for the elevators. It was unconfirmed, but Bolan suspected the choppers were grounded on the casino's roof. The Serb was obviously a sacrificial lamb, meant to eventually die there but not before he'd given Ceasuvic enough time to fly away.

Bolan intended to deliver the Serb all the death wish he could ever ask for.

The Executioner was twenty feet or so from linking up with Grimaldi when the Serb whipped around the corner and hurled a grenade. Bolan glimpsed the Serb taking hits in the upper chest from the relentless cracking of semiautomatic pistols, then saw the grenade bounce up and ahead, deep into the baccarat pit. It was a wild toss, well beyond the line of Feds, but the grenade landed a few feet from a woman paralyzed with terror. Bolan knew he couldn't reach the woman in time to save her.

Grimaldi could, and did, sweeping over the woman and hauling her to her feet. Bolan could only hope Grimaldi had enough seconds available to secure cover.

The blast trumpeted new chaos. Bolan hugged cover behind a craps table, riding out the explosion as glass and other debris blew over his position. He looked up, running, angling for the bar. Beyond the cloud of smoke he picked out Grimaldi rising from the woman, a roulette wheel mangled to giant jagged teeth by shrapnel.

"Jack! Over here!"

Stowing the mini-Uzi, the soldier palmed both the Beretta 93-R and the mammoth .44 Magnum Desert

Eagle. While he waited for Grimaldi, Bolan raised Williams, ordering him to hold his fire.

"I know that look, Sarge," Grimaldi said, crouching beside Bolan at the lip of the landing leading up to the bar. "You have something in mind to break the tie."

"Time to swing for the fences."

Quickly, Bolan told Grimaldi about the Serb tactic for charging and clearing out an entrenched enemy position.

The Stony Man pilot showed Bolan a grim smile. "Definite risk factor, but it sounds like a winner if you connect for the homer. I'm ready whenever you are."

Bolan saw the Serb, bloody and snarling out curses, pivot around the corner, then the warrior rolled onto the landing. The Serb started to turn his way, looking confused by the abrupt lull in pistol fire. Bolan triggered both weapons as fast as he could, spraying the cornerstone as the Serb jumped behind cover. A primal scream ripped the air, the hardman figuring his clips were nearly empty, when the Serb danced out into Bolan's gunsights.

The Executioner charged, tracking his adversary with both weapons. As he scored flesh with a 9 mm-.44 Magnum combo, Grimaldi cut loose with his mini-Uzi. The Executioner burned out both clips, but Grimaldi finished up, his long burst of subgun fire driving the Serb down the hall, the hardman firing even as he took the hammering force of the 9 mm storm. The Serb toppled under a rain of his own blood and shredded silk.

Bolan reached the elevators, glimpsing the huddled mass of terrified casino guests spread down the long hallway. Groans, cries and soft whimpering filtered into the Executioner's ringing ears. Three elevator cars stood on each side of the hall. It would be a gamble, riding up in the elevator. If Ceasuvic had a shooter waiting up top, Bolan was dead as soon as the doors opened.

"Now what, Ballard?"

Bolan turned, seeing the grim anger on Williams's face. "We ride to the top."

CHURYBIK STOOD in the middle of the living-room floor, staring at nothing. He was finished in America.

He laughed out loud, the sound seeming to hit his ears from a great distance.

Like from Moscow.

There were no excuses, no justifications, no bullshit left to hand to Viktor Tokinov. Churybik knew he would be held accountable for this string of disasters, for the madness of the Serbs. How could this have happened? He decided it was pointless to stand there and wish he could reach back in time and fix it all. Fix what? Change what? What was the use agonizing now over something he couldn't change? Still, it was all so incredible, the questions kept coming.

There was FBI in the casino? The Olympus was about to be stung by an army of Feds, a major money-laundering operation uncovered by the Americans, on the verge of being shut down? How could he or any of his associates have missed a bunch of federal suits strolling the premises? The Olympus was Viktor's pride and joy. What was he going to tell the man?

Little did it all really matter now.

Ivan Churybik was going to Greece. Before the shooting started downstairs, he had called Viktor. The Serbs would get what they wanted. Ceasuvic had raised his troops before going below and igniting hell, his backup maybe an hour or so from the private airport.

Churybik felt like the loneliest, most miserable man on the planet. Again he laughed. The train, he thought, called the good life was leaving the station. He pictured himself running after the caboose, charging hard, screaming out his pleas for the conductor to stop. He was just about to touch the ladder's rung when his legs gave out and he landed flat on his face. It was a strange image to dwell on right then, but he had to admit all he had worked for, fought and even killed for was now for nothing.

He was nothing.

And, of course, Viktor would choose a fall guy. Guess who, he thought, would be the scapegoat—no, the sacrificial lamb—for this disaster in America? He imagined Viktor would have another Duklov on hand. Only next time some thug would march him out to the nearest field and pump a bullet behind his ear.

When Ceasuvic swept through the front doors, snarling out his demands, and Churybik spotted their hostage boy, he didn't even feel the first flash of anger or surprise.

Nothing shocked him anymore where the Serbs were concerned.

Churybik suspected his troubles would soon be over. He wanted to feel something, outrage, fear, anything, but he was completely empty inside, his soul used up by stress, by the constant anger and worry of fighting to hold on to his empire.

Well, the empire was crumbling all to hell, falling fast and hard all over him.

"Did you hear me?"

Of course, Churybik had heard the Serb. He just didn't feel like answering a bunch of questions, didn't feel like jumping at the Serb's bark to move out.

Despair, he thought, was funny like that. A man was no longer afraid. He was deep in his own dark pit, no way out.

Well, dead men didn't have to care, think or feel. Even more strange to Churybik right then was that he found a sense of peace in hopelessness.

Very strange. It was going to be a long flight to Greece, and Churybik decided he would share these feelings with the colonel. He was curious to learn what train was leaving the colonel's station.

CHAPTER FIFTEEN

The elevator ride to the top, followed by the brisk march out onto the rooftop of the Olympus proved another exercise in futility for Bolan.

The soldier stood, clenching his jaw, Grimaldi and Williams by his side at the far edge of the roof. In angry silence, they watched the distant choppers shrinking from sight.

"I can scramble some flying eyes..."

"Forget it," the Executioner told Williams.

"What the hell you talking about, Ballard? Forget it? I got three dead agents in the casino, not to mention God only knows how many civilians shot up, dead or dying. This bastard Serb on some rampage..."

Bolan let the man vent. He understood his anger, but the Executioner had enough bad feelings at the moment for twenty men. Somehow, the setting sun felt to Bolan as if it mocked his dark mood. When Williams was finished unloading his anger, the soldier told him, "I'll handle it from here."

"How? Handle what? Look, Ballard, I don't want

to get into some pissing contest with the Justice Department, but we've been all over this casino for months, so I'll spare telling you how this operation just got wasted all to hell. We know about the Russian Mafia owning this place. We know Ivan Churybik is the big shot out of Brighton Beach, the mover and shaker for Viktor Tokinov, Moscow's imported version of John Gotti. Hey, how about you guys sharing a little information with us poor, ignorant FBI types? Because I'm getting a bad whiff here, remembering your Alamo charge below. It struck me as something other than your standard-issue G-man. Skip the ask no questions, I'll tell you no lies. Let me ask you at least what is it you think you're going to do? I mean, tell me, am I crazy, or stupid? Or has the Justice Department got some expendables, black-ops types they deny having at the CIA, top-secret assassins out headhunting these bastards, you know, something you'll never read about in the papers?''

Williams was on the money, even though Bolan could read through his sarcasm. ''You're neither stupid, crazy nor ignorant.''

''And that's that.''

''That's that.''

Bolan needed to touch base with Brognola ASAP. The Farm had its own cybernetic knack for tracking aircraft, reaching overseas to various American military bases and aircraft carriers stationed around the world; the cyber warriors ironing out the way for Bolan to resume his campaign with a little help from the military and various intelligence agencies. If he could get a general lead even on where the enemy might be headed next, Bolan could place himself within striking distance.

"We go down to the casino, see that the wounded are taken care of," Bolan told Williams.

"What a guy. Bleeding civs shipped out and the dead rubber-bagged, while you guys stroll off into the sunset. Have a nice day. That how it's gonna be?"

"We'll talk, put our heads together."

Williams grunted. "Sounds like on my side of that Ping-Pong table the ball's gonna shoot past me."

Bolan didn't have time to dance with Williams. An idea was taking shape, one that on the surface sounded so crazy not even he was sure he could pull it off.

But the Executioner knew that in his world, life was a gamble. One day he knew those dice would roll up, crap him out of the game. It wouldn't happen this day, and he would do his damnedest to see he kept winning tomorrow.

Which meant seeing his enemies trampled underfoot like the poisonous snakes they were. And, of course, there was always the little matter of surviving to come out the other side.

That was something Bolan never took for granted.

THE SIGHT OF Dragan Ulrok's broad, flat ugly face fueled Ceasuvic with confidence and hope.

It was good to be back among his own kind.

Any other time and place, and he would have embraced Ulrok, passed the smokes and vodka.

Instead he ran an appreciative stare over the grim faces of twenty brother Serbs, nodded his gratitude and told them to split into groups of ten for each of the two jets. Naturally they looked at his hostage, eyes questioning the presence of the terrified boy. There was no need to explain. The mere absence of his Pittsburgh platoon spoke grim volumes, even though Ceasuvic had already informed Ulrok of his problems.

By the time they flew back to the Russian's private airfield, darkness covered the New Jersey countryside. Turbofan engines were now screaming in Ceasuvic's ears, the sound fanning his sense of urgency. He found Churybik striding across the tarmac, coming from the squat white office. Strangely enough, the colonel hadn't heard the first outburst from Brighton Beach about what he had had to do back at the casino. No whining about this latest round of slaughter causing still more grief for the Tokinov bunch. No squawking either about how their jets could be tracked by American radar, this unlogged illegal flight pointing still more suspicion Moscow's way.

The colonel was well aware his enemies had all manner of aircraft that patrolled the skies around the world, satellites orbiting the earth, capable even of pinning down a crow in flight. He had come this far on anger, his hunger for vengeance, burning will-power and the ability to kick ass and kill. Who, what could stop him now?

"The guns?" he asked Churybik.

"Already on both jets. Just as you wanted."

"RPGs, also?"

"As the Americans might say, you are good to go."

This was beginning to feel all too easy to Ceasuvic. There was something in Churybik's eyes he didn't trust. What did he see in Brighton Beach? Despair? Cunning?

"The boy stays with us until we are safely in Greece. Will that be a problem for you?"

Churybik shook his head. "I do not see any problem with that."

Deciding he would watch Churybik closely, Ceasuvic turned and found his men boarding the jets. He would feel great relief once they were flying over the Atlantic Ocean. Once they landed in Greece, though, he was aware new problems, new challenges would arise. He knew it could get worse before he turned the corner. He dreaded some fouled-up repeat performance of what he had forged and agonized through the past day or so. But there was too much reward waiting on the other end to concern himself now with all the suffering and death they had endured.

Revenge would see all dead Serbs finally rest in peace.

Suddenly, the colonel was weary to the bone, ached and throbbed from head to toe, feeling the full brutal effects of the combat stretch now that the adrenaline had left his body like a mist thinned by the wind. Handing the boy off to Cviic, he boarded the jet and settled into his seat, his dry, tired eyes grateful for the dim overhead light.

Greece. Delivery of the two items.

Victory was just around the corner. It was good to be in motion, everything falling into place. Too much blood had been shed, too many good soldiers had lost their lives for him to fail now.

The next day held promise, bright as the next rising sun.

Tired as he was, Ceasuvic felt supercharged with renewed hope, determination, purpose. He would be reunited, he thought, with the cell that had killed those NATO worms who had sat behind the lines with their pointers and their paper and their propaganda mouthpieces spewing their lies to the world, those master planners of that air war, safe and sound, always giving the orders to bomb, bomb, bomb Yugoslavia. How many women and children had those people killed while they sat, sniffing brandy, puffing out their chests as they announced another day of so-called successful NATO bombing?

How much bullshit was he supposed to swallow? None, he answered himself. Never had, never would.

Ceasuvic couldn't wait until he showed NATO he could play that same strategy of death from above. And far better, far more horribly than anything they could envision in their worst nightmares.

Then there were his own nightmares, and they were all too real. His heart ached, as he thought about Karina.

He tried to free himself of his anguish, breathing deeply, squeezing his eyes shut as he felt the jet rolling, then lifting off, tilting and flying east. He wanted to enjoy rest, but his mind kept racing, burning up with sudden rage. One American bastard's grenade had not only killed his woman, but so disfigured that angelic face.

He ground his teeth together. Well, the cowboy, whoever he was, whoever he worked for, was dead.

This night he only wanted to see his dream of vengeance when he slept. He smiled as he fantasized seeing Karina's face, smiling above the horror he would unleash.

His angel, yes, soaring and laughing above the mushroom cloud.

His nerves raw, desperate to relax and sleep, he cracked his eyelids open, believing if he forced himself to stay awake that soon he would drift off into deep, much-deserved slumber. He found his men comfortably settled in, the boy no longer sobbing, just sitting there, looking numbed by terror.

"Son, listen to me. Look at me," Ceasuvic said, his angry voice jolting the boy out of his limbo of shock and fear. "You will live. You will be returned to your family. You have a mother and father?"

The boy gave the colonel a shaky nod. "Y-yeah. Are you...going to kill me?"

A loaded question, if ever Ceasuvic heard one. He was never a man to make promises he couldn't keep, but he figured in this instance the last thing he needed was a hysterical kid. The boy would live, unless, of course, he was forced at some point to use him again as a shield, or if they pressed him to the wall and he had to kill the boy.

"No. You will make it. Get some sleep, boy."

"Trains."

Ceasuvic wasn't sure he'd heard Churybik right, and threw Brighton Beach a curious look. The Russian underboss stared out the cabin's window, starwatching, as if he were praying to some god up there, or wishing he was worlds removed from the present. There was an oddly distant look in Churybik's eyes, and the Russian's bizarre somber mood was starting to disturb Ceasuvic. Was that self-pity in the eyes of Brighton Beach? Not that he cared, but it didn't escape him that Churybik had lost everything that meant anything in the world to him.

Tough.

Ceasuvic had his own losses to grieve over, but he wasn't about to sit around and brood.

"What, may I ask, is your particular train, Colonel?"

Gaze narrowing, Ceasuvic stared at Churybik, thinking Brighton Beach was just about pushed over the edge.

"Trains?"

"Life is a train, you see," Churybik droned, his gaze staying fixed on the darkness beyond the jet. "It rumbles toward us, big, powerful, unstoppable, unless it crashes into something or is derailed by an event beyond its control. Train stops in the depot. Some board, some wait for the next train to come along, perhaps to take them to their next destination. Trains, they have names. Hope. Joy. Greed. Love. Money. Power. Can't you see, Colonel?"

"I am afraid you are making absolutely no sense at all. Are you drunk?"

"Stoli. In the back. The wet bar. The train named—"

"Spare me. The train named Stoli. You are very much beginning to irritate me."

"The train named Irritation."

"Goddamn it, shut up with the trains!"

Ceasuvic felt the eyes of his men boring into him, suspected they were either curious or concerned about this babbling fool among them.

Churybik lapsed into a long and grim silence. Ceasuvic hoped he had ended the Russian's strange rambling with his outburst. All he wanted was sleep. He was just about to close his eyes, when he sensed Churybik wanted to say something else. Sure enough, as he looked back at the Russian, he saw the man staring at him with laughter in his eyes.

"Colonel. Allow me to say one last thing and I will be silent. Your train, it is called Death. And, unlike myself, you will manage to grab the ladder and pull yourself aboard."

THE SCENIC VIEW of Washington at night didn't impress him in the least. This town was divided straight down the middle, the men and the mice, even though they were out there, running around sugarcoating everything with political correctness. By day, he thought, it was the stuffed suits and the self-impressed strutting, playing their power games, telling the world what they thought and believed was the Gospel truth.

They gave the impression that they were the elite and the privileged, better than everyone else because they had the power, the cameras, the right amount of money.

Well, they could kiss his ass, and then some.

By night another crowd came out, only they were armed with guns, pumped on anger, desperate for money. They were ready to kill at the slightest insult, maybe waste some crackhead ten bucks short on a debt or mug some congressman out for a jog to show the Hill bunch what tough really was all about. The night crowd didn't have all those other benefits, and they were hell-bent on letting the other half know all about it. A part of him could sympathize. The world he used to be an integral and critical part of had shunned him, tossed him away like trash.

But whoever said life was fair? And why bother with the world beyond himself? They would all go on doing whatever they were doing out there, and there wasn't enough money, power and fame on the planet to keep them from it.

He pulled the drapery over the hotel-room window, shutting out the Potomac River, the Washington Monument, all that crap the tourists came here to see, swelling the ranks of an already overpopulated city.

The Gray Man puffed on his cigar. The cell phone with its secured line was pressed to his ear. There had been a long silence on the other end after he got the man up to speed. Long enough for him to take a look at the world beyond his hotel, pump himself up with his own anger over the past. Finally, he felt compelled to say something to get the voice from overseas talking.

"You know how it is. The human factor is always the loose end."

He listened to the deep raspy voice on the other end, scarred by years of stress, Bombay gin and Camel cigarettes.

"So, our fat friend who just became SecDef has a bad case of small testicles."

He liked that. The analogy worked. The guy should have been a scriptwriter for Hollywood instead of the brains, brawn and, yes, balls behind NATO.

"That gives me serious pause."

"He'll go with the program," the Gray Man said.

"Will he? You're sure of that?"

"He's scared, sees his whole future going up in flames unless he asks me how high he should jump. I like those kinds of guys."

"They don't make you just a tad nervous, my friend?"

"Okay, I'll grant you that."

"You said he wanted to get his hands on a gun, but you took the liberty to dump one in his lap?"

"Makes him feel safer, I guess."

"All this glossing over and glibness makes me somewhat jumpy."

"What do you mean?" he asked the man who used to run the U.S. Army Military Intelligence.

"No man, no matter who or what he is, doesn't want a gun unless he feels threatened, unless he feels fit enough to use it. Not only that, but you tell me you simply roll right into the hottest Hill restaurant, in full public view and shake his tree.''

He heard the criticism, understood the concern on the other side of the Atlantic. ''I made a judgment call.''

A grunt. ''Next time you decide to make such a call, kindly run it past me first.''

''Understood.''

''Now that we're clear on that, I still have this gut feeling there was another reason why you did what you did.''

He drew a breath, paced the room. ''You're right, there was. Our boy is of use only up to a point. His use all along has been intended to be, well, what I call the chaos and terror factor. I wouldn't worry about the gun bit. The way I read him, when the heat blows his way, he'll stick that gun in his mouth.''

''And his suicide is meant to aid us? How?''

''Voids, gaps, limbos. First, he'll attempt to put out the fire that our Russian friends have granted the Serbs to start. He'll be unsuccessful, and there'll be a scandal, complete with film at eleven. I mean to sow distrust, fan the flames of a potential holocaust.'' He felt his heart pumping confidence through his blood, now that he was on a roll. ''I want the average American looking harder and with more suspicion and cynicism than ever at their elected officials. It's about power, right?''

''That, and control. Mine.''

''So, you agree. Soon we'll walk as gods among mortals.''

"Part of it. Yes, we leave the world to its own madness. Understand, my friend, that all I want is out of this farce over here. I don't want to finish my career, much less my life, attempting to change things, make some statement, or go down in history as the good guy warlord of the Balkans."

"What do you want?"

"Peace of mind. My own."

He paused. He could appreciate that particular concept, even if he only believed it was fantasy.

"I can almost hear your mind at work," the overseas voice said. "You're thinking everyone has their own agenda in this. You're right. But we are only a larger version of all men. Greedy, self-serving, yes, but I see a difference. In our deal if everyone stays the course, everyone wins, everyone walks and the everyday woes of everyday men are left for others to fret over. I want paradise on earth—my own.

"But I also understand your doubts, your worries that it could come crashing down on our heads at any moment. Why don't you sit back and enjoy your forced retirement for the moment? Soon enough we'll point our fingers and say I told you so. Yes, it's truly a damned shame, the two of us having fought for a country we once believed in. Thing is, it's an ideal, this freedom and justice and equality for all men. We fought for principle. You fight for the principle, not necessarily the people. Sad truth is that what I've seen going on in America, the corruption, the greed, the crime, a society out of control, where even the children are murderers and rapists—I can no longer believe in that sort of people. Only a fool would. The wise wake up, shake their heads at the futility, the insanity, hopefully have a nice fat nest egg of cash tucked away to see them walk away from it. Let the animals eat one another.''

He found himself nodding. Where he was in it for revenge, and, of course, the money and the totality of the vindication he would feel from the coming power play, he came to see this viewpoint of angst. Only he heard the warrior on the other end rising out of his own ashes of hopelessness, prepared to save himself because he was more worthy than those he fought for in the past.

Principle, right.

''I want you to stay on top of our boy. I tell you what, I have business in Washington anyway. I'll be flying in the next day or so. Maybe the two of us should arrange a little rendezvous with this guy?''

''It can be worked out.''

''See to it.''

''Beyond that?''

''Beyond what, setting the SecDef straight, you mean?''

''There's always the Russians to consider,'' he told the man overseas.

''They won't matter soon, not to us anyway. Stepping-stones to our own heaven, that's all they are. Yeah, I know, I took their money, but I also sought it out. Do I sound nervous to you about the Russians?''

He chuckled. "Was it the second or third wife that drove you over the edge?"

"Whoever said it was anything about that?"

"Well, your personal woes were always a matter of public record."

"Do I sound woeful to you? No criticism intended, but what happened with me was job-related, my long workdays heaping pressure on my family."

"No criticism felt on this end."

"Good. Because we are almost seeing the daylight. As for the Russians, they'll be on their own in short order, I don't give a damn if that whole town shuts down."

"At least we have proof, plenty of backup."

"Yeah, well, whatever dirty pictures, videos you have exchanged with them, kept, whatever, I don't especially care for an advanced, front-row screening."

"It's insurance, and I do have plenty of ammo on hand. Talk to me, while we're on that subject. Should I hand it all over to the Russians, just in case the wrong people, by freak of happenstance, come sniffing around?"

"No, don't do that. Whatever you have could be of critical importance some day. Why trump when you don't have to?"

"Makes sense."

"Of course. Hold on to that high joker."

"Consider it in my pocket."

"Well, I would find a safety deposit box."

"I feel more comfortable keeping it all right where it is."

"Whatever."

"But if it eases any concerns, I have long since made copies. Spread around."

"Always cover your ass. All right, I can't think of anything else we need to discuss, but as we're both aware, during the next days and weeks to come we need to stay close."

"I don't think I'll somehow just lose this secured cellular."

He listened to the long silence on the other end. Finally, the voice spoke. "I was just thinking about our boy. When it hits the fan, well, I can see him running straight to the President, probably crying and begging forgiveness, pleading for the attorney general to be merciful."

"I hear you. He'll want a long pleasant vacation in the Witness Protection Program."

"It would definitely fit his style."

"You're headed somewhere with this, I take it."

"You take it right," the raspy voice said. "If it looks like he's going to crack...well, do I have to spell it out?"

"Not at all."

"Sounds to me like you're sitting right in his backyard."

"My Ivan comrade who is on it can even tell you when his wife goes to the bathroom."

The raspy voice chuckled. "On that note, I think I'll sign off. I'll be in touch."

When the line went dead, he punched off and set the cell phone on the dresser. He felt so amazed by progress, how everything was so beautifully dropping into place, he was light-headed, believed he could damn near walk on air.

Or water.

Yes, he was beginning to see just what real power and miracles were all about. It all came down to a man's will to shape his destiny, his iron hand to dictate his own terms, either up close in the other guy's face or from a thousand miles away.

If he excluded the SecDef, his own small circle of iron men made the entire rest of the world look weak and pathetic. There really was nothing divine about life, nothing supernatural or mystical, he concluded. Those who didn't have the guts to stand and take what they wanted were always muddying the minds of others with all that nonsense, as if there was some answer only they—the religious, the mystic, the political schemers, the rich—held a claim to.

The bottom line was his own circle were gods.

He found himself laughing at the world.

The Day couldn't come soon enough, but it would happen. When it did, he might even call the President of the United States himself, chuckle, tell the guy what smart and tough was really all about.

Let him know what it was like to be a god.

CHAPTER SIXTEEN

"The bottom line, Striker, is that we have on our hands the makings of the worst international incident since World War II, one of epic nightmare implications. And that in itself could be the understatement of the new century. I've been in touch with the Man," Brognola said, referring to the President of the United States, who secretly sanctioned all of Stony Man Farm's covert operations. "He said, and I quote, 'Pull no punches. Tell your man do whatever he thinks necessary to terminate the madness.' Not that you ever need to be told that, but I don't think he'll sleep again until this is over, especially after I brought him up to speed with the latest revelation from our Serbian songbird. And I'm staying planted right here in the office until this thing is resolved, one way or another, and I don't think I have to tell you how I want this to end."

"Wrapped up, nice and neat."

"Put a ribbon on it for me," Brognola grunted, an edge to his voice. "A big surprise Christmas package. Right. Only in my dreams of a perfect world."

Seated in the jet's cabin, Bolan was on the military jet's sat link with Brognola. He heard the big Fed heave a breath, followed by long silence on the other end. He could only imagine the new strain Brognola was under, after swallowing the bombshell Radin had dropped under intense interrogation. But with the latest bad news, the soldier was more determined to follow through with his next step of the campaign. On top of what they now knew, there was also the boy to consider.

Of course, Ceasuvic's kidnap victim would prove the colonel's last trump card, Bolan knew, if all else failed. The boy was never far from the soldier's thoughts. Given the Serb track record in America, or Bosnia or Kosovo for that matter, he knew they wouldn't blink when it came to killing innocent children. No matter what it took, Bolan would stop Ceasuvic. Thousands, maybe tens of thousands of lives, both of them knew, were right then on the line, perhaps even entire cities of innocent people faced a sudden extinction that could happen in eye-blinks.

As he waited for Brognola to continue, Bolan suddenly felt his own raw nerves, his body wound as tight as a coiled spring with tension. His mind wandered for a moment, as he silently cursed the ten-hour delay before they were finally airborne over the Atlantic Ocean. Even though he didn't have to like it, Bolan knew that sometimes waiting was all part of a campaign. There was intelligence to gather and sift through, logistics snags to work out, all of it landing him temporarily on the sidelines even as he burned to get back out there in the game. And, of course, there was damage control when it went to hell, as it had back in Atlantic City.

After the Olympus debacle, Bolan and Grimaldi were forced to hang around the carnage and destruction, dance through more verbal sparring with the FBI. Williams's general suspicion was that Bolan knew something about a series of gangland killings in Pittsburgh, since the same Serbs in question were part of another ongoing FBI surveillance in that neck of the woods. Now Williams had three FBI agents and seven civilians dead at the casino, dozens injured, some critical, downed either by Serb bullets or smashed during the mad rush to clear the killing ground, not to mention the boy Ceasuvic had grabbed. It had taken six hours before they untangled themselves from the FBI's grasp, Brognola burning up the FBI's ear from Williams on up to his superiors, the big Fed going to bat for his men, while fighting the whole time to maintain their Stony Man cover. After a quick drive back to the Gulfstream jet, Grimaldi had flown them to JFK where Brognola had arranged a refueling stop before the Stony Man pilot began their overseas course, heading for Aviano Air Base in Italy. After another refueling at Aviano, they would fly to the American military base in Incirlik, Turkey, which would put them as close as possible to the dicey venture Bolan would take into Russia.

Time, the soldier feared, wasn't on his side.

This was Bolan's third call to Brognola since the cleanup began at the Olympus. Once they were caught up on Bolan's side of things the first time around, the soldier informed Brognola of what he thought the next logical course of action should be, even though it could throw already-brittle U.S.-Russian relations back to cold war status.

Such was life. Bolan had his own headaches right then, suspected he was moving next into one of the most dangerous twenty-four-hour periods of his life. If VIP egos were trampled along the way, political careers sent crashing out the window, so be it.

Bolan wasn't about to drop the ball now, let anyone on his side down, least of all himself. Brognola and the Farm were hard at work putting the logistical pieces into place, the big Fed having already marshaled his own agents overseas to keep an eye on Bolan's next target. With the President's full blessing, it was Bolan's show from that point on, and he would have the full resources of the U.S. military in that part of the world at his disposal.

"Shifting gears for a second, Hal, what's the story on the boy Ceasuvic snatched?"

"As if our plates aren't overflowing with enough trouble, the FBI and my own office may come under some media fire, because the parents are threatening to go to the press. I understand the hell they're going through, but in a kidnap situation you can make all the promises you want, but you have to prepare yourself for a worst-case scenario."

"I'd have to say we're way beyond worst case."

"And then some, given where this is headed. I spoke personally with the parents, did my damnedest to reassure them everything possible is being done to see to his safe return. How can you explain to anyone's parents their kid's just a pawn in some sick bastard's bigger scheme?''

"The boy is Ceasuvic's ace. He'll only kill him as a last resort, but I intend to be all over the Serb before he even twitches a gun toward the boy. What's the boy's name?''

"Jack Percivall. Parents were on vacation from upstate New York. They call him Jackie. Their bad luck they picked the Olympus, and I'm sure they didn't know it was run by a bunch of Russian gangsters. As far as we know the boy is still alive.''

"Only one man I can think of to lay the blame on. Ceasuvic.''

"Understood, and what's done is done. But the way I read in between the lines from Williams, one of his men took it upon himself to approach Ceasuvic, in defiance of a direct order. The way this psychopath operates, if he even thinks he smells a problem he'll just start blasting away. At any rate, if there are any points in the plus column on that fiasco, the Russian Mafia cleaning up its money through the Olympus is history.''

"And Viktor Tokinov will get word soon enough that he's through in America.''

"Which will make him even more dangerous, Striker. This guy was bad news before his world started crashing down in the States. He's an ex-KGB killer and runs the top Mafia family in Russia. I can't even begin to imagine how many people he has in his pockets over there, or how many bodies have littered his path to riches. Which makes my job a little harder trying to get some cooperation with the Russians, especially the SVR.

"We both know the Russian Mafia is made up mostly of former KGB and Spetsnaz. Trained professionals, driven, determined, many of the bigger families connected to the current power structure. Tough nuts, if you'll indulge me once again understating the matter.

"Okay, I'll keep shaking it up on this end, I'll get you there, but once you start the ball rolling, understand you and Jack will pretty much be on your own. Tokinov losing his action in America may have him circling the wagons, hell, if he's as connected politically and militarily as my sources inform me, he could right now be screaming for legit backup at home. And straight from the Kremlin, or the SVR."

"Whatever he has I'll see it for myself when I make the house call."

"And now that he's apparently handed, or is about to hand over to Ceasuvic the means for Serbia's ultimate revenge—"

"Radin say what the targets might be?" Bolan asked when Brognola abruptly stopped talking.

"Ceasuvic never told him. I guess he wanted to keep that little juicy tidbit to himself until his great moment."

Bolan paused, massaging his dry, tired eyes. The soldier knew who and what he was up against, had long since weighed the odds, well understood Brognola's own problems, his anger and outrage, the stakes involved all around. A sudden swell of yet more angry determination hit Bolan's chest. "I'll nail these animals, Hal. And I'll see the boy gets home safe."

Now it was Brognola's turn to weigh the situation in thoughtful silence. Finally, he said, "If anyone can do it, Striker, I know I count on you to pull off what always looks like the impossible. All I can do on my end is keep tugging strings, smooth the way for you best I can. And pray."

"What about the traitor angle?" Bolan asked.

"You mean these shadows behind the scenes Radin mentioned? Some guy or guys over at the White House, key NATO members who have been aware all along what the Serbs intended to do, while taking money from the Russian Mafia? Well, Aaron's hacking all over the place, running with your hunch to follow the money. Needless to say that covers a lot of offshore banks, not to mention the legit ones here at home, plus the fact every and any guy on the take has a million-and-one ways to hide cash."

"Suggestion. Start looking at recent arrivals on the White House scene."

"Can you be a little more specific?"

Bolan had given it some thought during the latest hiatus, and if the President didn't want him to pull any punches, then why stop the swinging at heads within the Serbs and the Russian Mafia? "Political 'superstars' who have climbed the ranks almost overnight."

"Guys finding Larry King and Geraldo and all the other cable talking heads kissing up to them? Like they're the Messiah?"

"Something like that. Someone who is more style than substance. Just a feeling, someone shady who gets your instinct telling you they're all smoke and mirrors."

"A phony?"

"A pretender to the crown. Compare salaries against lifestyles."

"You're saying to try to smell out somebody who looks too good to be true?"

"It can happen that way. If there's a traitor or traitors in our own backyard, Hal, it wouldn't be the first time."

"And, unfortunately, I'm sure not the last. Okay, I can also have another talk with the President. Maybe he feels something's a little strange under his own roof, or maybe there's some rumors he's caught wind of, but wants to play hush-hush with the press. If I feel I have anything remotely resembling a suspect, I'll put a team on him, her, them, whatever."

"Sounds like the only plan that can be reasonably put on the table."

"I think all reason has gone the way of the dinosaur on this one."

"I have to agree. From here, it may only get worse before it gets better. Just keep pointing me in the right direction."

"On that note, I know you hate the delays, but give me at least twelve hours, hopefully less, to get you situated on the other side. Meaning airborne for Russia."

"At least we know Tokinov is bunkered down in his Kiev dacha."

"For now, right. As I mentioned, I've already scrambled some agents whose specialty over there is organized crime. He'll be watched around the clock, until you're in place. One last thing. The blacksuits you requested are on the way to Incirlik. I understand they'll be there hopefully to transport the boy, not to mention Tokinov, back to the States, and if that happens that's another series of headaches. Whatever, dump Tokinov off on my doorstep if it falls that way. Anyway, if it turns out you need the blacksuits in any other capacity than transport of human cargo, they're coming to you, armed and dangerous."

"Good to hear the old fire back in your voice."

"Yeah, well, my nerves have been working overtime on me. Tends to cool that fire some. I don't know, maybe it's just age."

"You're only human."

"Back at you. Which is always another worry of mine. I'll stay hard, bet your ass and, by the way, I am. You can be sure I won't sleep or even have time to spare for any creature comforts until I hear some good news. Bring me some, Striker, and real soon. Oh, while I'm on the good news and bad news, there's another piece of bad news. The Serb cell in Cleveland? Gone, vanished, apartments cleaned out. My men never even got a look at them. Made me think Radin was lying from the start until the other team I dispatched in Detroit made definite confirmation of the other cell. I'll spare you the long details on procedure of how we nailed them down, ID'd them, but we're looking at another small army of some of Yugoslavia's worst."

"I'm becoming all too familiar with the breed."

"Wanted war criminals all, once again, only I doubt they'll ever see The Hague on this bunch. No military background on the Detroit cell. Common thugs who were let out of prisons over there for the purpose of ethnic cleansing. Now they land in America, making fat money selling drugs, guns, porn, hustling prostitutes. Go figure. They owe the good life, I guess, to Tokinov."

"They better party hardy tonight, because the party's coming to an end. My guess is the Cleveland cell has left the country. Ceasuvic was running short on troops last time we made contact."

"We're on the Serbs in Detroit. They go down the street for a six-pack, we'll know about it."

"Keep me posted. I have another nagging suspicion Ceasuvic has them waiting in the wings just in case his own plans fall through."

"See that they do. You'll be the first to know if something breaks in Detroit. For right now, I've covered everything I can think of. Raise me when you reach Incirlik. Stay frosty, Striker, we need the win on this one. Missed the knockout in the first few rounds, but I'll gladly take a KO next time you step in the ring."

No argument there.

Signing off, Bolan's gut started churning as he thought about what they now knew the Serbs were trying to get their hands on. If Ceasuvic was successful, Bolan knew such a holocaust would touch off a firestorm of rage and horror and a call to arms across Europe, and even beyond, the likes of which hadn't been seen in maybe sixty years.

That Ceasuvic could even take it this far didn't surprise Bolan. He knew Russia's armories, missile silos, weapons caches and nuclear power plants were many and undermanned, the personnel at each of hundreds of such sites all too ready and willing to accept money from gangsters who wanted everyone to look the other way while they made long and repeat shopping trips through the store. He'd seen the new and allegedly democratic Russia. It was a runaway juggernaut of crime, corruption, alcoholism and suicide, the average Russian starving, out of work and wondering where the next meal was coming from.

It would never come from the Russian Mafia.

And if Bolan couldn't find or get to Ceasuvic in time…

Slowly, shutting out any grim visions of a future that had not yet happened, the Executioner walked toward the soft lights of Grimaldi's instrument panel, stepped into the cockpit and claimed the copilot's seat.

"Let me guess, Sarge, more bad news."

Bolan knew his new batch of worries showed as clear through as glass to his friend. "The stakes just got higher."

"How high?"

"Nuclear."

Grimaldi let out a soft whistle.

For long moments, while gathering his thoughts, Bolan stared beyond the Plexiglas as Grimaldi pushed the jet at top speed through the vast darkness, twenty-five thousand feet above the ocean.

"Seems one night," Bolan told Grimaldi, "Ceasuvic had a head swimming in vodka."

"And maybe told this Radin Hal's sitting on that he wants to go nuclear."

"Apparently, Viktor Tokinov agreed after he pulled the Serbs out of Yugoslavia—reasons for that peculiar move still unclear—that he could deliver them two, maybe three ADMs."

"Atomic Demolition Munitions. Nuke backpacks, like the Green Berets have."

"Spetsnaz version."

"Meaning what? More punch? Easier to set off?"

"Hal has the Bear digging up the particulars now. If I were to bet on the answer, I would say yes to both questions."

"So, the plan is?"

"Same one I put to you earlier."

"Fly into Mother Russia and kidnap the Russian boss of bosses. Sounds like that should keep both sides of the East-West diplomatic aisle busy for some time."

"I suspected all along the Serbs were out for something more than a rip-off of their criminal connections. Now I know why they went on their killing spree. It was and it wasn't about the money.''

"Wanted to turn around and buy some ADMs from Tokinov who, essentially, cut them loose on American civilians to begin with. Unbelievable, but maybe it isn't given the present state of world affairs.'' Grimaldi shook his head. "Serb vengeance against NATO, a mushroom cloud or two, maybe set off in a country surrounding Yugoslavia…well, the Balkans are still a mess, Sarge, probably worse than ever. And if the opposition's plan is to set off ADMs, in say Kosovo…''

"Or it could be along the border with Macedonia.''

"Or Albania. Turkey even, since there's still bad blood between the Serbs and the Turks, the Serbs unhappy about the Ottoman Empire kicking their butts in Kosovo six centuries back, settling in a majority Muslim population that has fought to this day for its own autonomy.''

"Long time to nurse a grudge, granted, but it's not too unlike the situation in the Middle East.''

Grimaldi nodded. "Power. Dominion over thy neighbor. An ever-shrinking landscape as more people swell a dwindling horizon, the few grab up more, while the rest are left to slug or shoot it out. That part of the world, the Balkans, stays a powder keg just waiting for the wrong someone to light the spark. We both know every country over there has been fighting for centuries, everyone believing the other guy's piece of real estate is rightfully theirs and they're all too willing to engage in wholesale slaughter to get it. It wouldn't be hard to touch off a full-scale war if one country suspected another country of setting off ten kilotons or more in one of their cities.''

"I hear you. But I'm thinking Ceasuvic has something on tap that could be worse than that.''

"Such as? Nuking a Kosovar refugee camp? NATO troops?''

"No, I'm thinking he's looking to set off one ADM each in several countries, depending on how many he gets his hands on.''

"Okay, after seeing him in action,'' Grimaldi said, "I don't think our Serb colonel would settle for anything but a body count in the six figures.''

"My guess is he would want to see nothing less than several countries surrounding Yugoslavia taking up arms. Pick any one of six countries over there; they're all willing to go for one another's throats if they feel threatened enough.''

"Getting nuked would definitely present itself as a threat. And if the colonel claims responsibility on behalf of his country for setting off the ADMs?''

"It isolates them even more,'' Bolan answered. "But it would rally the Serb people together if, say, Macedonia or Bulgaria declared war on Yugoslavia with the intention of full-scale invasion. Then, maybe the Russians would step in. Maybe that's part of Tokinov's twisted thinking. Maybe he's an old hard-line Communist who wants to see his country roll the tanks through Europe.''

"Sounds to me like this Viktor Tokinov already has the world he wants.''

"He may be rich, powerful and connected, but maybe he wants more. Just the nature of his beast. Maybe he wants to see his own country either join forces with Yugoslavia, a country Russia has always been sympathetic toward, back them up with Russian soldiers, supplies and hardware. Isolate the Motherland, bring back the Communists and his own vision of some new world order."

"Kind of goes against his obvious capitalistic urges."

"Who knows? Maybe he's insane. Maybe he's bored."

"Or just plain evil."

"That, too."

Grimaldi fell silent for several moments, then said, "Ceasuvic could be anywhere by now, Sarge."

"Hal's scrambled every available AWACS or Hawkeye he could. The Bear's taken the reins on the satellite databases. The skies where we're going are being watched. We'll know something soon."

"One can only hope. From what you told me earlier, we both know Tokinov has his own air force. He does business in a half dozen European countries. You can be sure if he builds his own aircraft to specs, with pretty much the sole purpose of transporting contraband, he will have state-of-the-art radar-jamming for starters, then you figure he's ex-KGB but still connected to his own intelligence resources. He knows all the right smuggler's moves, how to slip through satellite flyovers, radar nets, flying blind with lights out at night even. Fly out a decoy plane or two."

"That's why I need to meet the man personally."

Grimaldi nodded. "Snatch the boss, persuade him to tell us where the ADMs are, or where he plans to have them delivered."

"That's the plan. Follow the nukes, and we'll find Ceasuvic."

Grimaldi dropped into grim silence. They had been fighting together long enough for both men to know how fragile plans were when put to the test. But the Executioner intended to keep his plan as simple as possible.

It was a plan of the killing kind, and it didn't get much simpler than that. Grimaldi knew the deal, had been there, done that. Enough said. It was time to do it, plain and simple, politics be damned.

It was time for a grim face-to-face with what Bolan knew was a chunk of the real power behind Russia.

Viktor Tokinov was a savage, who worshiped only money, crime, power and his own pleasure. Too many times before Bolan had seen the Tokinovs of the world. Death was the only thing they respected, and feared.

So far, in his War Everlasting, his enemies never made it any farther down the road than a few steps in the wrong direction, once Bolan singled them out for an accounting.

He always saw to that in the past.

But now was now. Anything could happen in the near future, the unexpected, for one thing, and it usually did. They would show their fangs in all their bloodthirsty rage, and if that didn't work they might even try to con him with promises of money, vows that the world could belong to him, if only he would let them live, go with the flow, fall in as part of the team.

In Bolan's world he could ill afford sympathy for the Devil.

THE ADRENALINE ride was long over. Cviic was now so exhausted that he started to believe if he slept at all he would have one of those out-of-body experiences he'd heard them talk about on the American talk shows. Oh, if only he could just float away, he thought, or at least be alone, no more killing, no fear of dying, just a little slice of some peace of mind.

He knew it wasn't going to happen.

He could see clearly now, and he saw nothing but more death and destruction ahead, primarily his own, and that vision of the immediate future made him want to abandon ship.

Hell, the ship was already sinking, only his brother Serbs didn't know it yet.

What brave fools they were, just the same, he thought. He wished he could still share their thirst for vengeance, their zeal for NATO blood, but he found himself all used up.

From the start he had a fair idea of Ceasuvic's goal. Now that the colonel was on the way to getting what he wanted, Cviic had more than just serious reservations about the scheme. He sensed the mounting urgency and desperation all around him, as if everyone except himself believed they could pull it off, light the fuse to Armageddon in the Balkans.

They were doomed, he was sure, sailing on toward a fool's last murderous errand. It wasn't something he could quite put his finger on, but the facts of the past twenty-four hours had spoken volumes, as far as he was concerned. It was a feeling in his gut that quite frankly told him they were all, simply, fucked.

Surely, someone in the American military or intelligence community had discovered what they planned to do. Their nameless adversary who had tracked them and decimated their numbers in Pennsylvania certainly seemed to know who they were, and worse, always seemed to know where they were going next. And after all the killing and mayhem they left behind in America, knowing this part of the world was teeming with American military bases, Cviic was amazed a few F-16s hadn't blown them out of the sky yet.

Well, there was still plenty of time left for that to happen. If he wasn't so tired he would have laughed out loud at the fluke that had gotten them to this point of tasting the bitter fruit.

They had been in the air, three hours after setting down at an airfield outside of Marseilles to refuel, he figured. Apparently, Tokinov had connections in France, drug business, no doubt. The Russian boss also did business in Greece, Italy, God only knew how many other countries in Europe, if everything he'd overheard from Churybik and Ceasuvic was true.

And who was he to doubt these master architects of mass destruction at their word? So far he had survived, where too many of their own had died. Well, the mere fact he was still breathing didn't mean he had to take everything at face value.

Men always lied to advance their own agendas.

Cviic wanted to keep breathing, that much hope he clung to. Dying to help a madman fulfill his dreams of annihilation was no longer an option. He had already survived too much to risk tossing it all away when the next adrenaline roller coaster of combat slid in to pick him up for the ride.

It was over, plain and simple, and he wanted out.

But the scheme was already well along, surging ahead like a runaway train, no stopping it unless it was derailed.

He could feel the derailer, out there, somewhere. That guy just would not give up.

Try telling Ceasuvic that.

There was a long delay for some reason while they were grounded in Marseilles, Cviic eventually learning Ceasuvic and Churybik had been consulting with Tokinov's cutout who would deliver the packages. With each passing minute beyond that point, the look in the colonel's eyes increasingly frightened him. Ceasuvic would spare no one to see his plan succeed.

No one.

Everyone around Cviic seemed very sure of themselves, as if they had all the right answers, no move too risky, no horizon too far to reach, their fates meant to streak ahead, unstoppable as they flamed along on some divine comet.

It made Cviic question his courage, his reason to keep living.

Had he lost his stomach for killing, living on the edge? Had he ever really even believed in the insane plan? Perhaps he had just gone along with the talk, didn't take seriously the overheard rumors, the loose tongues flapping from too much vodka. Just like that, it felt as if his weary mind was starting to throb from all the uncertainty, his nerves ready to snap into wild sparklers and firecrackers from all the questions for which he had no answers. What was he going to do?

Cviic looked out the cabin window and found himself wishing he'd never left Serbia, despite the allegations made against him by NATO of being a crazed, barbaric war criminal. Propaganda. What did they know, anyway? He was a young soldier back then, simply acting under the orders of the politicians, the older men of influence, power and control. A naive kid who was forced to grow up too quickly, and too mean, his former fate dictated by the hatreds of others. Any old men, women or children he'd killed in Bosnia...well, he had the recurring nightmares to prove his remorse.

Blinding sunshine washed over the expanse of the Mediterranean Sea far below. Cviic stared, long and hard, as they soared over the glassy-looking green sea, sparkling in his sight like countless diamonds. Was that a ship down there? A frigate, cargo vessel, what? Was there even a parachute on board? What was he thinking? Executive jets were made to stay in the air, constant maintenance, repairs, a low-risk VIP way to roam the planet on a whim. Even if he could parachute out the hatchway, he would slam into the wing, broken in two, or maybe sucked through the turbofan engine, ground into hamburger, spit out in a thousand bloody pieces, raining bloody flesh, eventually eaten up by whatever found him a meal in the sea.

Why bother with such fantasy?

No, there would be no mad dash to the door, parachute drop to the sea or quick swim to whatever floated so far below, so far away, scooped up by a passing vessel, lying to the crew, as he was whisked to a safe far-off land.

Dream on.

No, he was trapped, forced to take this ride to the end of the line, serve out his own personal sentence, the war criminal who had so far managed to escape hell on earth.

It hurt his eyes to look out the window any longer. He looked away, shut his eyes. He figured they were no more than a few hours from landing at the site in Greece that Ceasuvic had worked out with Zadar.

A lurch, as the jet hit some sort of turbulence, and Cviic opened his tired eyes. He saw Ceasuvic emerge from the cockpit. The colonel looked around with new savage determination. He began to inform them that Zadar would be ready to greet them when they landed. Delivery was late, but Tokinov's envoy was on the way to Greece. Then, caught up in the excitement of the moment, Ceasuvic began laying out the rough edges of the master stroke. Cviic started to think about all the men they'd lost just to get it to this point, felt the urge to point that out, but figured why bother? The dead had been friends of his, all of them believing in the colonel as a great man of vision, a man who would avenge the bombing of Yugoslavia by NATO. If only they could see the psychotic in Ceasuvic now.

He couldn't help but wonder where it had all gone wrong for him, how he had ended up at the threshold of staring his own death in the face. Perhaps it had been simply the money at first, or the hope to escape capture by some black ops headhunters from an American intelligence agency, the desire for a new life of freedom which had lured Cviic out of Yugoslavia when the Russian Mafia came calling, offering Ceasuvic and a select group a way to become rich men.

It had been an easy enough life in the beginning, a dream come true for the son of a poor farmer. The truth was it was so easy—with some daring, balls and smarts, of course—to live as a criminal in America, that he came to believe anyone who didn't lead a life of crime was simply a fool, playing out a slave's game, since money was really the only god in America he could see, and the more money the more of a god a man was.

And the best money he could have ever dreamed of holding in his hands came as a soldier in the Serbian Mafia in America. Fine food, good drink, beautiful women all the time. The best clothes. A name for himself, and respect. Other immigrant business owners from Poland, Germany, Yugoslavia, were all too eager to hand over their money to him to keep their establishments from burning down, or worse, just so they could stay in America.

"Are you listening to me, Cviic?"

Startled, his head shot up and he found the colonel boring that penetrating stare into him, the one that warned him the end was near. "Sir?"

"I said, once we land and I hand out the final orders, you and a few others will stay with the boy."

The kid. Cviic found the boy cowering in his seat, but gratefully he was no longer crying. All those tears simply reminded him they had kidnapped an American citizen. No way would the American authorities let that ride. One more reason to bail.

Cviic listened carefully as Ceasuvic laid out his role, relegated to baby-sitter. He listened to the colonel talk about Plan B, in the event that Plan A failed. Ceasuvic made a point to let Cviic know he was to contact the cell in Detroit if he didn't hear from him within six hours once they were in the air with Tokinov's transport planes, prepared to drop doomsday on the capitals of Albania and Macedonia. Detroit would know what to do, the colonel said.

There. That was it. Cviic had just made up his mind. He was a lackey now. Maybe the colonel had read through all the doubt and fear in his eyes and didn't want him anywhere near the big event. Fine, whatever.

Somehow, some way, he would find the window that would allow him to slide out, land on his feet on the other side and run far away from this insanity. So what if he would never again know the good life he had in America, the easy money allowing him to indulge his every pleasure? It was better to keep breathing than living simply to sate his own animal wants.

Tomorrow could end up proving some blessing in disguise if he set out on his own, rediscovered himself. Once he was free of this madness he could figure out the future. He always had.

He was no Milenko, no hero ready to give up his life for Ceasuvic, and he never wanted to be.

Ceasuvic had plenty of Milenkos anyway, and the colonel could have them all to do with what he wished.

Cviic only wanted back his freedom to call his own shots.

CHAPTER SEVENTEEN

Colonel Milak Zadar was suspicious. Plan A was perhaps hours away from being executed, a half day at the outside, but it all felt too easy, everything was happening so fast there was a stink of desperation to it all.

And that meant trouble of some kind, flying in behind Ceasuvic. Or was he simply edged out by all the travel, the cloak-and-dagger routine, the eternal waiting, the constant worrying over if and when armed shadows would leap out of nowhere, guns blazing, end of game?

Zadar moved for the doorway of their large wood-and-stone dwelling. If Ceasuvic raised them again by radio, then Citnec or one of the others could handle the call. Zadar needed space and privacy, a moment alone to think. He left his AK-47 behind, aware some shepherd in these parts of Thessaly may be tending the flock near their safehouse. All he needed now was some Greek shepherd to go running to the nearest authorities, raising hell about armed foreigners taking up residence on this quiet but enormous sweeping stretch of monasteries and small villages.

He stepped outside and lit a cigarette.

Yes, he thought, everything was running along very smoothly, all the key pieces falling neatly into place. Why should that bother him so much? It wasn't that he didn't trust Ceasuvic. No, the man had engineered this plan, worked hard, sacrificed too much, killed too many to set the stage for the main event. Zadar couldn't imagine Ceasuvic simply bailing out on the final act, leaving Zadar and his men hung out there to fend for themselves. Of course, stranger things could happen, a whole list of disasters could unravel their plans, in fact, scrap the mission, but he had to trust Ceasuvic to get there, pick up the merchandise, hand out the orders and get them rolling.

He had to believe.

It was the shadow man in NATO Zadar worried about. But what could he do about that, if something went wrong and it looked as if they had been betrayed? Hunt down and a kill a man he had never even seen with his own eyes? No, they had come this far, hadn't they, forced to trust their enemies, the few traitorous bastards they were, and it appeared as if it was all running like clockwork. The NATO man was proving up to this point he could, indeed, move mountains.

He took a moment to check the vast and rugged plain, get his bearings, savor this brief moment of solitude. Mountains ringed the great plain of Thessaly in all directions. Without their four-wheel-drive

Jeep—another gift delivered by the mystery NATO man—travel in this part of Greece was nearly impossible, unless, of course, Zadar wanted to ride a donkey or a horse.

With the sun setting over the Pindus Mountains, the plain was quickly gobbled up by long shadows. Just to get to this lonely, desolate land, he thought, was a nerve-racking chore in itself. First the long boat ride coming south down the Adriatic Sea, finally docking in the port city of Parga. Weapons had already been stowed in large black nylon bags on the way down, but once Zadar set off in search of their cutout, he feared that at any second Interpol, CIA or American Special Forces commandos would swarm them, arrest them on the spot before they had the chance to haul out their AK-47s and defend themselves. Of course, the standing orders were to die on their feet, and if there was any confrontation with their enemies Zadar knew he would follow those orders through to the bitter end. If they allowed themselves to be taken prisoners the game was pretty much finished for Ceasuvic, the dream of Serbian vengeance all but dead.

The cutout had been where Zadar was told he would find him in Parga. A small bag of drachmas was handed over to the cutout, and they were on their way in their Jeep, armed with phony passports and visas, just in case they encountered some unfortunate delay while driving east through the mountainous terrain of Epirus. The cutout had also delivered the promised radio console, and his directions to the safehouse in Thessaly were impeccable. Not only that, but the arrangements with the owner of the small Meteora airport, just beyond the pass that cut through the Kamvounian, had already been taken care of. Whether that particular matter had been seen to by the Russians, Ceasuvic or the NATO man, he wasn't sure, didn't even want to know. It was handled, one less headache for him. And there were a half-dozen vans or Jeeps waiting for the others at the small airport to drive them the twenty-five-mile distance to the safehouse.

He was turning, pitching his cigarette away when he saw the older model Chevy van bounding toward him, coming from the dirt road that led to the mountain pass. Watching eyes somewhere out there or not, Zadar raced back into the safehouse for his AK-47.

"On your feet! We have company!" he bellowed at Citnec, Zipidu, Triglava and the new addition, Vidu Draklic, his Aviano eyes and ears, who had been picked up during the evacuation from Italy.

They were scrambling to their feet, Zadar snatching up his AK-47 when he heard the van's engine growing louder. He was outside, his assault rifle cocked and locked, when he counted two grim faces behind the windshield. They had thick, sloping faces, crewcut heads. Cautious, his men falling in behind, Zadar approached the van. The vehicle jerked to a stop, a spool of dust boiling up from its wake. Passenger and driver doors opened, and two big men in black bomber jackets stepped out.

The passenger scowled at the hardware, and said,

"Is this any way to greet your Russian bearers of potentially good news?"

Zadar relaxed. "The merchandise is here?"

"Not exactly."

"Then what, exactly?"

"We flew ahead of the two transport planes. They are grounded in Bulgaria."

Zadar bristled with undisguised anger. "I am afraid I do not understand."

"My Serb comrade, there are many small, very fine details Viktor had to work out, using cutouts, of course. So much was last minute, seat of the pants, you might say. Besides, I look around and Ceasuvic is not even here yet."

"Soon."

"As you say. There were bribes that had to be paid at the last minute. There are the Americans and their radar and tracking aircraft to consider. There is a schedule of satellite flyovers in the region that we must factor in."

"How much longer?"

The big Russian shrugged. "I am hoping twelve hours. I do not want to be involved in this matter any longer than necessary. Viktor is a careful man. One mistake on this, one error in judgment, a hasty or reckless delivery, American fighter jets forcing us to land, or worse. Well, I believe you have the picture of the logistical problems."

"And you trust the Bulgars?"

"No choice. And they have been paid handsomely. Now, you say you have a man to fly the transport."

Zadar nodded over his shoulder at Citnec. "He flew all type of aircraft during Bosnia's war. Two others with Ceasuvic are also capable pilots."

"That is good. Because we dump off enough fuel bladders from the second cargo plane, then fly off. You will be on your own. I realize Ceasuvic wanted two such planes, but there are some problems your man has created in the past day over in America. These problems have reached Russia in the form of FBI and Justice Department agents, maybe even CIA, who can say for sure? You might say Viktor has about reached his limit with you people."

Was this where it all started to go bad? he wondered, choking down his outrage over this sudden breach in their agreement with the Russians.

"And what will you do in the meantime?" Zadar asked.

"I have brought a secure handheld radio for you. I will drive back to the airfield and contact you when the planes are off the ground. I have detailed maps of Greece, the Balkans, surrounding countries, just as Ceasuvic requested. Complete with airfields, both private and military, American AWACS and Hawkeye flyover schedules for the regions, radar installations to stay away from. Everything Ceasuvic will need if he intends to stay in the air to do whatever he is going to do with the merchandise."

Zadar shook his head, irritation and anxiety swelling his gut. Twelve hours? That could prove another lifetime, where anything and everything could go wrong.

"What else can we do?"

"Nothing," the Russian said. "Except wait and hope all goes well."

"The way you say that, it does not exactly give me peace of mind."

The Russian chuckled. "From where you stand, it should not."

VIKTOR TOKINOV stared up through the skylight and found himself wishing he was somewhere up there, far removed from the madness of his own world. The stars were especially bright and beautiful that deep into the night, so many countless worlds up there, so far away, with so many other stars and planets in distant galaxies invisible to human eyes.

Working on his sixth double vodka, he wondered if there was, in fact, life on other planets. If there was, did they visit the earth? What did they see? Or did they even care if the human race marched on to the oblivion it seemed to him humankind so desperately sought? Why would they even bother to concern themselves with the madness and the foolishness of men that covered the earth from all four corners?

He kept staring up to the heavens, scratched his huge, hairy belly, then hoisted the pink boxer shorts a little as the elastic wanted to slide down with the sudden movement.

This was his time of night to enjoy peace, solitude, indulge his fantasies, to think whatever he wanted and even speak out loud to himself. This was a nightly ritual, something—the only thing—he looked forward to after a long day of handling all manner of everyone else's problems and gripes, dealing with greed and duplicity all around him. Everyone he came into contact with on a daily basis demanded his time or needed his money to launch this or that business pipe dream. Then there were his spoiled, ungrateful children, disappointing him more every day, probably longing for the moment when he dropped dead, so they could charge in and start squabbling over who got how much. Then he had competitors in Moscow lurking about, scheming to bring him down, claim his throne as the head of the largest, most powerful crime Family in Russia.

Family, he thought, and laughed out loud. Maybe he should change his will, he considered, then decided to leave it as it was. That way he dreamed he could return to earth, a ghost roaming his Kiev dacha or wandering his Moscow mansion, enjoying himself immensely as he watched his children squawking and scheming, carving up an empire he had spent twenty years building. He'd watch it all fly from their clutches because of their greed, treachery, their lack of resolve and the deadly martial skill it took to keep the other savages in the other Families from taking it all away from them in a few eye-blinks. When he was long gone, they would provide themselves with adequate enough hard lessons.

Alone in his massive study, he suspected he looked a grotesque caricature of his former self; a bald, half-naked pig in the eyes of his ten-man security detail, he'd heard the whispered insults on occasion. Well, screw them, they were overpaid as it stood, and it had been some time since he cared about what others thought about him, if he ever had. And why should he bother with the manipulative, cunning, lying ways of others? Russia was a land of insanity anyway. It was sad to see, but too many Russians these days didn't understand the meaning of hard work. They had become too much, he thought, like their Western counterparts, always chasing the quick easy money. Sure, it was easy enough these days for this tired old man, he thought, to stand around in his skivvies, get drunk and curse and judge the world. But he had earned his riches, and there was never any walk down Easy Street for Viktor Tokinov. He had shot, stabbed, beaten and extorted his way to the top, using his skills learned as a KGB agent to blackmail the right politician or policeman when it would advance his cause. He had created his world, and if he wanted to destroy it then that was right, also.

Just the same, he didn't want to see it all go up in smoke, but he wasn't sure how much he really cared any longer if he maintained his iron grip on the reins of power. All this work and worry, the meetings and deals, bribes to be paid out on a daily basis, people to keep in line, slackers, connivers and thieves under his own nose to monitor. It was exhausting, fighting to keep it all together, especially when he should be out enjoying life in his final years, sitting on a beach in the South of France, leaving the headaches to associates he could trust. Sure, he kept up appearances during the day, ranting and raving, if only to keep his associates off balance and wondering about his state of mind. Crazy men were unpredictable, and they made people nervous.

His own time, precious and quite rare these days, belonged to him. And if wanted to walk around his own house naked, scratching himself, drunk out of his gourd, talking and laughing to himself, he would. Let those who spread gossip about him try walking in his shoes for one day.

He was vaguely aware the doors to his study had opened.

"Comrade Tokinov?"

Recognizing Zolkov's voice, he said, "What is it?"

"Phone call from Moscow. It is your son."

"I am asleep."

"He says it is urgent."

"Tell him I already know about the Olympus casino."

"He says he must—"

"I do not wish to be bothered!" he roared suddenly.

When he was alone again, he waddled his hefty bulk to the bar and poured another drink. Even at this late hour they still wanted to disturb him. Yes, he knew there was grave trouble in America. Initial reports named the Serb colonel as the one responsible for turning his Atlantic City casino into a war zone, shooting FBI agents, killing tourists, hurling around grenades, even seizing some young boy as hostage to insure he safely flew from America. Strangely enough, he was no longer angry that his American businesses would be shut down, that the FBI would tie the casino's money laundering operation to him. Madness seemed simply to be the way of the world these days. Greed and envy were all around him. They always wanted to kill the king, didn't they? he thought.

And even if the American law came looking for him, so what? What the Americans didn't understand was he had powerful friends in high places in Moscow. This was Russia. What were they going to do? March into his home and arrest him, whisk him back to America to face racketeering charges, toss him in a cell? The very notion of such nonsense made him chortle with contempt.

The Americans believed they could go anywhere in the world, do anything they wanted, arrest foreigners, bomb cities, wave extradition papers around and demand justice. It was just that sort of superior nationalistic warmongering attitude the Americans displayed that had Tokinov seek out and save the Serbs in the first place, insert them into his American pipeline, even though he always knew what Ceasuvic wanted, that someday the Serb colonel would seek out only his own goal and hunger for revenge against NATO. And now that he had handed over the ADMs, he felt a great heaving weight inside, a feeling he didn't really understand. Was it self-pity? A gnawing gut instinct warning him of impending doom? Was this Serb business originally some form of suicide, a death wish creeping in his subconscious, urging him to deliver nuclear power to them? Had he been longing for his own destruction, knowing that if they used the ADMs they could easily be traced back to Russia, where someone who felt they hadn't been paid enough to keep their mouth shut could start pointing the finger his direction? Who could be sure of anything these days?

He had told the Serbs he would come to Greece, but since Churybik was with them he had decided to stay in Kiev and wait to hear the news. Whether it was good or bad, it didn't matter to him. Eventually, Churybik would be brought to him, and the man had some serious explaining to do. The flame may be flickering out, but some fire still burned inside him, Tokinov knew. He lived on somehow, wishing for something different to happen in a life that had become too predictable. Churybik most certainly qualified as unpredictable.

He shuffled back to the skylight. Looking up, he searched the twinkling heavens, hoping to spot a shooting star, a comet, something falling to earth that might stoke his fantasy about visitors coming to him from up there.

He stood, neck arched, chin up. He imagined those alien visitors falling from the sky, coming to earth only to speak to the great Viktor Tokinov. Perhaps even enlightening him with some of their own divine wisdom. These days, he knew he could sure use some.

THE EXECUTIONER was minutes away from plummeting to the earth from six miles above. The Starlifter C-141, borrowed out of Incirlik, was thirty thousand feet over the Ukraine, flying at its top speed of 566 miles per hour, bearing down fast and hard toward the outskirts of Kiev.

Bolan was alone in the gloomy shadows of the cargo bird's cavernous belly, the turbofan engines rumbling like distant thunder peals in his ears. The parachutes, both main and reserve, were thoroughly checked and packed by his own hands. Still once again he checked off his equipment and hardware. Goggles, insulated ski mask and oxygen bottle. Check. GPS module to guide him to Tokinov's dacha in working order, with backup batteries in a pocket of his combat blacksuit. A layer of thermal insulation beneath that blacksuit would help him survive the freezing cold air this high above the earth once he hit the ramp. Set for two different frequencies, his hand-held radio was fixed firmly on his hip, next to his .44 Magnum Desert Eagle. One was for Grimaldi, the other for the special agent sent in by Brognola to watchdog the Russian boss.

Bolan had already made contact with Special Agent Babbitt. As of thirty minutes earlier, Tokinov was still on the grounds of his dacha. Babbitt had also done some homework for Bolan on the numbers: ten security guards armed with AK-47s, working in five-man shifts, a changing of the guard every three hours for the outside sentry detail. Satellite photos had already provided Bolan with the dacha's layout, and it was now filed away to memory.

As for the hardware, the soldier would go in with

his M-16 with an attached M-203 grenade launcher, hanging now, muzzle down, in its boot strap. A Kabar combat knife in ankle sheath, the Beretta 93-R already threaded with a sound suppressor in shoulder rigging, six frag grenades and spare clips for his weapons, and Bolan had about as much weight adding to the rate of the descent for his six-mile plunge that he cared to carry.

This was a HALO jump—High Altitude Low Opening—and he knew any one of a dozen or more things could go terribly wrong, leaving him squashed as an unrecognizable puddle of goo on the Russian steppe. Once he hit the ground, hopefully somewhere in the general vicinity of Tokinov's dacha outside Kiev, he knew any number of problems could arise and keep him from snatching Tokinov, linking up with the Justice man and his team, and driving like hell for the rendezvous with Grimaldi.

He checked his chronometer. Once he left the aircraft, he had two-and-a-half hours to get the job done, reach the farm country that had been singled out as the best possible landing site by sat recon, before Grimaldi landed. Four F-16 fighter jets would provide escort for the Gulfstream jet.

Brognola had proved himself to be no small part in this operation. Bolan had been met with full cooperation at Incirlik, everything set to go as soon as the jet landed. But the big Fed had opted to leave the Russians in the dark about this most peculiar covert foray into their backyard, which left a gaping hole of chance for Bolan if the SVR or any other Russian problems showed and objected to his kidnapping one of their citizens.

There was no sense dwelling on what might happen if the Russians were somehow alerted ahead of time to what he was going to do. For all he knew, the SVR could already be crawling all around the area of his drop.

The green light flashed on near the cargo ramp.

"Sir?"

Bolan punched the button on the intercom. "I'm here."

"Two minutes and counting, sir," the Air Force pilot told Bolan, who was simply a nameless passenger to the five-man crew. "Our screens are clean at present. No sign of bogies, sir. All systems go. Good luck."

The Executioner copied, signed off and headed for the ramp. He tugged the ski mask over his head, slipped the goggles over his eyes, then readied his oxygen bottle. He didn't have long to wait before the ramp opened down to a blast of icy air and impenetrable darkness beyond.

Time to fly.

CHAPTER EIGHTEEN

Mica Zolkov wondered if he was stupid, crazy or just desperate for the money that Tokinov paid him to head up security and make sure the Old Man kept breathing. For what meaningful purpose was a mystery to him. The Old Man did little more than indulge himself like a pig, while growing predictably fatter by the day.

It was sickening to even look at him, he thought, forced to view the self-indulgent whale of a man with nothing less than contempt. And this was the most powerful gangster in Russia?

Maybe it was time to move on, he decided, find another Family to sell his services to. As a former Spetsnaz commando, there was plenty of work for a hired gun with his talent and experience in Moscow. He was long since fed up with the Old Man's strange and erratic behavior anyway. And if he had to endure one more tyrannical outburst from Tokinov...

Why did he stay on? he wondered. There was no glory, certainly no career advancement here. The two daughters, he chuckled bitterly to himself, had already seen fit to marry a couple of Moscow shooters employed by the father, cutting him out of the loop for any sort of inside power move.

Vasily and Boris may have thought themselves clever, devious enough to secure their own futures, but Zolkov knew those futures were shaky at best, given the current state of affairs under the Tokinov roof. He considered himself the lucky one, after all, for not marrying into this crazy family.

Still there was his job to hate, brood over, the thought of simply quitting getting closer to becoming reality. Maybe tomorrow. He was a soldier, not some nursemaid.

It angered him even more to see that his duties amounted to little else than something a peasant could, and should, do. He answered the phones constantly on orders from Tokinov, as if he were a secretary, or bartended, pouring drinks for the Old Man when he was too drunk to do it himself. He changed the water in the hot tub on a weekly basis, since the Old Man seemed to think the water may be poisoned by some jealous rival, maybe even the hired help had dumped enough sulphuric acid in the tub to burn the considerable flesh off his bones. Then there was the verbal abuse, Zolkov all too often made to endure the savage tirades, as if he'd signed on to be the Old Man's personal punching bag. And he had to play middleman with the children, forever dreaming up new excuses, lies, whatever he had to tell them to keep them from ringing the phone off the hook, day and night, their voices rife with the kind of desperation and insincerity that told Zolkov they wanted money.

Again he found himself disgusted at the sight he'd just left in the study. Every night at this time Zolkov was forced to watch the Old Man shuffle around the dacha in his underwear, that hairy white fish belly hanging out, so low, he figured it took a mighty effort alone to hoist it up just so Tokinov could relieve himself. Then there was the drunkenness, not such a big deal in Russia, which was swimming with alcohol, the city streets at night jammed with staggering, wild-eyed, raving lunatics who would kill someone just for enough rubles to see them through another bottle. No, it was the staring up at the sky with that irritating longing look—the Old Man babbling to himself, as if he were urging angels to fall from the heavens and save him from his insanity—that really made Zolkov wonder about his future in this house of madness.

Tomorrow. It was time to quit. He almost envied Duklov for getting the assignment to go to America and straighten out the Serbs. Enough of this madness.

If Kiev, he thought, was considered the mother of Russia, then Viktor Tokinov was the father of fools. Zolkov was better than this.

He walked outside, stepping through the kitchen door, which led to the patio. He needed fresh air, safe and sane distance to the freakish spectacle in the study. He stared into the dark woods that lined the north side of the hill on which the dacha sat. As security chief, Zolkov had many times urged Tokinov to beef up the latest monitoring equipment, alarms, surveillance devices, a list of items by which the boss could better defend his dacha. Tokinov wouldn't hear of it; he liked it all just the way it was. There was no security wall around the compound, which made his duties doubly perilous. Say a rival sent a killing crew here, well, there was nothing but open ground leading to the estate, long stretches of rolling fields east, west and south, pockets out there where an enemy could drop, wait, then advance again. Yes, there were security cameras mounted on a few trees, but they were easy enough to spot from a distance if an invader was looking for them. All laser and motion sensors were placed inside the building proper. There wasn't even a guard dog on the premises, since the Old Man had long ago made known how much he despised dogs, calling them messy, noisy creatures. Tokinov was so bullheaded, Zolkov wondered if the man didn't secretly harbor a death wish.

And talk about morale. It was nonexistent, Zolkov always having to stay on top of his men, silence their loose tongues, which were always flapping away with gossip and contempt for the Old Man. They were paid to do a job; it was as simple as that. But as much as he tried to run a tight ship, Tokinov's outrageous behavior always derailed any attempt on his part to see to it his men remained professional, alert, ready to tackle danger. These days, too many of them were clearly just putting in time, watching the clock, waiting for the next shift to step in and send them on their way.

Zolkov heard himself grunt at all the insane eccentricities of the Old Man. Perhaps money and power did that to some people. They felt they could do and say anything they wanted, thought themselves invincible, believed they could walk all over what they considered the little people—

What was that?

Zolkov checked the east end of the dacha where the shrubbery was strung out from the building, creating a tangled dark wall. He would have sworn he heard something hit the ground from that direction. Pulling the AK-47 off his shoulder he took several steps off the patio, angling away from the far end of the shrub wall. He cursed the nearly nonexistent lighting that shone from the back, a covered bulb, here and there. Another one of Tokinov's ridiculous quirks, the Old Man always complaining how the compound was too bright, always ranting he wanted less lighting, not more. What could Zolkov do, other than take the cash and keep looking for a way out?

Zolkov knew who was patrolling the grounds in that direction—or should be. He crouched at the edge of the shrub wall. He couldn't hear anything other than the chirping of the crickets. Instinct warned him somebody was there who didn't belong on the grounds. Or was it simply his imagination, tweaked by agitation with the Old Man?

"Isitlin? Komiskov?"

He was about to pull the handheld radio off his belt, then decided to explore further before he sounded what might be a false alarm. He slipped around the corner, was taking several steps ahead when he saw the two bodies. There was a moment of hesitation as he heard the bitter laughter in his head, cursing the Old Man for his negligence, but he knew it was over. Before he could bring the AK-47 to bear, a tall shadow came out of nowhere, sliding into view like a wraith from out of the narrow break in the shrubbery. Funny how Zolkov could gauge the distance to the shadow—twelve feet—at the instant when he knew his own death had come calling. Even more strange, with all his training and experience, was how he already knew the tall stranger with the sound-suppressed pistol would beat him to the draw. The strangest thing of all was how he had time enough to register one last thought, something about how Tokinov's outrageous behavior had killed him. That was right before he heard the soft chug of the shadow's weapon and the lights went out.

BOLAN RACKED UP three quick and relatively soundless kills. After wiping the strange look of surprise crossed with something like self-mockery off the face of number three with a 9 mm round between the eyes, Bolan swiftly moved to the edge of the shrub wall.

Crouching, he took a moment to get his bearings, the M-16 now slung over his shoulder, a 40 mm frag grenade up the snout of the M-203. He checked the rolling field to the east from where he'd made his advance. The soldier had taken the prescribed scenic route following his departure from the Starlifter, falling and cutting his course north to south past the lights of Kiev, ending with his drop in the field, a few hundred yards east of the targeted dacha, his GPS module steering him in the whole way. So far, everything had gone off without a hitch. Free of goggles and oxygen bottle after shedding the chute, Bolan had crawled across the field for the most part, making a short dash ahead in spots, watching the single-story block-shaped dwelling as he advanced. The dacha appeared dismally unprotected, if his first assessment was on the money.

But what did they say about appearances?

Realizing there was no point questioning any luck thrown his way, Bolan was on the premises, already rapidly shaving the odds. Three down, seven to go if the Justice man's intel was anywhere close to being in the ballpark.

Peering through the slits in his black ski mask, the Executioner was about to make his move for the patio, when Number four stepped outside. Bolan would have preferred taking out the sentry with his Ka-bar combat knife, a silent kill, where he could gently lay the body down. There was too much pottery scattered around the patio to risk a head shot with the Beretta, then see the guy crash into something that would jolt any troops close by. But the distance was too great to his next target, and there was no cover beyond the shrub wall, no way in to the patio except for a straight-on charge.

Bolan sighted down the Beretta. There was no choice but to risk some noise.

The shadow slipped his arm through the AK-47's sling and was lifting a cigarette to his mouth when

Bolan caressed the Beretta's trigger. A crack of bone, as the 9 mm Parabellum round cored through his temple, and the shadow toppled. Sure enough, deadweight crunched hard to the brick patio, way too loud for Bolan's liking.

The soldier was up and running for the open doorway, grimly aware he was on Grimaldi's clock, and it was ticking down fast. There was no plan now other than to bulldog the play from there. He needed this wrapped within minutes and would blow half the house down, if necessary, to get to Tokinov.

He was through the door, took in the hanging pots and pans, searching for live ones, when he glimpsed the armed shadow boiling out from a door to his side. Perhaps the hardman had heard the thud of his fallen comrade, or perhaps instinct was simply warning him something didn't feel right, or maybe he had just tried to raise one of the dead men outside.

Knowing he could never get off a clean burst with his M-16, Bolan was forced to cover behind a long counter as the hardman cut loose. As the slugs whined off the metal cookware above Bolan's head, the soldier heard the shooter screaming in Russian. The shooter kept sounding the alarm, bellowing for several heartbeats, and Bolan hoped he was sufficiently distracted enough with his call to arms to allow him even the narrowest window of opportunity.

The soldier knew he couldn't stay put, no matter what. He saw the stream of lead tearing into his former position, bullets still clanging off pots and pans, and knew it was now or never. He popped up, a mental picture of where the shooter was, in relation to the din of autofire, etched in his mind. The shooter was trying to readjust his aim, the AK-47's flaming muzzle swinging for the ski mask, but Bolan was already holding down the M-16's trigger, drilling a short burst of 5.56 mm lead into the shooter's chest.

Even before the hardman hit the floor in a twitching crimson heap, Bolan was racing for the corner of the hallway from which the shooter had emerged. He braced himself for return fire, caught footsteps pounding his way, voices shouting in anger. At least two, maybe three more shooters were on the way. The Executioner plucked a frag grenade off his webbing and armed it. He peered low around the corner, glimpsed two shadows suddenly skid to a halt midway down the hall, their AK-47s coming up. The Executioner counted off two seconds, then gave the steel egg an underhanded toss around the corner as bullets slapped at the wall above his head. Bolan rode out the thunderclap, hugging the corner as smoke and dust boiled over his position. If there were more shooters headed from that direction...

Too late to consider anything but another roll of the dice.

Bolan broke his cover and charged through the smoke cloud, his nose stung by cordite and leaking gore. Seconds later, M-16 fanning the dimly lit opening at the far end, he made out the frantic voices ahead, beyond the archway. On the run, nearing the end of the hall, he found a tight pack of hardmen in the living room. Four shooters were grappling with an enormously fat man, who was sporting nothing more than a pair of underwear. If he hadn't seen the intel photos, Bolan wouldn't have believed his eyes at the ridiculous sight of Viktor Tokinov.

The Russian boss of bosses would have made a walrus skinny by comparison, but the soldier had no time to make snap judgments about the man's weight problem.

The four shooters were engaged in a wrestling match with Tokinov, who was slapping at their arms, cracking open-handed palms off their faces. The shooters were stunned and angry at this sudden assault by the man they were paid to protect. Bolan didn't understand the odd scene he was presented with, but Tokinov's lashing out at his men gave the soldier all the opening he could have asked for.

Two shooters were skittering away from Tokinov, aware of the danger, their AK-47s on the way up to track the invader when the Executioner went on with his grim work, seizing the moment. He marched a line of 5.56 mm slugs across their chests, the air above the hardforce turned into a crimson halo as the next two victims on the receiving end of Bolan's death charge toppled backward. Hardmen three and four were still torn between grabbing whatever blubber they could to haul their boss away or bringing their arms to bear when Bolan finished them off with two 3-round bursts that slashed open their chests and sent them falling away to leave their boss on his own.

Cautious, Bolan moved for Tokinov, his senses alive as he made a quick but hard search of the living room, the adjacent hallways, took in the open double door to what he assumed was the study.

He took the handheld radio, his M-16 trained on Tokinov in a one-handed grip. The crime boss stood his ground, his expression alternating between defiance and despair. Whatever was churning through Tokinov's mind, Bolan could ill afford to trust the man, or the moment. He was far from being home free.

"Condor to Groundhog, come in."

"Groundhog here, Condor."

"The snatch is done. I need you here on the double. Copy that."

"Affirmative. We're right down the road, Condor. Moving now. Over and out."

"American," Tokinov spit, "what is this? You come to kidnap me? Do you know who I am? Do you know where you are?"

"Yes and yes. Move it outside."

"Like this?"

"I don't have time to dress you. You go as you are."

"No. I have a coat in the closet. Coat, or kill me."

Bolan knew the man could have a gun stashed somewhere in the closet, or a weapon in a jacket pocket. He figured if he indulged this one request, maybe Tokinov would cooperate later when Bolan put a few choice questions to him. Maybe not. There was no time to argue.

"Show me. Make it quick."

Tokinov moved for the foyer, but was anything but quick as he dragged his bulk along, his belly jiggling, shoulders slumped in what Bolan read as defeat. He stopped at a door and pointed.

"Open it, step back," the Executioner ordered.

When that was done, Tokinov backed away and said, "The mink one, if you don't mind."

Bolan grabbed the long fur coat and was handing it to Tokinov when his handheld radio suddenly crackled, the Justice Man's voice barking through in clear panic. "Groundhog to Condor, we've got a problem out here...."

The Executioner froze, heard, "Get out of the car," over the radio, then the transmission was abruptly cut off. Dammit! Now what? Some type of Russian backup was outside, no doubt armed and waiting. He could stand around and question Tokinov all he wanted, but he was aware the man could simply lie to him.

The Executioner snatched the Russian and locked an arm around his throat. It occurred to him he was prepared to borrow another page from the Serb colonel's manual, this time regarding hostages and their use as a shield to freedom.

Whatever was waiting outside, Bolan had no intention of getting knocked off Grimaldi's timetable, not even by one minute. He would make that evac site, Tokinov in tow, or Russia would prove the last place on earth he ever saw.

ZADAR HEARD Ceasuvic snarling for him to come in, but Citnec received the call. Zadar already suspected what the colonel wanted to know, and he wasn't looking forward to telling him the news about the delay of the ADM delivery.

Grim, Citnec held the radio mike out for Zadar. It took some time before the man felt capable of making his way across the room. The problems seemed to keep mounting, and Zadar feared an avalanche of some kind was poised to drop on their heads. If nothing else, he knew Ceasuvic was still alive, but where was he? It had been six, seven hours since the Russians had left for the airfield, and still no call from the Russians that the cargo planes had even left Bulgaria.

Zadar felt his guts knot with dread, his mind tumbling with questions for which had no solid answers, every fiber of his being screaming at him that disaster was just around the corner. And Ceasuvic and the others should have already landed.

Zadar steeled himself, then took the mike. "Yes."

"We have had another delay."

"May I ask where you are?"

"With some associates of the Russians. Italians."

"You are in Italy?"

"Unfortunately. Seems our radar has picked up too much air traffic in the area at this time. I cannot say too much. I fear this line is not secure. They have their ways of listening in. Do you have it yet?"

Zadar drew a breath. "No. Not yet. But our friends have arrived ahead of the packages. They claim delays on their end, but say it will be soon."

The silence was deafening, Zadar's ears filled with the sound of his pounding heart.

Ceasuvic's voice finally crackled back. "Be ready to meet me when I land. If I must wait too long beyond that, I will become very unhappy."

Zadar listened to more silence as Ceasuvic didn't bother to sign off. He dropped the mike on the console, wheeled and strode across the Spartanly furnished room. Suddenly he felt the urge to be alone, far away from the watching eyes of the men in his cell. He could feel their tension, crackling like sparking electricity, heating up the room the longer they sat, waiting. Zadar needed clean, crisp air, all right, if only to get the smell of fear out of his nose.

Both their fear, and his.

CHAPTER NINETEEN

The Executioner found a welcoming committee of armed, dark-clad shadows amassed around two ZIL limos and two sedans at the far end of the driveway as he emerged with his hostage from inside the dacha. Judging by the AK-47s and Makarov pistols aimed his way, Bolan was pretty sure they weren't there to congratulate him on a job well done.

They descended two flights of steps onto the driveway, with the muzzle of his M-16 pressed against the base of Tokinov's skull. Bolan growled, "Keep walking. If any shooting starts, you're the first to go. I'll take my chances after that."

"Do I look to you as if I care any longer? Everything I have…it's all finished. Gone."

That gave Bolan pause and made him search Tokinov's face, the soldier's gaze narrowing. This was supposedly Russia's most notorious and powerful crime lord, and now Bolan was hearing—what? Despair? If Tokinov was feeling like giving up, that he didn't give a damn, then the soldier knew the situation had just turned more precarious.

A man with nothing to lose could prove worse than a cornered rattlesnake.

The Executioner prepared himself for the worst, that sudden explosion of violence spelling out his own doom. Maybe Tokinov was inclined to break away, not caring who lived or died, as the shadows opened up with their weapons. If Bolan met his end here, then he could only hope someone else would quickly pick up the torch, and stop Ceasuvic.

Headlights washed a white shroud of light over the mob scene awaiting Bolan's approach. He picked out Babbitt in the crowd, recalling his face from Brognola's intel packet. Five other dark-suited figures stood up against the sedans, hands on the rooftops. Pistols were jammed against the heads of the Americans.

A tall figure with a crew cut stepped away from the light, taking easy strides and wearing an odd smile on his lips. He held his arms out, as if that gesture meant there had to be some misunderstanding.

Bolan took the lead to cut through any crap. "Listen up, I'm leaving with Tokinov. Or nobody leaves."

The shadow said, "Of course. Leave."

"What's that?" Bolan asked, his suspicion deepening as he moved Tokinov closer to the stone pillars that marked the front entrance to the drive.

"My name is Sergei Alanskov. I am with SVR. I am agent in charge. My department's specialty is organized crime."

"And?"

"You Americans must think we are stupid people.

You must think our radar is inferior to yours, just like our intelligence.''

"Maybe you didn't hear me, Alanskov," Bolan growled. If push came to shove, Bolan was prepared to drop a 40 mm grenade into the threesome farthest away from Brognola's people, then go for broke. He counted ten SVR agents and hoped the Justice men would take the cue if he started the fireworks and hurl themselves into the storm. "I'm taking Tokinov and leaving."

"I heard, I heard. You can have him. Feel free. I will not stop you."

"Is that right? Well, you can be sure I'm not up for any bullshit double-talk."

"No, I am serious."

Bolan watched as the SVR man ran a scornful look over Tokinov. "We found out about the stolen ADMs. We planted an informant within his organization months back. We were too late when we raided the armory, the ADMs were unaccounted for. Whoever you are, understand I despise what this…man is. He is what is destroying my country. His money corrupts everyone it touches, and the corruption keeps spreading like some virus in my country. Not Alanskov. He does not need nor want any dirty money."

Bolan's chuckle was grim. "Next you're going to tell me I'm free to go."

"Precisely. Before you say 'bullshit,' hear me out. I am smarter than you think, more honest, I may add, than many of my counterparts. Good enough to see your Justice agents staking out this dacha. Of course, as you can see, they were unaware of our presence.''

"The point, other than how slick you are?''

"I am under orders from my superiors right now to let you have Tokinov. We do not want some international crisis because of the ADMs he intends to drop off to some Serb war criminals. Ah, I see the surprise, the skepticism. We have known about Tokinov and the Serbs for some time. The man you hold your weapon to is a parasite. We do not care what happens to him.''

"Put your weapons away and I'll try to swallow all this,'' Bolan said.

"With, as you might say, a huge grain of salt?''

"Exactly.''

Bolan moved Tokinov along, then ordered him to stop. He was well within striking distance now. One 40 mm grenade, one clip of 5.56 mm lead, if it went to hell. Under the circumstances it was as good as it could get.

Alanskov barked the order over his shoulder. Pistols were pulled away from the Justice agents and disappeared inside suit coats and bomber jackets.

"So,'' Bolan said, "you're willing to let me take Tokinov out of your country in hopes of wiping some egg off your faces.''

"You could say that. Listen, we have already tracked the aircraft that allowed you to parachute. At this moment, our radar is following what I believe is your pickup. I feel you are in no position to not trust my good intentions.''

Bolan could feel fate squeezing him. The whole operation had been a long shot, from getting into Russian airspace without the Russians catching on their skies were being invaded, to Grimaldi flying them out, hoping their own course would remain free and clear without a few MiGs scrambled to intercept the intruding aircraft and blow them out of the sky. No matter what the long odds had been, Tokinov was a critical piece to Bolan's jigsaw puzzle. Without the Russian crime boss there would have been no Ceasuvic in America, no ADMs now out there, ready to blow who knew where and how many up in a mushroom cloud. He needed Tokinov to answer the bigger questions. If not, the hunt could be over.

Unless, of course, the ADMs were already delivered to their destination, simply waiting on Ceasuvic to arrive. In that event, Bolan knew Brognola would call on all available resources, the skies over Europe swarming with American fighter jets, all military personnel on full alert to find, take out the Serb colonel and recover the ADMs.

"Listen, American, if you do not believe I am sincere, I offer to go with you while you fly out of Russia."

"In exchange for what?"

"Nothing. You can keep Tokinov. We know he has helped to create quite the mess in your country. He is responsible for much death and misery. He is an embarrassment to Russia."

"I suppose I don't have any choice."

"There is no time for suspicion. You will miss your flight."

That much was true. Bolan wasn't sure what to believe, but he didn't see where there was any other option than to go with whatever flow the SVR was offering. Grimaldi was on the way. Ceasuvic was at large.

And perhaps the next world war was one madman's touch away from becoming reality.

"You leave with or without me, I promise you no MiGs," the SVR agent said, "will follow you. I already know you have your own fighter jet escort. If the time ever comes for your country to return such a favor...there you have it."

"Prigavda, you know it?"

The SVR man was nodding. "Farm country, thirty kilometers east of here. It is good land to set down your jet. Come, I will escort you there."

"LET'S NOT GET too happy," Bolan told Grimaldi. "I don't hear the fat lady singing yet. This mission is a long way from being finished up."

"Roger that. But mind if I stay hopeful?"

"Keep it alive, no other way."

"I'm already striking up the band for the fat woman. I see daylight. At least as far as getting the hell out of Mother Russia in one piece. If that SVR man is being straight with us."

"What's your ETA, Partyhawk?"

Bolan held the handheld radio to his ear, watched as the stark black, flat landscape of the Ukrainian steppe unfolded beyond the sedan. Babbitt was riding shotgun, another agent behind the wheel. The two ZILs with their SVR load were riding point, the Russians leading the way down the paved road that cut through what Bolan could only view as poor farm country. The soldier had informed Grimaldi how fate worked in mysterious ways, as far as the SVR man went. It was a definite boost to their confidence, although both men knew they wouldn't breathe easy until they were well out of Russian airspace. Their luck had taken a turn toward the better, for a change. Like Grimaldi, Bolan only hoped that good fortune was both real and held up.

"Two minutes and counting to touchdown, Sarge. By the way, you need to phone home ASAP. You might say special news report. Talk to you about that when you've boarded. Along the hope angle, let me just say, the parties in question have been made."

"I copy, Partyhawk. See you on the downside."

"You mean upside, don't you?"

"Stay ready for the worst case."

"Always."

"Greece."

Bolan looked at Tokinov. The Russian crime boss was now cuffed, and appeared to be resigned to whatever fate was in store for him.

"What was that?" Bolan asked.

"The ADMs are en route for Thessaly, Greece."

Bolan found Babbitt watching him during the exchange. "The Russian is already looking to score brownie points," the Justice agent said. "I hear deal."

"No deal. Nothing matters anymore," Tokinov said. "Whether I spend my life in a jail in America...and believe me, we still have gulag in Russia."

"Doesn't sound like much of a choice," Babbitt said.

Bolan felt another sense of urgency jolt him. He was already putting together the logistics, flight time, knew they would still be in the air for several hours before a refueling stop at Incirlik. From there, Greece wasn't that far away, but it might as well have been the other side of the earth as far as Bolan was concerned. If Ceasuvic beat them to the punch.

"I don't know how we missed them, Ballard," Babbitt said, shaking his head, embarrassed.

"It happens. No sense in beating yourself up."

"Yeah, if the SVR man was in a hostile mood it would have gone down a lot different. You don't think the SVR guy is being a little too cooperative?"

"I think he's covering for his superiors. I think he'll play ball."

Bolan searched the black skies to the south and made out the dark bulk of the jet coming in for a landing.

"Those nerve gas warheads that were used on the NATO people in Italy?" Babbitt said. "Well, we've got a line on the armory where they came from."

"A break for a change."

"Maybe I'll find out just how cooperative my Russian counterpart will prove in the near future."

"Sounds like a plan," Bolan said.

"Find these Serb bastards, Ballard. I don't think I need to tell you what will happen if they set off those ADMs."

Bolan nodded. "Oh, you can count on me nailing them."

"Only if you find and get to them in time."

"The clock is definitely ticking down."

"And toward the beginning of doomsday maybe," Babbitt mumbled to himself. "God forbid."

LICKING HIS DRY LIPS, running a hand over his skull, Ceasuvic felt paranoia stretching his nerves like rubber bands about to snap. Finally they were putting Italy behind, the pilot gathering speed and altitude, pushing them for the darkness over the Adriatic Sea, the other jet lifting off to fall in behind. It hardly eased his agitation to know they were on the way.

They were flying blind, lights doused on the outside of both jets on his order. A ghost ship, he thought, but flying on to what?

The tension around Ceasuvic was unbearable, the silence excruciating. He was beginning to think he was seeing F-16s everywhere beyond their jets, little streaking black bolts on the distant horizon. Anything could happen, he knew. There were American military bases everywhere in this part of the world. He imagined missiles flaming for the jets, saw B-52s up there, dropping their payloads, blowing them all into a million pieces.

It was taking way too long to get to Greece. He

understood the need for caution, the pilots maintaining constant vigilance on the skies around them, watching the radar screens for any sign of aircraft in the immediate vicinity.

But he needed to get there.

Only now there was some delay in the delivery. His mind buzzed with grim possibilities. Maybe Tokinov had lied. Maybe the American military had seized the aircraft in Bulgaria. Maybe they were already made and being tracked by an AWACS. Stop it, he told himself, he was making himself crazy.

He pulled the shutter over the window. The soft overhead lights glowing over the faces of his men, he clearly read the strain on their faces. Then there was the boy, staring off into space, making Ceasuvic wonder if he was maybe in shock. And Churybik just sat there, some strange peaceful expression on his face that the colonel didn't trust, as if the Russian underboss was immune to all the pressure.

Ceasuvic paced the cabin. He felt trapped, confined, like some wild animal on a leash. He turned and growled, "Listen up, especially you, Churybik." He searched their faces, read their concern, his men wondering why he was wound so tight. "When we land, if I have to wait much longer than sunrise…if I believe we have been betrayed, we will kill the Russians." He looked at Churybik. No reaction. "And I will start by shooting you."

Ceasuvic watched Churybik closely. Incredibly the Russian just shrugged, then looked away. It was feeling more wrong by the minute. Ceasuvic had just issued a possible death sentence, and Churybik acted as if he didn't give a damn whether he lived or died.

The colonel went back to pacing. Any moment now he felt as if he were going to explode right out of his skin. Finally he headed for the cockpit, wanting to know how much longer before they landed in Thessaly. He knew whatever answer he heard wouldn't be nearly good enough.

CHAPTER TWENTY

"It's a suicide run, Hal. I don't think they plan on just walking or driving into Kosovo, or Macedonia or wherever, and setting the things off. It's the planes. My guess is they'll drop them, maybe by parachute, the ADMs set to go off, according to altitude and rate of descent. I don't think they even care if they get shot down in the process by some F-16s. They'll set them off in the air, go down with the ship."

"Yeah, and up in their mushroom clouds of glory."

"Which is why it's critical they aren't approached by anyone other than myself. I've seen what happens when Ceasuvic goes into a panic. In the unfortunate event, though, I can't get to him and he does go airborne, you'll need a contingency plan. Fighter jets on standby, ready to blow them out of the air."

"Let's just hope it doesn't come to that. This is messy enough without the public having full knowledge of how something like this could happen, that anyone with the right amount of money and connections can run around setting off nukes. Although the public relations and the diplomatic nightmare are really the least of my concerns.''

Bolan drew in a deep breath, his body wracked with the strain of what he'd been through already during this campaign. But as run-down and weary as he felt, he knew he would have to dig even deeper if he was going to catch Ceasuvic and finish it.

In the coming hours, Bolan knew the sat link to Brognola would prove either his ally or the bearer of the worst possible news. So far, Grimaldi was holding them on a steady course southbound for Incirlik, the Stony Man pilot pushing the jet at its maximum 561 mph. Smooth sailing, it looked as if the SVR man was true to his word, as Grimaldi's radar screen was free of approaching aircraft. Bolan looked away from the sat link, stared at the slumped bulk of Tokinov, the Russian's massive frame spilling over the seat. Minutes ago, the man had dropped three names on Bolan.

The American traitors.

It was the toughest possible knowledge for Bolan to digest, and he needed Brognola to process the information, run it down, find if there were any holes in Tokinov's story. At the first possible chance, Bolan would give the big Fed the latest grim news.

"Okay," Brognola said. "The AWACS and the Hawkeyes are nearly breathing in their exhaust fumes. We know Ceasuvic has just left Italy, two jets, straight off the Tokinov Aerodynamics assembly line. Our satellites even read the serial numbers. Just to double-check, there's an envoy from U.S. Army Intelligence going to that particular airfield to have a chat with all personnel concerned. The two transport planes were made flying into Bulgaria. I'll fax sat photos as soon I get them, just so you know what you're looking for, but Aaron tells me they're scaled-down versions of the Russian Antonov AN-22 transport. Built for speed. They're still on the ground for some reason. My guess is the pilots have picked up too much air traffic over the Aegean and are waiting for it to clear so they can make that last leg in. I've passed the word along to all commanders running the various American bases from Turkey to Greece. Hands off, let the aircraft in question fly and land safely. That's straight from the President. It's still your show."

"It's been a race from the start."

"I hear you, Striker. I only hope you beat Ceasuvic to the finish line. I'll have that attack helicopter waiting for you when you two reach our base in northern Greece. Now, about those ADMs. Aaron did his homework, pulled this straight from Pentagon databases. These particular Spetsnaz versions were built to be idiotproof, meaning a twelve-year-old can both crank it up and shut it down. Keypad. A seven-number code activates it. If they're the same ones we think were lifted out of this particular armory, then they are housed in a canvas backpack. If, and I hope to God it doesn't reach this point, you have to shut the things down, there's a switch at the back, left bottom. In a way it's so simple it makes it clever. Anybody who didn't know what they were looking for would never dream of either just pulling the ADM out of its pack or taking a knife and tearing open a hole in the back.''

''You're saying the switch is an off button?''

''Simple as that.''

''What's the verified yield?''

''It packs a five-kiloton punch.''

Bolan could only imagine the destruction they could wreak, not to mention the radioactive fallout that would contaminate an area of about twenty miles in all directions, depending on the wind.

''Hal, I'm going to need you to scramble a CIA team in Greece. I need the area in question reconned before we arrive. I'll work out the particulars on radio contact with the CIA men when we get to Greece. I can't go in blasting away, without knowing exactly where the boy is.''

''I understand. I'll get right on that.''

''There's something else,'' Bolan said, and gave Brognola the three names of the traitors.

''Unbelievable,'' Brognola said. ''He's sure?''

''He says one of them has the proof.''

''Our new Secretary of Defense…''

''Yeah. Dirty pictures tell the whole story. Seems the Russian Mafia was looking to buy influence into the next White House. A couple of those names I just mentioned are either in it for the money or, from what Tokinov tells me, they're looking to create a war in the Balkans, for whatever purpose, I can't say. Some sort of sick idea about making their mark in history, if I'm inclined to believe Tokinov.''

"Like I've said. Anything is possible."

"It appears so. Find out where they are. If we come out the other side in Greece, I intend to pay them a personal visit."

"You're going to have to. If it's true, these bastards are responsible for helping murder our own citizens. So, what's Tokinov's angle? I've already got Radin crying all over the place about his sweetheart deal."

"Despair."

"How's that?"

"The way I read Tokinov, he's close to the edge. He's given up, maybe it's as simple as that. A tired, defeated old man, I can't say for sure. But I don't think he wants to be handed back to the particular SVR man who gave me a personal escort to Grimaldi."

"Well, Tokinov's a whole other situation. The list of charges against him and the rest of his people in New York we've been rounding up are growing by the hour."

"I think you should go ahead and bust those Serbs in Detroit. But go in with big numbers on your raiding party, and they better be ready for a fight. They won't go quietly, that much I can tell you."

"This could be a job for Special Forces, I'm thinking."

"Whatever it takes. Any developments..."

"I'm on top of it."

"Never any doubt on this end. You know something, Hal, I can almost feel Ceasuvic out there, waiting for me. So far, he's been one step and a few bullets ahead of me. This time...I can feel it. He's finished.''

"Make me a believer, Striker, just one more time."

Bolan signed off. Silently he urged the Gulfstream on, knowing it could all go either way, depending on an hour here or there.

The Executioner would hold on to the hope that he could beat the clock. There was nothing else to do but wait, and feel his nerves and tension some more.

And hope the news on Brognola's end didn't get any worse.

"IF YOU ARE FINISHED with your temper tantrum, would you like me to show you how to activate them?''

Ceasuvic brought his anger under control. The Russian named Zominiki might have thought it was enough that they had landed safely in Greece with the ADMs, but Ceasuvic didn't see it that way. For one thing, he had been forced to wait five hours after their jets had landed at the airfield owned by the Greek. Now it was midmorning, the sun was up and there wasn't a cloud in the sky. Flying the cargo plane in full daylight was especially dangerous when Ceasuvic meant to invade Macedonian and Albanian airspace. In the event it looked as if they would be shot down by American fighter jets, he would order a crash landing, setting off the ADMs on the way down.

Feeling the paranoia tweak his nerves again, the colonel gave his surroundings a quick search. The seven Russians, including Churybik, and his Serbs were gathered at the foot of the ramp leading up into the belly of their transport plane. Ceasuvic didn't want to linger any longer than necessary, but he was told by Zominiki nobody was moving until the money that Churybik had brought from America was counted. Not only that, no one had seen fit yet, he noticed, to roll the fuel bladders out and top off their transport plane's tank.

Time was killing all of them.

Ceasuvic wanted to believe another hour or so on the ground didn't matter, but as he scanned the mountains around the airfield, he had an uneasy feeling they were being watched. Cviic and four others had taken Zadar's Jeep back to the safehouse. Worst-case scenario—Plan B. It would be up to Cviic to make the overseas radio call and order the Detroit cell to initiate the fallback mission. Ceasuvic then decided he might just go ahead and order Cviic to make the call anyway. This had begun with several acts of terrorism against their enemies. Why hold back one final assault on America now?

"Proceed," Ceasuvic told the Russian.

The Russian rattled off two sets of seven numbers, designating which series of numbers belonged to the ADMs he called number one and two. It sounded simple enough to Ceasuvic. The ADMs were set inside backpacks. He hefted one, the Russian telling him they were eighty pounds, five kilotons each, capable of knocking out half a small city. With fallout, radiation poisoning, they could cause suffering and death far beyond ground zero.

"Any questions?"

Ceasuvic looked at the wooden crates in the transport's rear. "You brought the parachutes I requested?"

The Russian nodded.

Ceasuvic ordered his men to fix a chute to two of the smallest crates they could find.

"What's in those crates?"

Zominiki smiled. "Some extra weapons for you. Courtesy of Viktor Tokinov. AKs, RPGs, grenades."

Ceasuvic nodded, pleased with progress, but burning to get on with it. Then he gave the order to roll out the fuel bins, told his men he wanted them assembled in thirty minutes for the final briefing. As anxious as he was to get going, Ceasuvic knew there were still maps to pore over, routes to their targets to discuss with his flight crew. Just a little longer, he thought, and they would take to the air.

Soon enough he would give his enemies all the death from above they could handle. It was worth the wait.

THE BOY WAS SHAKING in his chair, sobbing quietly, but Cviic had long since made up his mind about both the boy and his own salvation, aware his next course of action required simply the will to do it.

He was going to set them both free by the barrel of his AK-47. Then what? There was one Jeep outside. Okay, he would take the vehicle and just drive. Somehow, someway, he would dump the boy off in a village, then keep moving. Anywhere was preferable to remaining stuck in this madness Ceasuvic had created. And if anyone attempted to stop him, Cviic would fight to the death. If he had to wait any longer, he would fight and kill for only himself, his run for freedom. And if he had to die in the near future, then he would at least die for himself. Selfish? he thought. Damn right. He had learned selfishness well during the past few days. He had been schooled at the foot of the master of "self," Ceasuvic.

He wondered briefly about his change of heart, but knew it had started when he'd witnessed the colonel's bizarre behavior over Karina. Up to that point he had wanted to believe Ceasuvic cared about his men, whether they lived or died. But he had come to see that Ceasuvic only wanted Ceasuvic, had cared only about Karina and getting what he wanted. The lives of his men didn't matter to him, unless they advanced his own purposes. Well, too many Serbs had died in order for Ceasuvic to attempt his insane plan of dropping a nuclear backpack on Skopje and Tiranë. And what about that particular insane scheme? The colonel would never succeed; it would prove a final act of suicide. Once the transport plane broke Macedonian airspace, the Americans would send out their fighter jets and order Ceasuvic to land. And when it became obvious he wasn't about to comply, the Americans would shoot the plane into a thousand pieces.

Time to free himself, he thought.

There were four brother Serbs inside the safehouse. Yomanic and Ptleva were chain-smoking, Zomic and

Manjaca hovering around the radio console, looking hungry for news from the colonel.

Cviic suddenly found Manjaca giving him an odd look.

"Cviic, the way you keep staring at the boy, I am beginning to wonder about you."

The others chuckled. The boy's sobs filled his ears, fueled his heart with cold anger.

Now, he decided, pulling the AK-47 off his shoulder.

"Are you crazy?"

Manjaca's cry of alarm caused the others to jump. No one was laughing now. They were turning his way, when he held down the assault rifle's trigger, letting it rip, their deaths, he knew, signaling his freedom. The AK-47 bucked in his hands, as he chopped them up with the 7.62 mm leadstorm, raking his autofire left to right and back. A few wild rounds pounded into the radio, turning the instrument into sparking and smoking ruins. So much for Detroit, he thought, firing on.

The boy was screaming now, holding his ears, trying to drown out the din of autofire as Cviic pounded his comrades into the far wall, their blood spraying the hostage before they landed in a heap. For a moment, he stood, staring at the carnage in disbelief. He had done the deed.

"Boy, get up! Follow me!"

Cviic cursed, the boy was glued to his seat. Cviic nearly ran across the room, yanked the boy out of his seat and dragged him through the door. He was heading for the Jeep, when he caught the scuffling and groaning from behind. Wheeling, he spotted Manjaca, his chest tattered crimson ruins, the horrible wheezing betraying a punctured lung.

Manjaca staggered, pitched into the doorjamb, the AK-47 up and spraying lead.

Cviic shoved the boy to the ground and darted several feet in the opposite direction, as the bullets snapped past his face. Manjaca managed to scream a vicious curse before Cviic hosed him down with the last few rounds from his AK-47.

A hissing sound. Cviic looked at the boy, who once again had his hands pressed to his ears. Looking on, Cviic saw the front and back tires on the driver's side deflating.

"Dammit!"

He had no idea where the closest village was, but one look around at the vast desolation and he knew a long hike was ahead for both of them.

Cviic reached the boy and hauled him to his feet. He was about to move out, when he caught a faint noise he quickly thought he should recognize. Straining his ears, he marked the familiar whapping sound, coming his way from the south.

Chopper.

Cviic fed his AK-47 a fresh clip, grabbed the boy by the arm and shouted for him to run.

CHAPTER TWENTY-ONE

Grimaldi cleared the mountain ridges, directing the Kiowa Warrior OH-58D helicopter on an arrow-straight course for the Serb safehouse. "There he is!"

Bolan stared through the reinforced, bulletproof cockpit Plexiglas. A lone Serb gunman was half pulling, half dragging the Percivall boy, just as their Company eyes in the foothills had informed them minutes earlier. As the Serb made his desperate scuttle across the plain, he kept glancing over his shoulder, fumbling to hold on to his AK-47 while wrestling the boy along. Fate had seen fit to throw Bolan his one chance to save the boy. A lucky break for a change, for once his timing beating the enemy to the punch.

"Drop me off directly behind them," the Executioner told Grimaldi. "Then hover right over them."

"Dust bowl, I copy."

The CIA man's voice crackled over Bolan's walkie-talkie. "Watchman here. You fellas better hustle. According to my man on the other side of the mountain, it looks like the main event's a few minutes from getting in the air. Wrap it up here ASAP. I know how you don't want to be late for the show.''

Bolan copied. He felt his heart pumping, fresh waves of adrenaline coursing through his veins. All the intel-gathering, interagency cooperation and aid from the U.S. military would mean next to nothing if Bolan blew it here. He had come too far to see Ceasuvic escape his gun sights now, to leave it for somebody else to finish. In the event the Serbs flew off, a squad of American fighter jets was ready to shoot down any aircraft that left Meteora.

M-16 in hand, Bolan was out of his seat, moving for the fuselage doorway as Grimaldi began his descent. It was plenty enough attack chopper, Bolan knew, to get the grim job done on the Serb aircraft: four AGM-114 Hellfire air-to-ground laser-guided missiles, plus air-to-air and antitank missiles, two pods with 70 Hydra 2.75-inch rockets, as well as a gunstick at Grimaldi's fingertips for two .50-caliber machine guns in the war bird's nose. The Kiowa was part of the Army's Helicopter Improvement Program, and Grimaldi had jumped at the chance to "borrow" the attack bird the second he laid eyes on it back at the American base.

The Executioner kept hope alive that the Stony Man pilot would see the Kiowa help make his day.

Bolan opened the boarding door to a blast of rotor wash and grit.

"Go!" he heard Grimaldi yell.

The soldier didn't hesitate, leaping out the doorway and landing on his feet like a cat. He was running ahead when Grimaldi shot the chopper forward, then lowered the Kiowa over the Serb and the Percivall boy. The anticipated dust storm swept over their position. The Serb staggered around in the whirlwind, firing his AK-47 at the chopper, blind for the most part as the rotor wash blew the dust storm in his face.

The boy broke free of the Serb's grasp, distracting the hardman, giving Bolan all the room he needed. Eyelids slitted against the driving grit and dust, Bolan moved into the storm and dropped a 5.56 mm hammer of doom over the man. Blood spurting from his chest, he hit the ground as if he'd been poleaxed.

The soldier moved in front of the Kiowa, waving his arms for Grimaldi to back it up. Quickly, as the Kiowa peeled off and the dust storm slackened, the Executioner checked on the Percivall boy. He feared the worst when he first saw the blood on the boy's shirt.

"Easy, son, take it easy. You're going home. We're the good guys," he said in a tone and language that seemed to calm some of the boy's fear. Gently he checked the boy for bullet holes and grazes, then realized the blood belonged to somebody else. He looked back at the safehouse and spotted the body sprawled in the doorway.

"Vuk...Arkan...Cviic...serial number..."

Bolan looked over at the dying Serb, who repeated his name, rank and serial number. This particular Serb had snapped, slaughtered his own, and had been in pursuit of some mindless run for freedom. But why Bolan could neither venture a guess, nor did he care.

The boy was still alive.

As the Serb rasped out a death rattle, the soldier raised the CIA man, told him to get down there and take the boy back to the American base.

Seconds later the soldier was bounding through the Kiowa's doorway. Grimaldi didn't have to be told to get the chopper up, full speed ahead.

IVAN CHURYBIK settled back in his seat. Finally, he was putting behind this madness. But what was next? His future was as grim as ever. There was so much wreckage left behind in America, he feared Tokinov would simply hand him a death sentence as soon as he set foot on Russian soil.

As his jet started to taxi, he glanced out the window and saw the Serbs moving to board their transport plane. He chuckled. The fools. Ceasuvic had his precious tools of revenge.

Before long, he suspected the Serbs would go up in flames, all right, but it would happen because of missiles fired from F-16s and not the mushroom clouds Ceasuvic so desperately wanted to see boil up from Skopje and Tiranë. It was small consolation, but the cause of his own grief would be dead soon enough.

Churybik looked at the grim faces of the Russian shooters Viktor had sent along. They were almost carbon copies of Duklov. Silent, eyes hard, but watching him with the same contempt Duklov had treated him with.

Forget them. Churybik knew he had his own problems, no doubt, once he reached Russia. Tokinov, despite the rumors the man was senile, mad, whatever, was still in charge. He would want some answers, and somebody's head would have to roll. It was a safe bet that Churybik's neck would be the first one on Viktor's chopping block. Still, maybe he could blame the Serbs. There had to be some excuse he could hand Viktor. But what? Churybik was searching his mind for those excuses, ways to save himself when—

He jumped out of his seat. All the time he had spent with the crazy Serbs, he knew the unmistakable sound of explosions and weapons fire by now. He was racing for the starboard window, peering outside when he saw the helicopter shoot past them. His mouth gaped wide at the sight of the missiles on the aircraft. He heard the anxious voices shouting and cursing all around him, Viktor's men jumbled beside him.

Churybik urged the jet to gather more speed, but as he watched the chopper hover at some intercept point two hundred yards ahead, its nose started swinging toward their jet, and he was pretty sure he would never have to worry about answering to Viktor Tokinov.

A second later, Churybik watched in horror, as a missile streaked from the chopper and confirmed his final fear.

WHATEVER CAUSED all the lingering and delays, forcing the Serbs to stay grounded up to that point, was really moot. Bolan could hazard several guesses, but why bother? he figured.

All that mattered was that he was inserted, and sprinting hard for the transport plane. Moments earlier, Grimaldi had dropped him off at the far southern edge of the airfield. The Stony Man pilot then quickly introduced himself to the enemy. The Kiowa swept over the Serbs gathered on the cargo plane's ramp, the .50-caliber machine guns flaming, kicking a few hardmen off the ramp and onto the runway. It was air support enough for Bolan to pick it up a few notches, close the gap and go to work.

On the run, as the transport plane's propellers spun to life, Bolan triggered his M-203, the muffled pop all but drowned out by the return fire directed his way from the Serbs clustered in the mouth of the cargo hold. It was risky, granted, the soldier aware the grenade blast or a stray bullet could touch off the backpack nukes.

Ceasuvic had left him no choice.

At the other end of the airfield, Grimaldi was unloading missiles and rockets on the jets and the other Tokinov transport special. Grimaldi dropped the sky on those aircraft, the series of explosions shaking the earth beneath Bolan's feet.

He left Grimaldi to it, the soldier's own plate overflowing with Serb problems.

The Executioner's 40 mm round boiled a fireball through the Serbs near the ramp, kicking the enemy back from the smoky thunderclap. The way ahead looked clear for a moment, Bolan pumping his legs, twenty feet and closing on the ramp, when two Serbs, wounded by Grimaldi's initial strafing, chose that instant to rise from the ground.

A quick burst from his M-16 and the Executioner dropped them for good.

He loaded the M-203, then triggered a 3-round burst from the M-16 as a Serb emerged from the whirling smoke, his finger reaching for the button that would close the ramp. The burst went wide, Bolan seeing the sparks flash over the Serb's head. Another burst, making the adjustment, and Bolan nailed him in the chest, the 5.56 mm tumblers knocking the Serb off his feet.

Then Bolan went for broke. They were screaming from deep inside the belly of the transport plane, flailing shadows beyond the swirling smoke cloud. With the aircraft's turbofan engines shrieking in his ears, Bolan tapped the M-203's trigger. The 40 mm round streaked on, a near perfect line before impacting against the partition to the cockpit.

It was the home run Bolan needed, as the transport plane lumbered on, its roll slowing enough for him to make the ramp. He cracked home a fresh 30-round magazine, then forged ahead, searching for live Serbs.

CEASUVIC HEARD himself gagging on the smoke, choking, as he tried to suck air into his raw lungs. He looked up, made out the chatter of autofire and saw what remained of his men getting chopped up by whoever was doing all the shooting from the ramp.

He couldn't believe this was happening. How? Why? So much time and effort now wasted, he raged to himself. The cockpit was in flames, he saw, his pilots dead.

The shooting stopped as the last of his Serbs pitched to the floorboards. Where were the ADMs? He peered through the smoke, grabbing up his AK-47, kicked something and nearly toppled on his face. Looking down, he discovered he'd almost tripped over one of the ADMs. Should he try to set it off now? He would get a few seconds. And to what avail? A suicide blast? Take out the shooter...?

He froze. No, it couldn't be. A lone shooter.

"Don't do it, Ceasuvic."

"You bastard!" he roared.

He'd seen that face several times before, filed it away to memory, then forgotten all about the bastard once he believed he'd blown him off that hilltop in America. He caught only a glimpse of that face now, but it was the dark man, the nameless adversary who had killed Karina, shot up his men and was now on the verge—

Ceasuvic bellowed and held down the trigger of his AK-47.

THE SERB COLONEL was making his suicide charge when Bolan came low around the crate, his M-16 blazing on full-auto. The soldier braved the rounds chewing up wood above his head, saw his hasty burst chop off Ceasuvic at the knees. By then the transport had come to a full stop, the cockpit eaten up by fire, the smell of roasting flesh biting into Bolan's senses.

Ceasuvic snarled, sounding like a wounded animal

to Bolan, as the Executioner rolled up and away from the crate.

He had the man dead to rights, but the colonel still wasn't a believer.

Ceasuvic roared, his voice ripped with all the agony and hatred that burned in his soul. He rolled onto his back, his AK-47 sweeping up when Bolan held down his M-16's trigger. He riddled Ceasuvic with a long burst, not satisfied until he'd burned out the clip.

Bolan checked the transport's belly, stem to stern. All dead, present and accounted for, he slipped his arm through the M-16's sling. He hauled up both ADMs, went and kicked open the side door, then pitched them to the ground.

Ahead, Bolan found that the airfield was a long wavering wall of flames. There were a few survivors out on the runway, but Grimaldi was swooping over them, his .50-caliber machine guns cutting them down where they stood.

The Executioner hit the ground, one hand each pulling up the backpacks. He kept his eyes peeled for any movement, but after a long search, he could tell they were finished here.

When the Kiowa set down, Bolan walked into the rotor wash, leaving the backpacks on the ground. Boarding, he told Grimaldi, "Raise the cleanup crew, Jack. We're out of here."

They would have to wait a few minutes until American military personnel arrived to retrieve the ADMs, but Bolan was grateful for the brief respite.

Beyond Greece, the Executioner had his own mop-up detail waiting.

THE GULFSTREAM JET was taking them home. Bolan watched the sunlight glittering off the seemingly eternal expanse of the Atlantic Ocean, far below.

"It's hard to believe," Grimaldi said, "our own people helped engineer the possibility of a major war in the Balkans. Why?"

"I may or may not get some answers."

"But the one guy is...I can't say it. It makes me sick to my stomach."

"I'll give that one guy a choice. The other two, I'll let them call the play. But I have a feeling they won't just hand themselves over."

"You're going need backup."

Bolan showed his friend a grim smile. "You've come this far with me. I don't think I'll just drop you back off in Miami, go my own way."

The Executioner saw his friend shaking his head and could guess what he was thinking. It always sickened Bolan, too, when a traitor walked among their ranks, using the blood and suffering of others to either fatten bank accounts or further some twisted agenda.

"Well, the ADMs are safely in American hands. And the Percivall boy is on the way home to his parents," Grimaldi said.

Bolan nodded. Something had gone right for a change.

The Executioner settled back in his seat and shut

his eyes. If he slept at all, he knew he would see the faces of three traitors in his dreams. Little did they know he was about to turn their lives into a nightmare.

CHAPTER TWENTY-TWO

The alarm was wailing all over the house, but Bolan had gone in, prepared to make plenty of racket. The man was stirred up, all right, throwing on lights, racing around his living room, as frantic as hell, his silk robe whipping about him like a bird's flapping wings.

It had been easy enough, scaling the wall, moving into the back, the guard dog chained, barking at the black-clad intruder as Bolan moved up the deck, broke the window to the kitchen door and let himself in.

Simple, but what waited for him at the end of this particular ride was anything but easy to witness.

Brognola had set the table for the first of two pick-ups of the traitors. Once again the big Fed had taken Bolan this far. The rest was up to him. Earlier, one of the traitors had chosen to eat his gun.

The Executioner sat in the shadows of the dining room, the Beretta 93-R in his hand. The man punched off the alarm, started flying around, throwing back drapes, talking to himself. Peter Fritch was on the edge. The Glock semiauto pistol in his pudgy fist didn't escape Bolan's eye.

"We're all alone," Bolan said.

He thought the man was going to faint as he spun, then spotted the intruder.

"You sent your wife packing for a long weekend. Problems on the home front shipped away. It's just the two of us."

"Oh, God, who are you...are you going to kill me?"

"Not unless you point that weapon in my direction. It doesn't have to go down that way. It's your call."

The soldier rose from his seat, moving out of the shadows.

"Who are you? FBI? Justice Department? God, I've been seeing shadows all day. I knew I was being followed!"

He was losing it, Bolan could tell, hysterical now that his world was shattered.

"This is a roundup," Bolan said. "Plain and simple, at least on my end."

"Some choice," Fritch snarled, shaking uncontrollably. "A lifetime in prison. Or what...you shoot me?"

"You're a traitor."

"I've got names."

"The general's already dead. And we know about your man in Virginia Beach. I don't see what else you have to offer."

The guy was quickly coming unraveled, and Bolan could almost read his thoughts.

"Why, Fritch?"

"Fear."

"Of what?"

"Not…getting what was mine. They had me, the Russians…I couldn't lose all I've worked for…the shame and disgrace…my new position…"

"We know about the dirty pictures, the blackmail. Tokinov's a done deal."

"Then maybe you can cut me some slack?"

"I don't think so. Drop the gun. You'll never be able to put it to your head in time, or in your mouth. I'll shoot it out of your hand."

"A fate worse than death—no way, I won't go to prison. I can't! I'll never make it a day!"

Fritch broke under the strain, perhaps all those images of prison life stoking his terror and despair, pushing him over the edge for the swan dive into his own abyss. But Bolan was ready as he lifted the Glock for his temple. The Executioner tapped the Beretta's trigger, drilled a 9 mm round into his hand. Fritch screamed, then hit the floor, clutching his wounded appendage.

The soldier moved forward and scooped up the Glock, then took his walkie-talkie and told Brognola's people to come inside and cuff the traitor.

The Executioner had seen enough, and the sight of Fritch made him sicker to his stomach than he would have thought possible. He could never understand men like this who would betray their own, sell out their country. Under the circumstances, the soldier figured his was not to reason why.

HE SAT in the shadows of *Winston*'s cabin. He kept the Beretta 92-F in his lap with one hand, the remote control in the other hand. One television was tuned to CNN, the sound off. So far, there had been no breaking news report about a nuclear attack in the Balkans, but he already knew it was over. A source of his inside Army Intelligence had passed on the word.

He chuckled. It had been a long shot anyway. He wondered what exactly had gone wrong. Well, too many people had been involved, tripping over one another from the start, everyone knowing too much about the other guy. And then there was Tokinov, word lately being that the Russian crime boss had become a self-indulgent pig, losing his mind, his will eroded by pleasure, his hold on his empire slipping slowly from his grasp with each day. The Serb angle had looked promising in the beginning, some ADMs handed over to them by the Russian, who had this strange affection for the Serbs. Some nuclear holocaust sparking a war in the Balkans. Then he and the general would just walk off into the sunset, laughing at the world at large while Fritch flew around, trying to put out the fires. Well, there wasn't going to be some in-your-face statement to America or those bastards in D.C. who had sent him packing so long ago.

He looked at the other television set in the far corner of the room, laughed to himself at the grotesque sight—the tape in the VCR, the screen showing Peter Fritch in all his glory, if anyone had the stomach to call it that.

Suddenly he felt the boat shift just enough to warn him an intruder was on the deck. This one was light on his feet, unlike Fritch, and he could sense the stealthy movements of a professional.

"Come on down," he called out.

Moments later a tall shadow materialized on the steps and walked into the cabin. He looked at the sound-suppressed pistol, a Beretta, like his own. He read pro and killer all over this one.

"Take a seat, I've been expecting they'd send someone like you."

THE EXECUTIONER was wary. He suspected the ex-colonel was holding a weapon in his lap, figured this one would go out hard. Bolan glimpsed the disgusting sight of Fritch, swung his Beretta up and sideways, then squeezed the trigger and blew out the image in a short blast of sparks and smoke. Another quick tap of the Beretta's trigger, and he shot out the screen on the other television.

"I'm afraid I won't be staying long," Bolan told the man.

"I guess you came here to ask me why."

"I'm not sure it matters any longer."

"Hey, but maybe it does. I don't know who you

work for, CIA maybe, but I've still got a list of players who took money from the Russian mafia. All on disk, right here in my drawer. Want me to get it for you?"

"That's okay. And it won't buy you freedom."

"Right, freedom. None of us is ever free, mister. So, what happens now? You terminate me with extreme prejudice. I'm not one to blow my brains out like the general. You know he was in line to be the next Allied Supreme Commander of NATO? Only he didn't want the job. Smoke screen. Jerked them all off, had plans to retire, disappear."

"Maybe I can spare a few minutes to hear the why."

"Because I was disgraced by my own, for starters, a long and distinguished career ruined by one mistake."

"It was your choice."

"There are no choices anymore. This country is going straight down the tubes, the world is more and more poised every day to go up in flames. We were simply lighting the spark. Humankind will get what it deserves, just like I got mine."

"I'm not so sure I share your opinion," Bolan said.

"I don't give a damn what you think! What we did, well, we just wanted to show all those bastards in Washington that we could do it. Use the Serbs to launch a major war in the Balkans."

"You were connected to the Russian mob all along."

"Of course."

"Tokinov won't be buying his way into the White House."

"There will be other Tokinovs. The Chinese only scratched the surface as far as buying influence. Money is the only god too many people pray to anymore. Wake up! The world's gone crazy. It's time to bail and let them consume each other. Don't you stand there and play high and mighty with me."

The Executioner saw it coming. Whatever madness burned in ex-Colonel White's mind, Bolan would never know. It was enough that he beat the man to the draw. White was leaping out of his chair when Bolan pumped a 9 mm slug between his eyes.

The traitor slumped back in his chair, an odd smile frozen on his lips, as if he'd been hoping all along someone would punch his ticket.

Bolan hardly felt good about obliging this man's death wish. Burdened by anger over the treachery of his own, the Executioner moved to the desk to find the disk, the one that supposedly had still more names of traitors to be tracked.

Well, the Executioner had done all he cared to do. The big game was hunted down, out of the picture. Someone else could pick up the ball from there.

But there was always tomorrow, he knew. More traitors, more savages like Ceasuvic out there. The hunting of those who preyed on the innocent, who engineered wholesale death and destruction would never end.

Not on Bolan's watch. As long as he was still breathing the hunt would always signal him to his own call to duty.

To his War Everlasting.

**Don't miss the high-tech, fast-paced adventure
of title #51 of Stony Man...**

Be sure to get in on the action!

DON PENDLETON'S

STONY

AMERICA'S ULTRA-COVERT INTELLIGENCE AGENCY

MAN

DOOMSDAY
DIRECTIVE

THE
ARMAGEDDON
PROJECT

BOOK II

Grant Betancourt wants to create his own technological
utopia and puts together a plan where three combat
groups of religious fanatics will attack the centers of their
rivals—thereby insuring the destruction of all three. Can
Stony Man stop Betancourt in time? At stake is only the
future of the world.

Available in February 2001 at your favorite retail outlet.

Or order your copy now by sending your name, address, zip or postal code, along with
a check or money order (please do not send cash) for $5.99 for each book ordered
($6.99 in Canada), plus 75¢ postage and handling ($1.00 in Canada), payable to Gold
Eagle Books, to:

In the U.S.	In Canada
Gold Eagle Books	Gold Eagle Books
3010 Walden Avenue	P.O. Box 636
P.O. Box 9077	Fort Erie, Ontario
Buffalo, NY 14269-9077	L2A 5X3

Please specify book title with your order.
Canadian residents add applicable federal and provincial taxes.

GOLD
EAGLE

GSM51

**A journey through the dangerous frontier
known as the future...**

JAMES AXLER
DEATH LANDS®
Zero City

Hungry and exhausted, Ryan and his band emerge from
a redoubt into an untouched predark city, and uncover a
cache of weapons and food. Among other interlopers,
huge winged creatures guard the city. Holed up inside
an old government building, where Ryan's son, Dean,
lies near death, Ryan and Krysty must raid where a local
baron uses human flesh as fertilizer....

On sale December 2000 at your favorite retail outlet. Or order your copy now by
sending your name, address, zip or postal code, along with a check or money order
(please do not send cash) for $5.99 for each book ordered ($6.99 in Canada),
plus 75¢ postage and handling ($1.00 in Canada), payable to Gold Eagle Books, to:

In the U.S.	**In Canada**
Gold Eagle Books	Gold Eagle Books
3010 Walden Ave.	P.O. Box 636
P.O. Box 9077	Fort Erie, Ontario
Buffalo, NY 14269-9077	L2A 5X3

Please specify book title with order.
Canadian residents add applicable federal and provincial taxes.

GOLD
EAGLE®

GDL52

James Axler

OUTLANDERS®

TIGERS OF HEAVEN

In the Outlands, the struggle for control of the baronies continues. Kane, Grant and Brigid seek allies in the Western Islands empire of New Edo, where they try to enlist the aid of the Tigers of Heaven, a group of samurai warriors.

Book #2 of the Imperator Wars saga, a trilogy chronicling the introduction of a new child imperator—launching the baronies into war!

On sale February 2001 at your favorite retail outlet. Or order your copy now by sending your name, address, zip or postal code, along with a check or money order (please do not send cash) for $5.99 for each book ordered ($6.99 in Canada), plus 75¢ postage and handling ($1.00 in Canada), payable to Gold Eagle Books, to:

In the U.S.
Gold Eagle Books
3010 Walden Ave.
P.O. Box 9077
Buffalo, NY 14269-9077

In Canada
Gold Eagle Books
P.O. Box 636
Fort Erie, Ontario
L2A 5X3

Please specify book title with order.
Canadian residents add applicable federal and provincial taxes.

GOUT16

**Gold Eagle brings you
high-tech action and mystic adventure!**

THE

Destroyer™

#122 SYNDICATION RITES

Created by

MURPHY
and SAPIR

The outgoing President has decided to strike up an odd relationship with a CIA analyst. Has the President decided to mount an eleventh-hour attack on CURE? Remo and Chiun are sent to untangle a mess that runs from the White House to the Mob and to a small maximum-security prison cell, where America's infamous Mafia don has hatched the ultimate scheme of vengeance and profit....

Available in January 2001 at your favorite retail outlet.

Or order your copy now by sending your name, address, zip or postal code, along with a check or money order (please do not send cash) for $5.99 for each book ordered ($6.99 in Canada), plus 75¢ postage and handling ($1.00 in Canada), payable to Gold Eagle Books, to:

In the U.S.
Gold Eagle Books
3010 Walden Ave.
P.O. Box 9077
Buffalo, NY 14269-9077

In Canada
Gold Eagle Books
P.O. Box 636
Fort Erie, Ontario
L2A 5X3

Please specify book title with your order.
Canadian residents add applicable federal and provincial taxes.

GDEST122

A journey through the dangerous frontier
known as the future...

JAMES AXLER

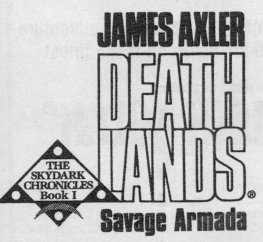

DEATH LANDS

THE SKYDARK CHRONICLES Book I

Savage Armada

Beneath the beauty of the Marshall Islands lies a battleground for looting pirates and sec men in still-functional navy PT boats. Ryan Cawdor and his warrior band emerge in this perilous water world, caught in a grim fight to unlock the secrets of the past.

On sale March 2001 at your favorite retail outlet.

Or order your copy now by sending your name, address, zip or postal code, along with a check or money order (please do not send cash) for $5.99 for each book ordered ($6.99 in Canada), plus 75¢ postage and handling ($1.00 in Canada), payable to Gold Eagle Books, to:

In the U.S.

Gold Eagle Books
3010 Walden Ave.
P.O. Box 9077
Buffalo, NY 14269-9077

In Canada

Gold Eagle Books
P.O. Box 636
Fort Erie, Ontario
L2A 5X3

Please specify book title with order.
Canadian residents add applicable federal and provincial taxes.

GDL53

Don't miss the action and adventure of Mack Bolan on these titles!

DON PENDLETON's
MACK BOLAN®

#61472-1	CONFLAGRATION	$5.99 U.S.☐	$6.99 CAN.☐
#61471-3	KILLSPORT	$5.99 U.S.☐	$6.99 CAN.☐
#61470-5	EXECUTIVE ACTION	$5.99 U.S.☐	$6.99 CAN.☐
#61469-1	VENGEANCE	$5.99 U.S.☐	$6.99 CAN.☐

(limited quantities available on certain titles)

TOTAL AMOUNT	$
POSTAGE & HANDLING	$
($1.00 for one book, 50¢ for each additional)	
APPLICABLE TAXES*	$ _____
TOTAL PAYABLE	$ _____

(check or money order—please do not send cash)

To order, complete this form and send it, along with a check or money order for the total above, payable to Gold Eagle Books, to: **In the U.S.:** 3010 Walden Avenue, P.O. Box 9077, Buffalo, NY 14269-9077; **In Canada:** P.O. Box 636, Fort Erie, Ontario, L2A 5X3.

Name: _____

Address: _____ City: _____

State/Prov.: _____ Zip/Postal Code: _____

*New York residents remit applicable sales taxes.
 Canadian residents remit applicable GST and provincial taxes.

GOLD EAGLE®

GSBBACK2